SNOWHOOK

SNOWHOOK

JO STORM

DUNDURN
TORONTO

Cover image: istock.com/AmpH
Printer: Webcom, a division of Marquis Book Printing Inc.

Library and Archives Canada Cataloguing in Publication

Storm, Jo, 1972-, author
    Snowhook / Jo Storm.

Issued in print and electronic formats.
ISBN 978-1-4597-4300-7 (softcover).--ISBN 978-1-4597-4301-4(PDF).--
ISBN 978-1-4597-4302-1 (EPUB)

    I. Title.

PS8637.T6753S66 2019   jC813'.6   C2018-903100-X
                                                C2018-903101-8

1   2   3   4   5   23   22   21   20   19

We acknowledge the support of the Canada Council for the Arts, which last year invested $153 million to bring the arts to Canadians throughout the country, and the Ontario Arts Council for our publishing program. We also acknowledge the financial support of the Government of Ontario, through the Ontario Book Publishing Tax Credit and Ontario Creates, and the Government of Canada.

Nous remercions le Conseil des arts du Canada de son soutien. L'an dernier, le Conseil a investi 153 millions de dollars pour mettre de l'art dans la vie des Canadiennes et des Canadiens de tout le pays.

Care has been taken to trace the ownership of copyright material used in this book. The author and the publisher welcome any information enabling them to rectify any references or credits in subsequent editions.
                                                — J. Kirk Howard, President

The publisher is not responsible for websites or their content unless they are owned by the publisher.

Printed and bound in Canada.

VISIT US AT

dundurn.com | @dundurnpress | dundurnpress | dundurnpress

Dundurn
3 Church Street, Suite 500
Toronto, Ontario, Canada
M5E 1M2

CHAPTER ONE

Hannah's parents would not let her go to town. It was barely a town anyway, Timmins. It was so far from Toronto that her friends would ask her, "Didja see Santa?" every time she came home. Timmins was essentially a crappy mall, a hospital, and a bus station. At eight, she hadn't cared; at ten, she couldn't go to town without an adult; at fourteen, she couldn't go because —

"Hannah," called her father. He stood by the woodpile, removing his mitts and pulling a hatchet from his belt loop. "Give me a hand?"

She went over and helped him lift the tarp that covered the kindling. It was birch kindling, the kind that smelled sharp and tangy when it burned, but the tarp had ripped overnight and now the wood was soaked and useless. Hannah looked up at the chimney stack that rose over the cabin. There was no smoke, but she could see waves of heat rising off the brick mouth. That meant the fire was burning well and they wouldn't need kindling.

"We'll need more kindling," said her dad.

"Why? The fire's already going. It hasn't been out since we got here."

Hannah's father looked at her with his Learning Face. That was what her younger sister Kelli called it, the Learning Face. It was a seriously annoying face. "What if we need a fire outside, to smoke fish?" he said.

"Gross."

"What if we want to use the wood oven?"

"What if we need to make smoke signals?" said Hannah sarcastically.

"Hannah, don't be smart," said her father. "Look, I'm going to show you something."

He dropped the tarp, hooked the hatchet onto his belt, and put his snowshoes back on, stuffing his mitts in his pocket. She could see the nametag, "G. Williams," that was sewn inside of them; hers said "H. Williams."

Hannah was already wearing her snowshoes, so she followed his wider tracks easily as he moved to the edge of the clearing where their cabin sat, past the tarped-over snowmobile and the SUV. They hadn't brought the other vehicle; it was a car and would never have made it down the back roads to get here. Even in the summer, they always brought the four-wheel-drive vehicle. Her parents called this place "camp." When she was younger, Hannah had fooled some of her friends by saying that she went "to camp" for almost every school vacation, but then stupid Kelli had blabbed and then everyone knew that it was just a cottage — a three-room, dingy cottage with an outhouse in the backyard, on the edge of a smelly pond.

They wended their way through the bush until they came to a little stand of poplar trees with a few frozen yellow leaves still clinging to them, almost hidden in the bigger, bushier arms of the blue spruce and waxy green hemlock. Her father looked up into the branches of the poplar. "These should work." He reached up with one hand and grabbed a branch, and with the other he loosed his hatchet and chopped the branch off. He held up the iced-over poplar branch, and Hannah noticed the nicks on his red knuckles. Her dad loved to work outdoors without gloves. "Can you burn this?" he asked.

Hannah rolled her eyes. "No, it's green wood. And it's wet. I'm not ten, dad."

"That's right," replied her father, "you're fourteen going on forty. But sometimes you have to make do with less, right?"

Hannah shrugged.

He knelt down and placed the branch on the flat part of his snowshoe, holding it on its end with one hand. "In the winter, all wood is wet — on the outside." With the other hand he brought up the hatchet and quickly made a series of downward motions on the sides of the branch until the bark bristled out like a skinny, grey-green porcupine.

"Instant kindling," he said.

"Great. Is there an instant travelling stick, too, so I can go back home?"

"You never know out here," he said. When he had his Learning Face on, Hannah knew, it was hard to get him to do anything but talk about the bush.

"I'm cold, and it's lunchtime," she said.

"Okay." He stood and brushed the snow off his coat, turning his head to the line of clouds that were being pulled toward them by grey, pouting tendrils. "Smells like another storm, eh?"

Hannah let her breath out loudly, but didn't reply.

They trooped back. The last two days had been warm and humid, but last night the temperature had dropped so quickly that the wet snow had chunked back into ice and broken through many of their tarps, and even Nook's doghouse. Hannah and Kelli had spent all morning scraping ice and snow off the porch, the woodshed, the cars, the doghouses, and the outhouse steps to see what damage had been done. The snowmobile tarp was also ripped, and a chunk of falling ice had broken the gas line. Fixing it was tomorrow's job. Hannah had volunteered for that one, mostly because it meant she could drive into town with her father to go to the hardware store.

They removed their snowshoes and propped them against the dogsled in the cold porch that separated the front door of the house from the elements. There were two more dogsleds behind the cabin, as well. The one on the porch was very small and was called a kicksled. The two behind the cabin were trail sleds, much longer and heavier.

Hannah's dad put the green kindling in the big wood-box just outside the door. The box slid from the cold outer porch to the inside of the cabin, right through the wall. The opening was protected by a thick piece of yellow plastic that swung inward, like a doggy door.

When they went inside, Hannah slapped a sodden woodchip-covered glove onto the counter that separated the kitchen area from the rest of the main room and stooped to undo the laces of her boots. From the doorway to the bedroom she shared with her sister came Kelli's voice. "Illegal manoeuvre! Illegal manoeuvre!"

"Calm down, dork," said Hannah. "It's just a glove."

"Unacceptable use of outdoor clothing!" Kelli ran in, snatched the glove off the counter, clambered up a folding stepladder, and placed it neatly on the glove dryer that hung above the big pot-belly wood stove in the centre of the cabin.

"Kelli," said their mother, "calm down. George," she continued, "put some wood in the stove, please."

Hannah's dad took two pieces of maple from the woodbox, opened the belly of the wood stove, and put them in. Kelli's exuberance had woken Sencha and Bogey from their napping spot by the couch, and the two house dogs ran over to greet Hannah and her father as though they had been gone for years. They kept a respectful distance from the hot cast-iron stove.

The two dogs were as opposite as could be. Sencha was a Dalmatian, but she had brown spots instead of black ones, and she shed on everything — pretty little white hairs that somehow corkscrewed into anything that wasn't Teflon-coated. Her ears sat high on her head and she watched everything with bright hazel eyes, investigating every sound or movement, no matter how small, with her gaze or with her nose, depending on how comfortable she was. Hannah's mom called her "Little Jane Austen."

11

Bogey, on the other hand, was square and big and had two coats of thick fur: an oily outer layer of beautiful dark brown, and a dry underlay of rust-coloured kinks that kept him warm even when he jumped into the cold pond to chase tennis balls or ducks, or just because he was a Labrador retriever and needed to remind everyone of that fact.

"Bogey, get down!" said Hannah, pushing him away. The big dog dropped back to the floor, his tail still wagging. Hannah's dad gave him some rough pats on his flanks, and the Lab nearly toppled him over, pressing into his legs like a cat. Sencha went back to her warm bed near the stove, lying down with an assortment of grumbles.

Kelli, still near the gloves, looked suspiciously at the bottoms of her sister's legs. "Are your pants wet? You should go change."

"You should shut up," retorted Hannah. "The floor's already wet from Lab slobber."

"Ha-neul," said her mother from the kitchen, "respect your sister."

Kelli, safely behind the wood stove and out of sight of her mother, stuck her tongue out at Hannah.

"Let's eat!" said her father, pulling out a chair from the kitchen table.

The table was *so* old and *so* ugly: the top was faded pink plastic with a terrible pattern of gold-speckled stars and rough metal edging. The chairs were a horrible flaky silver with plastic seats and no padding. Hannah hated the chairs, the table, and the ruined edges of all her sweaters from sitting at it.

"Set the table, girls," said her mother.

"I've been outside helping with chores!" complained Hannah.

Her mother did not say anything, just kept stirring the large aluminum pot on the ancient propane stove in the kitchen. Kelli slipped from her chair. Sighing, so did Hannah.

Kelli smiled widely, wobbling under the weight of the heavy crockery. She loved it when everyone pitched in and did things together. She put down the stack of dishes and divvied them up, racing around the table to the far side and back again with a single plate each time.

"You're gonna slip and fall," said Hannah.

"Kelli, stop running," scolded their mother. "Hannah, stop needling. George, we need salt and pepper."

Hannah's dad laughed and sprang up. "Probably not pepper, but I'll get them both anyway."

He got them and also grabbed the bread that sat under a tea towel — a sort of cornbread with eggs and bacon baked right into it. He broke the bread into big pieces with one egg in each, and put a piece on each plate. "I'm going to Jeb's tomorrow," he said as he added butter to the top of the egg. "The weather's supposed to turn later this week, so I want to get over there before we're stuck under another four feet of snow — that always makes us want to hibernate, eh, Mina?" He grinned at his wife.

"Maybe you should call first and make sure she's ready for visitors," she said.

Hannah's dad grunted. "Scott's there right now, and it looks like she's getting better, so it should be fine."

Scott and his sister Jeb and Hannah's father had all grown up together in Timmins. When Jeb had decided to sell part of her land and build a new house much farther down the road, Hannah's father had bought it — which was why they were now the proud owners of a shack in the middle of nowhere instead of a real cottage by a lake in Huntsville or Lake of Bays, like everyone else.

"But … we were gonna go to the hardware store! Can't we just go to town instead?" Hannah asked.

"We're not up here to shop," answered her father. "We haven't seen them yet and it's been almost a week. It's time to be neighbourly now that we're settled in."

"This is true," said her mother. She pushed back her long, dark hair with one hand while ladling the stew into the small bowls Kelli had placed on the table.

Hannah wrinkled her nose at the smell. "Is there kimchi in this? Yuck. I'll just have the bread."

"It's homemade kimchi stew," replied her mom.

"Kimchi is good for you," said her father.

"Yeah. Kimchi puts fire in your belly," added Kelli. That was what their mom always said.

Hannah looked at the dull white enamel bowl and its sharp-reddish contents. "I don't want fire in my belly. I want to go to the mall."

"We are not up here to shop," her mother reiterated, sopping up her own stew with the bread.

"We can take out Sencha and Bogey and play in the snow, if you want," said Kelli. "They don't even have American Eagle at that mall, anyway."

Kelli was only nine and didn't know good clothes yet. Hannah told her that.

"Hannah, be respectful," said her mother.

Her father said, "We can go to town Friday to get the snowmobile part, and on the way home we'll stop by the mall, okay?"

"But I'm bored *now*, Dad."

Her parents exchanged a look and then went on eating, ignoring Hannah. The rest of the meal passed in silence.

"You know, Peter will be there," said Hannah's father, pausing to butter one last hunk of bread after the meal was done. Peter was Scott's son. He was older than Hannah by a couple of years and his mother had died some time ago, when Peter was much younger.

"I hate Peter," said Hannah. "He's obnoxious. He doesn't know anything and he acts like he still owns this place."

Her mother rose and began clearing the dishes, nodding to Kelli to help. "He's just different. He was brought up here, Hannah, like your father. They learn different things here."

"He listens to *country music*," said Hannah.

"I like country," said Kelli. She started singing as she took the dishes to the big single sink and placed them on the washing side. "O give me a home, where the buffalo roam, and the deer and the antelope plaaaaay."

"You don't have to come," her father said to Hannah. "I just thought you'd like to see them."

"I don't," said Hannah. If she went she would be forced to call Scott her "uncle" and Jeb her "aunt," even though they weren't really her family. Peter never called *her* mother Aunt Mina. Jeb in particular gave her the creeps, with all her military stuff and the way she looked at Hannah as though she were a total stranger, even though they'd been going over there since she was five years old. She'd used to call her Aunt Jenny, but Jeb's Army nickname (the initials of her full name, Jenny Eliza Barrett) had stuck after she came home.

"You're going, Hannah," said her mom. "Don't be so unfriendly. It'll be good to see Peter, and you need to get outside every day."

Hannah stared at her mother, who was drying the dishes that Kelli was washing. Her mom had diabetes, and she was a freak about making sure she got lots of outdoor exercise. She was even more of a freak about making Hannah and her sister do it.

"Am I done?" asked Kelli. At her mother's nod, Kelli dried her hands and went to the picture window that dominated the living room. She looked out to where the doghouses could just be seen in the deepening shadows of the trees. Afternoon was passing swiftly. By five o'clock it would be fully dark.

"Dad," said Kelli.

"Hmm?" said her father. He was putting his parka on.

"Which is your favourite of all our dogs?"

Her father's moustache tweaked from side to side as he considered. "Nook," he said finally. Nook, like Rudy, was a husky cross — no one knew exactly where they were descended from, except that it was a sledding line. She was the daughter of one of the dogs he had owned before he went to teach in Korea, before he met her mother and they got married.

"I like Bogey," confided Kelli.

"Little Jane Austen is the best," said their mom. Sencha lifted her head and wagged the tip of her tail.

"People aren't supposed to have favourite dogs," said Hannah.

"Okay, enough bellyaching," said her dad. "Let's keep on keeping on."

The rest of the afternoon was spent doing more chores. Hannah dug out their SUV while her dad cleared the long, thin driveway that led back to the long, thin dirt road that led to the long, thin paved road that took them to Timmins. It was an hour to town by car in the middle of summer, an hour and a half in the winter.

After a while, Kelli came out with Bogey. She threw a pink tennis ball into the snow and the big brown Lab plowed after it, breaking a trail for her.

Hannah and her dad untied Nook and Rudy and tied them to the bumper of the SUV so they could work on the doghouses. They nailed a piece of tarpaper over the hole in the roof of Rudy's doghouse and poured cold tar on it — which didn't really pour so much as glop and glump onto the wet shingles.

Nook's doghouse was in worse shape. "Held together with spit and duct tape," said her dad. He looked at the two doghouses. The sides of Nook's kennel were scratched and splintered from her chain rubbing against it and from animals nesting in it during the spring, before they arrived for their summer vacation. "I guess we have our summer cut out for us, kiddo. Time for some new dog-houses." He knelt in the snow and began testing the other parts of the structure.

Now was her chance. Hannah took a deep breath. "Dad?"

"Hmm?"

"I want to go to camp this year."

He looked confused. "We're at camp."

Hannah shook her head. "No, like a *real* camp. Like, with other kids." She had thought about this for three months. She took another deep breath. "There's one called Tabigon, in Temagami. They have leadership courses," she offered, hoping it sounded adult and mature.

Temagami was pretty close to Timmins, only a couple of hours away. It took fourteen hours to get from their house in Toronto to the cabin in Timmins, so compared to that, it was very close. This was the sneaky part of the plan. Hannah's best friend, Lindsay, went to a sports camp, but it was many hours south, in Muskoka. They had their own lake and sailboats and jet skis and three tennis courts, including an inside one. They had boys and horses. They went rock climbing and kayaking. They had everything. *Everything.*

If she could just get them to let her go to any camp, she and Lindsay figured they could get her parents to agree to Lindsay's camp later. First they just had to get them to agree to let her go at all.

"What kind of camp is it?" asked her father.

Hannah tried not to yell with happiness that he hadn't just said no right away. "It's a sports camp. It's good for you," she said. She knew those were magic words. *Good for you* was always better than *fun*. "I looked it up. You get up early and go swimming in the lake and learn to rescue people in canoes." This part would particularly interest her father. He had wanted to show them how to do that himself, but their pond was far too small and shallow. "They teach you how to survive in the bush, too."

"You already know that," he replied quickly.

"But it's different, Dad. It's with other kids. I could … I could maybe help, too."

"Hunh."

"And it's pretty close. I could come here on weekends and stuff. It's only for two weeks. It's good for me. Please?"

"Sounds expensive."

"Dad, I'll give up my allowance *forever* if you let me go. I promise. I'll never ask for anything, and I'll help Kelli with her homework and walk the dogs every day."

Her dad frowned. "Sweetie, you're selling it a bit hard."

She stopped talking and held her breath.

Her dad pushed his toque back and rubbed his forehead. "It's not for a while, so let's keep our minds on the task at hand. Go grab Nook and Rudy." He paused and looked over at the two huskies. They saw him looking and began jumping and barking. "Poor guys. They think we're going out. They just want to work. You know what? Let's take them tomorrow instead of driving to Jeb's. Make a day of it. I'll ski and you can drive the sled. Tomorrow, guys!" he hollered as Hannah trudged over.

The dogs were pretty excited, now that her dad had talked to them. They also knew that whenever they were tied to anything other than their kennels, it meant they were about to run. They jumped and whined, and Hannah knew she'd have to take them over one at a time.

She decided to take Nook first. Nook was a true northern sled dog, with dense, thick fur that stood out all around her face like tinsel on a Christmas tree. Rudy was one of her pups and looked just like her, except his ruff was brown. When Hannah's mom and dad had come back to Canada and decided to move to Toronto, her dad's friend Pierre had offered to keep Nook for them. Pierre had thirty dogs — thirty! — and he competed in races all over North America, so Nook and Rudy stayed with him all year, except when the Williamses were at their camp.

"There's my girl!" said Hannah's dad as they approached. "Get up, Nook, there you go. Tomorrow, I promise." After he'd clipped her collar to the kennel chain again, he ran his hands over her fur and lifted each foot to look closely at the pads. "Still got it after all these years, eh?" he said, and he scritched his fingers through her age-whitened ruff the way she liked.

Nook was a veteran, a dog who had run big races and traplines both. She had trained other dogs to be leaders and rebellious puppies to run in a team. She had once, Hannah's dad said, gone after a black bear that got too friendly with his camping supplies. But she looked just like one of the house dogs as she sat on her haunches and thumped a foot on the ground in happy time to the scratching.

"Check Rudy's front left foot, will you?" Hannah's dad said.

Hannah started to object, then remembered her vow from only a few minutes ago. She went to Rudy and lifted his paw. She studied the heart-shaped pads carefully. One toe had a wide pink crevice running through it. Over that crevice was a sort of clear coating — the special glue that Pierre gave them to seal wounds on the feet to let them heal. Bandages would never work; they always fell off or got torn off by the dogs themselves, then the wounds would get wet and then become infected.

"It looks okay," she said.

"Any pus?"

"No."

If my friends heard this, they'd laugh until they peed themselves, thought Hannah.

George grabbed Rudy's head ruff and playfully wrestled him from side to side. "Stop trying to dig holes, idiot. The ground is frozen!"

Rudy licked his face.

CHAPTER TWO

After the doghouses were patched and an adequate area shovelled clear around them, Hannah and her father went inside to get a cup of hot chocolate. The cabin was empty; Hannah's mom was teaching Kelli how to cross-country ski outside on the deserted road.

"Dogsleds next," said her dad after they had finished their drinks.

They got their coats and boots and hats and mitts back on, took the shovels, and went around the cabin to the back porch, which was really a lean-to with sides, although someone had added a shallow front wall, like stables have. There were many pegs here, and different-size hooks, and they all held dogsledding equipment. Four large pegs held a heavy touring sled that needed many dogs to pull, and a smaller sled sat underneath it on a shelf.

"We'll use the cross backs tomorrow," said her father, after they had pulled out all the dog harnesses and inspected them for tears. The cross back harnesses were for racing and formed a big X across the dog's back. The other harnesses were square and had more padding on them; they were for pulling heavy loads.

Hannah and her dad checked the rigging: the long ganglines that the dogs were attached to, the short necklines, the thick tie-out line, and the tough, webbed snowhook line. The snowhook was used to anchor the sled. It was a heavy claw with two sharp prongs that were curved so that the more the sled moved, the more they dug in. The backs of the prongs were attached by a flat bar, so the driver could step on it and drive it into the snow quickly to stop the sled.

Then they set out a gangline for four dogs — Nook would lead, with Sencha beside her and Bogey and Rudy behind as the wheel dogs.

Hannah listened half-heartedly as her father rambled on and planned their short trip. Jeb had been in the Army proper, but both her father and Scott Purcell were Reservists. They both loved planning things "the Army way," which, as far as Hannah could tell, meant making a list and then adding or subtracting things a hundred times an hour. What to take, how to pack, what to eat, when to leave — endless tasking just to go to a neighbour's house.

The only thing that kept Hannah from freaking out was the fact that her dad hadn't said no to the summer camp idea. So, she dutifully laid out the rigging and helped tighten the loose screws on the frame of the dogsled, and oiled the wood on the handle and put wax on the bottom of the runners so they wouldn't stick to the snow. They also put new black hockey tape on the handle and replaced the bungee cord that held the drag mat and the attached metal brake off the snow. And it was all very boring and she felt herself floating away a little, worrying about what Lindsay was doing, and what she was missing, not being in Toronto.

Nothing ever happened up here; it was just endless days of fixing things and watching her sister get boringly excited about the forest. And more and more often, Hannah would go home and find out she'd missed something — a new person added to or an old one subtracted from their group at school, or a new routine in ballet that she hadn't been there to learn — and she would struggle to keep up, trying to learn everything in secret while making it look like she'd known it all along.

"Grab some ointment and booties, too, Hannah," said her father, so she packed into a bag the ointment and the fleece booties that protected the dogs' paw pads from the cold and the abrasive ice, as well as preventing snow from getting caught between their toes.

When they were done, it was almost dark. They stomped back to the front porch and once again shook off all the snow, then went inside and undressed. It seemed to Hannah that most of winter was about putting on clothing and then taking it off, and being wet in between. At school plays and meetings, when her parents talked to other parents, Hannah heard them say things like, "We like the simplicity of it." But it wasn't simple. There were more stupid things to do up here in one day than in a week in Toronto.

Her mom and sister had returned from their skiing, and as Hannah and her father undressed, the phone rang. Hannah snatched up the receiver. It was a ridiculous phone, a squat square of dull beige plastic, ugly and heavy. It even had a curly cord that attached the handset to the dialing part! And the dialing part was *round*, like one of those Fisher Price toy phones for babies. You had to stick your finger in and twirl it instead of punching buttons. The cord was ancient and duct-taped in several places, and so stretched out that only small lengths of it still retained their original spring-like shape.

"Hello?"

"This is Lieutenant Wagner. I need to speak to Mr. Williams."

"Just a moment, please," said Hannah.

She held up the receiver. "Dad," she said, then placed it on the counter. "It's the Army."

CHAPTER THREE

"Yes, sir … Yes, sir … No, sir, I'm at my family's camp in Timmins … Yes, sir."

Hannah stopped listening closely. She knew there were only two reasons for her father to talk like that: he was being called up, or he was getting a promotion. Either way, it meant he was leaving.

"Okay. Do we have an estimation of time? Yes, sir … No, sir, I'll leave the car for my wife and catch a ride with Corporal Purcell. What are the chances of mobilizing? … No, sir, just getting my family kitted out in case, since we're all up here … Yes, sir. I'll see you at the rendezvous … Thank you, sir."

He put the phone down and immediately picked it up again, speaking as he dialed. "We've been called up. Big storm in Quebec. They thought I was still in Toronto. I guess that damn answering machine isn't working again."

"Are you going?" asked Mina.

Hannah's dad held up a finger and spoke into the phone. "Hey. You get the call? … What? … Well, you could have called me, Homer … Okay. I'll see you in an hour." He hung up.

Mina's eyebrows rose. "You're going tonight?"

"Yep."

"I thought it wasn't that serious."

"It isn't," said George, "but he's going in now, and he's my ride."

"Is it a big storm?" Kelli asked.

"Very big," he answered, going into the bedroom. "There are power outages, and it's not just snow, but ice and freezing rain, too."

"An ice storm!" said Kelli. "I bet it'll be pretty. Like a forest that shines back at you. Pretty! Can I come?" she asked, coming to stand in the doorway to the bedroom.

"No, honey, you can't come. You stay here with Mom and Hannah and have fun, okay? I'll be back."

Hannah watched her mom in the kitchen, where she was wrapping up sandwiches. She stopped wrapping for a moment, and then when she started again, she was a bit slower, like she had to concentrate harder. "How long?" she asked.

"I don't know. Not long, Mina."

"But what about the sledding?" said Kelli.

"You're big now, you don't need to have everyone around when we do things," he said.

Kelli said nothing.

27

It wasn't long before the lights of Scott Purcell's truck winked through the trees down the driveway. Nook and Rudy ignored the vehicle, but the house dogs went wild, barking. When Hannah opened the door, Bogey went bounding out to the truck at full speed, jumping on Scott to lick his face and pressing and twirling against his legs, almost knocking him over. Scott laughed and thumped the Lab's sides, and both dog and human looked very pleased.

You're not that special, thought Hannah from the doorway. *Bogey does that to everyone.*

Before Scott had arrived, Hannah's parents had gone into the bedroom and closed the door. Even without seeing their faces, Hannah knew they were arguing. Her father hated to argue in front of people, hated yelling. He wanted everything calm and talked about reasonably. Hannah had met her mom's family only twice, but each time she had been shocked at the volume of their conversations. They spoke and laughed and cried at the same volume: deafening. Around them, Hannah saw her mom become a different person, argumentative and teasing, and much louder. Normally, she never raised her voice.

Scott came in stamping his feet, but didn't remove his boots, standing on the living room mat and dropping snow all around him. Kelli retreated to the folding stepladder again and stared at him from there, glaring at his feet.

"Hey, Hannah," he said, then, "Let's go, Williams, time's a-wastin'!" He nodded to Hannah's mom. "Hello, Mrs. Williams."

"Hello, Mr. Purcell."

"I've come to take your boy away," he said. He did not look sorry. And when Hannah snuck a look at her father as he came out of the bedroom carrying his duffel bag and coat, neither did he.

It was a quiet night after Hannah's dad left, driving off into the dark. Hannah's mom took her insulin injection and then they ate supper. Afterward, Hannah and Kelli cleaned up while their mother read a book about accounting. She was taking a course at the community college near their house in Toronto. She was tired of her job as a gym teacher at a private school.

The darkness outside was thick, as though it were pressing down on them. Kelli complained that her head hurt.

"It's just the low pressure," said her mom. She said it would be gone by morning.

The next morning Hannah's mom divvied up the chores that their dad usually did. Afterward, Sencha and Bogey came out to play with Kelli, who had strapped on snowshoes and wandered past the yard at the back of the cabin, tromping down the path she had made that went into the Moss Garden. This was a large open space under the tamarack and poplar and birch. In the summer, a thick, spongy moss grew on it, as well as harder, stiff, white crumbly stuff her dad identified as lichen.

Later, they came back inside and played a dice game.

"When's dad coming back?" asked Kelli, whirling the plastic cup that held the dice and dumping it upside down onto the table. "Ooh, a full house, one roll!"

"No one knows yet," replied her mom. "Don't worry, he'll let me know." She turned to Hannah. "Hannah, get the radio out, please."

"Why?"

"Just get it."

Hannah went to the kitchen and fished the radio out from under the counter. Like everything else in the cabin, it was old and ugly, with green metal casing on the sides and broken white plastic on the front. There was one dial to tune the radio — not even digital — and a single speaker. The back had a big space for batteries.

"Turn it on, please," said her mother.

Hannah shrugged, putting the radio on the counter between the phone and the small brown box that held her mom's insulin ampoules — small glass cartridges that fit into a special needle. Her mom had been prepping her lunchtime dose.

The radio crackled as Hannah turned the knob that doubled as both the on/off switch and the volume dial. As the speaker warmed up, the voice of the announcer became clear.

"*This is a CBC Radio One Special Report for north-eastern Ontario: Environment Canada reports that a massive storm system continues to develop in eastern Quebec and is growing larger, dumping extreme amounts of precipitation.*"

"Are we northeastern Ontario?" asked Kelli.

"Yes," said Hannah.

"Pre-cip-i-tation, pre-cip-i-tation," chanted Kelli.

It snowed a little again after lunchtime. The first fat flakes drifted down like friends, landing on their upturned faces as they stood in the front yard.

"I hope we get *lots*," said Kelli. Hannah said nothing, but she was hoping the opposite.

"Well, let's not let the work you did yesterday go to waste," said their mother to Hannah. "Let's go out for a sled ride."

They took the small kicksled out to the end of the driveway with Rudy and Nook and took turns racing up and down the empty road. The snow came and came and came, each piece part of a large wave of white.

"Can you hear that?" asked Kelli as they trooped back. Her face was mostly hidden by her scarf and the snow that clung to it, but the sides of her dark-brown eyes were crinkled, so Hannah knew she was smiling.

"What?" said Hannah.

Her sister spread her arms and twirled, landing on her butt in the snow. "The nothing between the flakes. It's snowing so hard, it's even taking away sound!" Kelli was delighted with the whole spectacle.

Her mom was not as happy. She spoke less and less as the day went on, and when Hannah's dad called again just before dinner, she spoke to him in short, angry sentences. "George, we're fine. Hannah is bored," she said, flicking a quick glance at her daughter. "We went out on the sled. Rudy is getting fat."

Hannah heard a scratchy, tinny sound and realized it was her father laughing. Her mom turned her body so that she was facing away from them, hunching over a little, but when she looked back and saw Hannah watching, she turned around again, straightening up.

"We're fine. Everything's fine. Good. You'd better get back to them, then. I'll see you at home."

She hung up and walked back to the table.

"Is he coming back?" asked Kelli.

"No, they're leaving."

"For Quebec?"

"Yes."

"How long will he be gone?" asked Kelli.

"Kelli," said her mom. Her tone said *stop bothering me*.

"Great," said Hannah. "Are we stuck here until he gets back?" Their vacation was supposed to end that week. It was Monday, and they were meant to leave on Saturday to be back in time for school.

"No. If he's not back, we'll close up and leave," said Mina.

"What about Nook and Rudy?" asked Hannah.

"Pierre will get them, Hannah, like he always does."

"It's not fair that he left us here."

"Hannah, be quiet."

Her mother shutting her up as though she were a child made Hannah even angrier. She went and sat on one of the backless stools that lined the counter, leaning an arm on it and staring out the window at the snow that continued to fall in fat, ugly blobs.

"I'm not coming here anymore after this," she said. "I can stay at home by myself or at Lindsay's. I already asked and she said it would be okay. I hate it here."

"You *will* still be coming here, Hannah. You're not staying in the city by yourself."

"Then I want to go to camp this summer," said Hannah. "I can't stand it here. I want to do what normal kids do."

"Normal kids wish they could do what you do, Hannah."

"No, they don't! They stay in the city and go shopping or to the museum. They go on the subway."

"They're cooped up indoors," answered her mother. "They never see the sun. All they see are strangers."

She was using the same voice with Hannah that she used with Hannah's dad, as though she were being exceptionally polite to spare her feelings, even though Hannah was obviously wrong.

Hannah was never right.

"They have *fun!*" shouted Hannah, sweeping her arm angrily off the counter. Her elbow hooked on the stretched-out phone cord and it shot off the counter; a loop of it was caught around the little brown case of ampoules her mother had taken out for her evening dose. Hannah watched as the case sped across the counter's surface and then crashed to the floor, striking the corner of the indoor woodbox on its way.

"Hannah!" yelled her mom, rushing over and picking up the box. When she lifted it, Hannah saw the corner darken, and then it began to drip as the contents of the ampoules leaked out. Her mom put the box carefully on the counter and sharply told Hannah and Kelli to stay away in case there was broken glass. The box made tinkling sounds as she righted it, like cold change.

CHAPTER FOUR

It stopped snowing just before they went to bed, but the wind rose, bending the laden trees and whipping branches against the cabin. Hannah had stoked the big stove in preparation for the cold night, but the wind brought with it warmer air, and the cabin began to feel uncomfortably damp — close and sticky.

The humidity inside rose, and with it the smell of wet wool, a wet dog scent, and a cloying, heavy feeling. Kelli slept deeply through it all, but Hannah lay awake, listening to the *scree scree scree* of the branches scraping against the walls, watching the low clouds race across the window-pane. As she looked up, the clouds got lower and thicker, and the wind slowed down, but then the snow came again, almost like the wind and the snow were arguing over who was more important.

The morning was hard to discern. All that really changed was that the grey of the clouds and the sky was more noticeable. Hannah pushed the snow away from the end of the driveway. The plow had not been by yet, and there was a neat line where her shovelled path ran parallel to the road. They were usually the very last road to be plowed, because there were only two houses, and then an endless swath of Crown land — land that belonged to the government.

Dimly, Hannah heard the crack of the screen door whacking shut, and a few seconds later two low shapes came hurtling at her: Sencha and Bogey. Trailing after them was her mother.

"There's no use shovelling the thing again, Hannah," she said as she got near. The snow was already puffing over the toes of her thick boots. "I'll call Jeb to come and clean us out once the storm has passed."

Sencha used Hannah and her mom as a bulwark, racing around them in a game of tag with Bogey struggling, mightily and happily, to catch her. In tight turns the Dal tucked her tail like a rabbit and changed directions very quickly, then leaped forward. For one moment she looked like a greyhound, racing low and fast. The next, she went head over tail as the big-boned Lab plowed into her side and they both tumbled through the snow.

"The first time you walked was out here," said Hannah's mom. "In the winter. At home, you'd sit upright and grab the railing, but never walk on your own."

Hannah watched Sencha jump up in mock outrage and pounce on Bogey, who lay on his back, tongue extended and paws waving.

"We were out here for Christmas, and I took you outside and put you in the middle of the driveway near the car, and you walked all the way to the cabin door because you thought we were leaving."

"Mom, do you even like it here?"

Sencha came up, panting and wiggly, and pressed against her mom's legs. Her mother paused, stroking Sencha's ear, pulling the soft flap out over and over.

"Who taught you to snowshoe?" she asked.

"You did," said Hannah.

"Who bought you cross-country skis?"

"That doesn't mean you *like* it here."

"Who went tenting with you in blackfly season so we could catch fireflies while your father," she motioned with her head to the cabin, "moaned about them like a little boy?"

Hannah smiled. "You did."

"I love it here," her mom said, pressing harder on Sencha's skull. "The trees ... so many trees, so much space. No one tells me I can't do something. No one tells me what to do at all."

"Dad does."

"Dad tries."

They started back to the cabin. The snow was getting heavier, falling now thick and wet, not light and fluffy. Hannah thought of the ampoule box skittering across the table and felt her chest constrict. Her mom bent down and picked up two handfuls of snow, then threw them at Bogey, who tried to catch them in his mouth before going back to racing after Sencha.

They got back inside just as the snow began to change to sleet. The sleet turned to a slick, hazy rain for a while, then back to sleet as the afternoon wore on. The trees began to bow under the weight of the accumulated snow and ice, bouncing whenever the wind rose.

Hannah helped Kelli feed the dogs. After struggling out to Nook and Rudy, she came through the door and saw her mother standing by the end of the counter with a wooden spoon in one hand and a boot in the other, as though she were torn between going to the kitchen and going outside. Her face was flattened of emotion. Beside her, the radio was on, an announcer talking.

"What's wrong?" asked Hannah. They had not spoken about Hannah breaking the ampoules since it happened.

"Another storm. Nothing to worry about, Hannah. We have everything we need."

Hannah called her sister in and Kelli and their mom emptied out the wood stove's accumulated ashes. The dogs slept. Kelli put the ashes in a big metal pail and Hannah helped her drag it out to the outer porch. Kelli stood and stared at the sky.

"What kind of clouds?" she asked.

Hannah frowned. "I don't remember. There's more than one, anyway." She pointed at the sky where the clouds looked like iron filings, all piled up and splintery. "I've never seen that kind before."

Kelli pointed at another part of the sky. "Those are snow clouds though, right?"

"Yeah."

"It looks like they're fighting in the sky."

"They're not fighting," said Hannah.

"Everyone else is," said Kelli, still looking up.

"We have to get back to Toronto, Kelli. Mom needs her insulin."

"We'll go on Saturday. She said she has enough. That's what she said."

"She doesn't have enough."

The cabin was prepared, the wood and water secured, candles and lanterns ready. They dug out the car and then Hannah drove it to the end of the driveway to make it easier to get out. Usually being able to drive the car was one of the most fun things she got to do, but today it was just another chore. Already the freezing rain had pushed down the last bit of snow, making the driveway a thin skating rink, and she had to drive very carefully. Above them, the whole sky turned grey, and the sun was a sickly yellow halo through it. Kelli and Hannah stood and watched the sky roil; the downward pressure of the incoming weather and the ugly clouds made Hannah uneasy. They went back inside. Their mother was washing her face at the sink, patting under her eyes to dry them.

"Mom, are you okay?" asked Kelli, hanging up her mittens and grabbing two graham crackers from the big cracked cookie jar by the stove. Cookies were allowed after each chore was completed. The radio announcer continued to talk in the background.

"I'm fine. The phone is down."

"Well, we still have lights," said Hannah.

"They're sending the Reservists back," her mom said. "I just heard."

"Why? They don't need them?"

Mina ran her index and middle fingers under her eyes. "No. The storm has moved."

"To where?"

"To here, Hannah. It's here."

CHAPTER FIVE

"We should go into town," said Hannah. "That's what we should do, Mom. We can get more insulin …"

"We don't need to go anywhere," her mom replied. "They haven't plowed the road. We're safer here."

"How about Jeb's place? We could go there. They have a satellite phone."

"Listen to the wind!" said Kelli.

Hannah heard the wind and then the fierce, driving sound of rain on the roof, so loud that sometimes she couldn't hear the rattle of the dice on the table. The broken pieces of the insulin ampoules rested in a chipped coffee mug behind the sink, up against the wall — not a single one had survived Hannah's mistake. Every now and then Hannah heard a faint clinking sound from it when the wind whipped up especially high and the walls groaned inward under its force.

"We're not going anywhere. We'll leave on Saturday," their mom said. "Kelli, it's your turn."

They slept in the next morning. Hannah got up first and went into the tiny bathroom and clicked on the light. Nothing happened. She clicked the switch again. Tipping her head out and looking at the ancient VCR under the equally ancient TV, she saw that the digital clock on the front of it was dark. *Great*, she thought.

"Mom," she called. "Power's out."

Her mom came out of her bedroom, tying a thick housecoat around herself. She joined Hannah at the living room window and they stood and looked out in silence.

It really was an ice forest. The trees were smothered by a thick coat of ice, their limbs bent down under the incredible weight. The driveway was littered with smaller branches sticking up, and Hannah could see all the paths they had dug out so carefully yesterday were covered in a thick sheet of ice.

"It's gross out there," said Hannah.

The sentence was barely out her mouth when she saw the first snowflakes begin to fall.

"We'll start with breakfast," said Mina. "You get a trail to the outhouse."

Hannah grabbed the metal pail of wood ashes that was sitting in the covered porch and wrestled the outer door open. It had frozen shut at the bottom, so she banged and kicked at it until it cracked open, laying down ashes right away so she didn't slip on the icy surface of the path. The air still felt heavy and thick. It felt ... wrong to Hannah, somehow. Usually winter air was dry and harsh on the lungs; this morning it was lumpy, almost, coating her throat with moisture as though it were still raining.

She came back into the cabin and stamped her boots by reflex, even though there was no snow on them. Kelli came out, sleepy and grumpy, and headed for the bathroom.

"You have to use the outhouse," said her mom, pointing at Kelli's oversize rubber boots.

Kelli circled the wood stove, looking first at her mom, then at Hannah. Hannah shook her head very slightly.

"Okay," said Kelli. "Are we having pancakes?"

"Yes, dear, we need lots of energy today," said her mom.

"I can warm the syrup," offered Kelli.

"All right."

They kept the radio on during breakfast. Their mom stopped chewing at the beginning of each new sentence the announcer started, as though she were concentrating very hard.

"*This is a CBC Radio One weather update: The massive storm in western Quebec that moved over into northeastern Ontario overnight is still present and active, as a cold front has stalled the storm over the region, dumping an extreme amount of freezing rain, hail, and snow, knocking out power and closing roads. Emergency responders are being pulled from Quebec to follow in the storm's devastating wake. Sudbury, Algoma, North Bay, and Nipissing have all declared a state of emergency.*"

"You're on dishes," said Hannah to her sister. "I did the path."

Hannah watched as her mom poured another cup of coffee and added a little sugar, stirring quickly. "I'll do the dishes," she said, "and you two go make sure everything's okay."

They got dressed and went out into the icy morning, Hannah balancing a heavy, thick porcelain carafe full of hot water. Kelli spread ashes as they went, first to the outhouse again, then to the well, where Hannah carefully poured some of the hot water over the pump handle to unfreeze it. They turned to see their mom coming out of the cabin with two empty water pails.

"I can get that," said Hannah, but her mom waved her off with a short chop of her arm and muscled past them.

"Dogs," she said shortly, heading for the pond. Whenever the power was out, they took water from the pond for washing.

Kelli and Hannah went to the doghouses, and Hannah poured hot water on top of the frozen water bowls, watching as the ice broke up and became drinkable. "Moss Garden next!" said Kelli as Hannah poured hot water into Rudy's bowl.

"Kelli, shut up, okay? There are more important things to do than go see your stupid fort."

"Mom!" yelled Kelli, "Hannah's being mean to me!"

"Hannah, for heaven's sake, stop acting like a child."

"You're such a *wuss*," said Hannah to her sister. She took her glove off to break up the chunks of ice in the bowl and poured more hot water in.

"No, you have to be respectful."

"Whatever."

"Mom, we can go to the Moss Garden, right?" called Kelli.

"Hannah —" said their mom.

"Mom, I'm not saying anything!"

"Help … once you're done the doghouses," her mother finished.

Her mom's voice sounded weird. When Hannah looked up, she saw that her mother was down on one knee, and one of the pails she was carrying had spilled across the unbroken snow, the water mingling with the thick coat of ice, making an ugly blue channel in the snow. Hannah had never seen so much ice in her life before. It was everywhere, glittering and angry: it hampered all movement and made it three times as hard to lift her foot out of the snow and place it down again. She finally ended up half crawling, half wading through the snow, using her gloved hands to break through the ice and pull herself forward toward her mother. The ice bit into the backs of her hands where the gloves came away from her cuffs.

"Mom! *Mom!*"

"I'm okay, Hannah."

Just breathe, just breathe, Hannah repeated to herself. She reached the pond path and scrambled over to kneel in front of her mother.

"Mom!"

Her mother looked up.

"I'm fine, I just … the path is slippery." Her mom struggled to her feet again. "I have to go refill this now. I want Kelli and you to bathe tonight. It's not good to be dirty out here."

"I'll get it," offered Hannah.

"Have you done the doghouses?"

"No, but I can do —"

"Your job is yours; my job is mine, Hannah. See to the dogs." Her mother stood up, grasped the pails again, and started back toward the cabin.

"But —"

"I'm not asking. Go."

Hannah watched her mother walk away and a picture of the broken ampoules arose unbidden in her brain. She thought again of how she had hooked the cord to the stupid, *stupid* rotary phone that wasn't even working since the telephone line had gone down, too — and there was no cell service in this stupid, *stupid* place, either — and she thought about her mother, who was now out of insulin, because they were trapped with no way to get to town.

And no one could get to them, either.

From his kennel, Rudy whined, eager to work, eager to run. Hannah walked over to him, and with each step the feeling of *doing something*, anything, became stronger. She thought of the dogsleds at the back, ready to go. Rudy quieted under her hand as Hannah stroked his ear, pressing against her legs. Both of them were quivering.

"All right," said Hannah. "We'll fix this mess. We're leaving tonight."

CHAPTER SIX

The snow continued to fall in great white sheets. Hannah's first thought was that she would go to town. But Timmins was far away, too far for a trip that wouldn't get her into trouble. But what else could she do? She needed to get to a phone or a person with a snowmobile.

That meant Jeb's place. Jeb was the closest — scratch that, the *only* other — person nearby, and even she was a long way away, five clicks down the road by car, probably twice that on the twisty back trails. So she would take the dogsled to Jeb's, and then Jeb would take her to Timmins on the snowmobile to get more insulin.

She would be a hero.

"I'm a fairy," Kelli said, coming into the living area that made up most of the front of the cabin. She was bulky and tottering, wearing at least four layers of clothing. "I'm metamorphosing, like a cocoon. Soon I'll be a real fairy! Then I can fly away to get Dad and bring him back!" She unpeeled a layer and dumped it on the floor.

JO STORM

"Kelli, don't just leave that there, put it away," said their mom from where she was standing at the kitchen window. She was pulling the hand crank on an emergency radio, *even though it's probably fully charged*, thought Hannah.

That was her mom, over-prepared. Hannah tried to see if there were any telltale signs of low blood sugar setting in — shaky hands, or being hyper. After her mom had first started insulin, she had taken too much by accident and had a severe episode of low blood sugar. Hannah had been very young, only about eight, but she remembered how scared she had been, how her mother had seemed both there and not there. How the doctor had spoken to her father only — ignoring Hannah completely — using terrible words like *seizure* and *coma*, and making Hannah cry right there in the hospital in front of everyone.

"I'll do it," responded Hannah quickly. She scooped up the thermal sweater that her sister had dropped and carried it to their bedroom. She stuffed it into her own packsack that was stowed over her bed. Their room was like an airplane cabin, or like the train cabin they had been in once when they travelled from Toronto to Timmins in a sleeping compartment: thin and long, with dark plywood on the walls, and all the cupboards had latches and were raised off the ground.

She heard the faint static of CBC Radio coming from the living room and hurried back out. If she was going to leave, she reasoned, she'd better know what the weather was going to be.

"*Accumulations of twenty-six inches or sixty-six centimetres of snow and ice buildup have been reported in*

48

the last twenty-four hours. Hydro One says it may take up to three weeks to restore power in some areas. Most roads in the Cochrane District are closed, including Highway 11. Both the premier and the prime minister have officially declared the region a disaster area. Stay tuned for more updates."

Kelli still thought it was all a game. She wanted to have points for being the best prepared, and the person with the most points won a prize.

"Should we check the emergency kit?" she asked. It had everything four people would need for three days, all in one bag that was only a little larger than a school bag. It was on Hannah's list of things to get.

"We checked it when we got here," Hannah said quickly. If they dragged it out in the open now, she'd never be able to get it into her packsack without one of them noticing.

"But maybe mice got into it!" said Kelli. "Oooh, or maybe a ... maybe a wolverine!"

Hannah made a disgusted sound.

"We have lots of food and water and wood," said their mother. "We could probably stay here until spring and be fine, especially since your father isn't around to eat us out of house and home."

She was saying things in the joking way she had when she was worried. Kelli hadn't noticed it yet, but Hannah had. Her mom would make things very fun and easy for them to keep their eyes away from real problems. She also wanted to keep everyone busy, so she took Kelli outside to dig out around the woodpile while Hannah cleaned the breakfast dishes and heated water on the wood stove in a big cauldron. As soon as they had gone, Hannah went into the living room and took out a toque and three pairs of gloves from the big communal glove box.

There were at least a dozen pairs to choose from. She chose quickly but carefully. The big difference between mittens and gloves was that mittens housed your fingers together, which was good for keeping your hands warm. When she went ice fishing, she wore mittens. When she went cross-country skiing, she wore gloves. When they had gone winter camping for her mom's birthday, she had worn mitts, even to bed. When she told that story back home, her friends laughed, Brittany especially. Brittany didn't care about the difference between gloves and mitts; she didn't wear either, not even on very cold days. It made getting change for the bus too hard, and it was impossible to use your phone.

Next was the emergency kit. It was on top of the closet in her parents' room. It had a first-aid kit, emergency blankets, and two flashlights, among other things. Then she opened the side of the dresser that her dad kept his things in and took two pairs of warm socks and the extra utility knife that he kept there. Along with a locking blade, it had a detachable hook, little screwdrivers, even a saw. She unzipped the emergency bag and threw in the knife and the socks as she left the room.

She was walking back into her own room when she saw the two dark blobs of Sencha and Bogey, then Kelli and her mother looming through the living room window, scaring her so much she almost dropped the emergency kit, still half-open. They came in the porch area and stamped their feet to get rid of the snow. The dogs padded around them, waiting for the front door to open. Hannah quickly tossed the emergency kit under her bed, closed her own packsack and stuffed that under the bed as well. She started lacing up her boots as the other two unlaced theirs.

"What are you doing?" asked Kelli.

"I'll go clear off the tack room," she volunteered.

Her mom looked surprised. "You will?"

She nodded. "In case it snows again. It's piling up a lot. I know we were going to put Rudy and Nook inside because of the storm, but I was thinking we could put them in there instead? I think they would be more comfortable."

"That's a good idea, Hannah. Very well."

Hannah got her coat and boots and hat and mitts on, took the shovel, and went around the cabin to the back porch. She shovelled out the bottom of the tack room and untied one edge of the thick oiled burlap that covered the sled she would take. The sled was almost three times as long as Hannah was, but most of that was the long runners that extended for the length of a ski behind the square, open area called the basket. The front of the runners curved up, also like a pair of skis, but they connected at the front, forming a bow that pushed past brush and over snowbanks. The brushbow had a hitch on it called a bridle, which was used to attach the sled to the gangline, the main line that the dogs were attached to. In the basket of the sled was a sealed container full of the dog food they used when sledding — a special mixture of meat and vegetables that Hannah's father cooked in Toronto, froze in brick shapes, and wrapped up airtight.

Hannah took out the line she would need and hooked it to the brushbow, ready to be hooked to the dogs. She placed an extra gangline in the basket, and two harnesses, and finally, a snowhook. She was so busy that she didn't notice Kelli until her sister spoke.

"We're going to the Moss Garden!" said Kelli from below.

"Crap! You scared me to death!"

"Why?" said her sister, leaning into the doorway. "What are you doing?"

Hannah debated telling her sister what she was planning, maybe even asking her to go along. The knowledge of her adventure burned in her, and she wanted to share it with someone so they could get as excited as she was. But Kelli would never be able to keep the secret, so Hannah couldn't tell her, and her sister was too young to go on an adventure like this, even if it was only for a day. "Nothing," Hannah said. "Where's mom?"

"Getting her boots on."

Hannah heard the crunch of snow as her mom stepped outside. She was wearing snowshoes and carrying Kelli's, which she handed to her.

"Okay," she said to Kelli. "Let's see what we can find today."

Hannah waited until they had become blurs in the forest before hurrying inside to grab both her clothing bag and the emergency bag. On her way out of the cabin, she opened the small cupboard over the stove and grabbed a handful of energy bars, too, stuffing them into the clothing bag, and finally, a closed tin of leftovers that sat in the back of the propane fridge: leftover spaghetti.

She placed the bags in the cavity inside the sled, a small three-by-three-foot space with slats at the bottom instead of a solid seat so it would weigh less. Finally, she put in a camp stove and canisters of fuel, placing them in their own small canvas bag at the top of the emergency bag. She covered the sled with burlap and then stood in front of it, looking for any suspicious bumps that might give away her plan — but there were none. She slapped her hands together the way her mom did after a hard day's work. She was ready to go and had everything she needed. She would be back and a hero before anyone even knew it. There was no way she could get into trouble.

Dinner was silent and quick. While Kelli and their mom were doing the dishes, Hannah grabbed the back-roads map and wrote the number of the pharmacy in Timmins on it. Everyone went to bed early.

Hannah waited in the dark that night after dinner until the cabin grew quiet with the sound of sleep and snow. She had volunteered to take the dogs out last thing and check on Nook and Rudy in the kennels. It gave her a chance to put collars on everyone, pull the sled off its hooks, and do a last check of the two big packsacks — the blue clothing bag and the black supply bag. The snow was falling thick and fast. On any other night she might have stopped to enjoy it, but tonight it was merely something she had to see through.

As she lay in the bed waiting for everyone to fall asleep, she went through a mental list of her equipment: the dogsled gear, her clothing, the first-aid kit, the knife, the camp stove and its fuel. She had everything she could possibly need.

Leaving the cabin was the easiest part. She crept to the door with her boots in hand, mitts and hat tucked in them already. Sencha, always curious, followed her, and Hannah opened the door and scooted the Dalmatian out, hoping she wouldn't start whining before Hannah was outside, too. Bogey quietly followed her, his Labrador instinct to stick with the group kicking in. Hannah tucked her long underwear into her boots and slipped a folded note on the counter right beside the radio, where one of them was sure to see it. It said simply, "Back with a snowmobile soon." She wanted it to be mysterious, although only Jeb's place was close enough to get to in a short amount of time, so they'd be able to guess where she'd gone.

The only problem would be noise: as soon as the sled dogs saw a sled, they'd get tremendously excited, barking and jumping. Heart in throat, Hannah approached Nook and laid her hand across the old dog's muzzle. "Quiet, now," she commanded, then led Nook to the perimeter of the clearing, tying her off to a tree near the buried car. Then she went back and did the same with Rudy. Leaving the two dogs tied and the other two roaming, she crept to the back of the cabin and grabbed the sled, looping the gangline across her shoulders and pulling it as silently as she could across the clearing to where Nook and Rudy waited. The thick snow, still falling like a heavy sweater over everything, muffled most of the noise.

Hannah was surprised to find that neither Nook nor Rudy began barking when they saw the sled. Perhaps they were thrown by the odd sequence of events, as they were in the dark and not wearing their harnesses.

This part she had planned carefully while lying in bed. She did not put on the harnesses, but merely transferred the sled dogs' leashes to the gangline so they would not run away. Then they all started out toward the road, Hannah balancing being pulled by the dogs with pulling the sled in a slow, measured way.

The driveway was buried in new snow up to her knees, and when they reached the road, Hannah was shocked at how the shape of it had almost totally disappeared; only a thin, treeless ribbon of white stretching out gave any indication that people travelled here. It looked like no one had been there in years, though it had only been a day.

At the end of the driveway, she stopped and set the brake by pressing it firmly into the packed snow and jumping up and down on it to make sure it would hold tight. As she sorted through the equipment, she ran through the sequence in her head. Nook and Rudy were her lead dogs; they would stand at the front of the line, before the wheel dogs, Sencha and Bogey. All four would be connected to the gangline, which ran straight from the middle of the front of the sled to the lead dogs. Each dog would be connected to the gangline by a tugline that ran from their harness to a clip on the main line. While Sencha and Bogey would also sport a neckline that attached each of their collars to the gangline, the lead dogs were attached to one another by a neckline that ran between the two dogs.

Hannah took a deep breath and laid out the gangline, put the harnesses on Nook and Rudy, and hooked them on. They stood still, used to it, but Bogey and Sencha were another matter. She got Bogey's harness on, but it took a little while, as he didn't know as well as the other dogs what to do. Finally, he was on the gangline. Then Hannah approached Sencha. The Dal slipped sideways, sensing the excitement that Hannah had been trying to keep down inside herself. The other dogs caught it as well, and Rudy began pacing — two steps left, whine, two steps right — tugging the gangline and the other dogs.

Hannah refused to be thwarted this close to the beginning of the trip, so she abandoned her effort to get Sencha into the harness, tossed it into the basket, and moved to the head of the sled. Sencha dodged in and out of the line, trying to get Bogey to play with her until Hannah's *go away* motions made her scamper off to a snowbank.

"Line out!" Hannah whispered, and Nook and Rudy pulled to the end of the gangline, lifting it out of the snow so that it was taut, the sled and the dogs held by the brake digging into the snow. Bogey was pulled haphazardly into place by their movements. He and Sencha had pulled the sled several times before, but this was the first time they'd gotten out to the cabin this winter, and he wasn't sure. He stood and half turned toward Hannah, his thick tongue hanging out of his mouth the way it did when he was thinking. Hannah pulled the snowhook out from the snow, stored it back on the sled, and then they started out, pulling slowly across the snow in the wan moonlight. Sencha's spots were a bobbing beacon in front of them as she raced ahead down the road, queen of their rebellion.

CHAPTER SEVEN

Hannah guessed that she would get to Jeb's cabin by mid-morning, lunch at the latest. She followed the thin ribbon of the empty back road until just past a tiny crooked bridge that was bookended by big, bulky shelves of snow with no trees. The rocky mantle of the Canadian Shield lay under everything like shin guards under socks; once the thin layer of soil had been scraped off, it shone hard and unyielding, no matter what the light was. The bush on either side had been trimmed back by surveyors who had come recently to see if there was any reason to mine the land, but still Hannah and the dogs had to skirt around downed trees across the road, thick with ice and leaving ugly, jagged stumps like broken fingernails at the forest edge.

Hannah stopped the team where the path was intersected by another, even thinner trail across the road — the bush trail for snowmobiles and ATVs. All the trails this far from Timmins had been made by locals, trappers and teenage boys who used them as a way to get into Timmins to get to work or the grocery store or the bar.

It was still dark. Hannah looked at her watch: 4:30 a.m. It would be several hours yet until her mother and sister found her note. She was tired, unused to being awake at this hour. It made her body feel odd, like it was floating. The snow fell on everything, so thick and heavy that it obscured the trail only a little past where the brush had been trimmed back. Hannah stood at the end of the bridge for a minute, allowing the last pieces of nervousness to wiggle around in her mind before gathering up Sencha's harness from the basket.

"Sennnnncha!" she called.

The Dal approached, head down and tail wagging furiously. Sencha was always torn between being in the centre of things with the other dogs and doing her own thing. Hannah started putting her harness on, getting her front paws through easily, but having difficulty stretching the long X down the length of her spine, as Sencha was a serious wiggler. Finally, she got it on. The Dalmatian pulled away and twirled, trying to see what was weighted on her back, then sat in the snow to see if she could pull or scratch it off with her hind foot.

Hannah knew that of all the dogs, Sencha would be the most trouble. She had the least experience as she had only been on a gangline once, last year, and though she loved running, she had only run while pulling once.

Hannah rearranged her team, leaving Nook at the front and putting Sencha beside her, then placing Rudy behind Sencha as the wheel dog, with Bogey's rough brown flanks and lolling tongue beside him. Rudy was like a larger version of Nook. He looked lean and lanky, but his chest was very long and tucked up sharply into a tapered belly and waist. His rounded breastbone reminded Hannah of an ice cream scoop.

Rudy lived for one thing: running. He would run all day, lie down, and get up and do it again, every day of the year. He and Nook still worked part-time on Pierre's sled. Pierre was a trapper, and he used the sled to get to places that a snowmobile couldn't — or to get there without a lot of noise — in Temagami. Her dad called Rudy and Nook "soft southern dogs," as a joke, because Temagami was south of Timmins, even though it was still far to the north of Toronto.

Rudy and Bogey would pull most of the weight, and Nook and Sencha would ensure the sled kept moving at the right pace, making the wheel dogs' job easier. Hannah was pretty sure that Nook would quickly show Sencha the ropes, but for now, Sencha would not be hooked to the gangline. She would run along beside with her harness on, learning; this was what the old mushers did with puppies or new dogs to get them used to one new thing at a time.

Hannah walked back and stepped onto the back of sled, on the long wooden runners that had a plastic strip screwed to them to give her boots something to grip. She called out the quiet "Hup!" that signalled the dogs to get ready. She had not run a dogsled by herself for a while. The last time had been a short race for kids when she was nine, five kilometres around a big snowbank, down a hill, and across a snowy beach to the finish line.

Nook and Rudy faced the trail, tails and heads low: a work pose. Bogey was looking back at her and Sencha was off on the other side of the road, sniffing at clumps of snow.

"Get up!" Hannah called, and Nook and Rudy pulled. Bogey, caught in the traces, stumbled and began to run, still looking over his shoulder at Hannah.

"Let's go, Bogey, good boy, let's go!" she called. But Bogey continued to look over his shoulder at her, and the line began to slacken on one side. Nook slowed down without looking back — *waiting for whichever dog is being bad to figure it out,* Hannah thought — but that made Bogey slow down even more.

"Come on, you stupid dog, get up!" Hannah half shouted, half whispered. But Bogey slowed down even more, convinced he was doing something wrong, since no one ever yelled unless he had done something wrong. The sled creaked to a stop.

"Stupid dogs!" Hannah hissed under her breath. It made her even angrier not being able to yell in case they heard it back at the cabin. But Bogey had never pulled a sled for long, and he did not take well to new things. In his mind, she imagined, he had just pulled for a long time and now he was done: perfectly acceptable behaviour.

She couldn't fail before even getting off the road. She just couldn't. She couldn't turn around and take the dogs back, either, because then everyone would wake up and she wouldn't be a hero, and they would still be trapped there, and her mother would still be in danger. She needed to get to Jeb's place and use that satellite phone or get Jeb to drive her into Timmins, by snowmobile if necessary, to get more insulin. Her mother's life depended on her being able to make Bogey run, on her making it off the road to Jeb, Peter, and that phone.

Hannah looked at her team. The two sled dogs had lain down, facing the trail, waiting. Bogey stood awkwardly, still staring at her with his anxious brown eyes, blinking away any snow that fell on them. She was hot under her layers — too many layers for the exertion of hauling dogs and a sled around. She unzipped the top of her coat, pulled off her toque, and let the winter air calm her for a moment.

Maybe she could run with only Nook and Rudy and leave Bogey off the line, too. Seasoned sled dogs could carry about twice their weight. With two dogs, she could carry about 220 pounds, she guessed. Hannah weighed 100 pounds, but she had no idea how much the gear weighed. She lifted the two packs again, considering. Maybe 30 pounds? They were hard to lift, and she wouldn't have been able to hike with them for very long by herself. There was a third lump, as well: the dog food that she had forgotten to split up. She had far, far more dog food than she needed, more than a week's worth. But she didn't want to dump it off the sled. She would get in trouble for wasting the food, and it could attract other animals, like foxes or even lynx, and they could cause trouble if they decided the cabin was an easy source of food — especially the foxes.

It didn't matter how much food she left, anyway, if she never got going. In the back of her mind, like an itch, a piece of her kept urging herself to *get going, get going*, to *do* something instead of standing around figuring out how much dog food weighed.

So she walked forward and unsnapped Bogey's neckline and tugline from the long, loose gangline and let him run free. The big Lab licked her mittens enthusiastically whenever she came near his face.

She took her snowshoes out of the basket and put them on, tugged her toque back onto her head, then tromped to the front of the sled.

"Okay, let's go," she said.

The green shoulders of the pines leaned down heavily across the little trail. Only the faint outline of old snowmobile tracks and the thick layer of accumulated ice underneath made them able to walk on the snow. Soon Hannah had taken off her toque again and unzipped the throat of her winter jacket. Closer to Timmins, the trails were very wide and even had signs like a real road, but here you had to already know where you were before you could get anywhere.

They walked for a while until Hannah's watch chimed the getting-up time of 7:00 a.m. Usually she left her watch on the small night table between her and Kelli's beds, and she would grab it and try to turn it off in a blurry haze, but this morning she turned it off as soon as it started to ring.

Hunger came then, almost knocking her down like a big dog greeting her after a long time away. Hannah had never felt hunger like this before. It did not wait quietly, but roared through her, leaving her gasping. All the walking, the excitement of being awake so early, and the hauling and tugging had left a hole where her stomach should be. In the lull of that roar of hunger, she felt almost giddy.

Then there were the dogs. The house dogs were used to eating twice a day, the sled dogs once, but Hannah thought everyone should get fed right now since they were working so hard. First herself, though. Hannah guessed she was about halfway to Jeb's cabin. It wasn't the best time, but the trail was thickly overlaid with snow, and she hadn't figured on Sencha and Bogey not pulling. Still, it was an adventure, and an adventure outdoors, with no parents; she wanted to have fun, too.

She walked back, set the snowhook, and dug out the camp stove from the pack. The heating element sat inside its own pot. Then she grabbed one of the fuel canisters and set the whole kit between the runners at the back of the sled so they wouldn't get knocked over by the untethered house dogs. Nook and Rudy, still in the traces, lay down, their front paws parallel and pointing forward. They were used to stopping, but Bogey and Sencha buzzed around, sniffing the sled dogs and the camp stove and the stumps and the jutting-up branch on the side of the trail and the frozen pieces of moss that hung from the tamarack. Sencha went over to sniff Nook, but the lead dog lifted her head until it was level with the Dalmatian's shoulder and silently lifted one side of her muzzle, showing a yellow canine tooth. Sencha wagged her tail rapidly and went away. She didn't bother Nook again.

Hannah cleared a patch in the snow and then dug down until she had a squared-off hollow. She screwed a canister to the bottom of the stove, placed it in the hollow — it was a backcountry stove, just a nozzle and a knob to turn the heat up or down, a heat shield, and three prongs that served as the "stovetop" — and lit it with the waterproof lighter that was in the stove pack. She filled the small pot with snow and set it on the stove, waiting for it to boil.

The waiting was the hardest. The heat from the stove woke her stomach again and it grumbled and clenched. She grabbed one of the protein bars she had taken at the last minute and opened it, but it had spent the last few hours sitting outside in the cold and was hard as a rock. She couldn't break off any pieces of it. She rewrapped the bar and placed it in an inside pocket, where it would warm up from her body heat. The snow in the pot wasn't melting. Then she remembered the silver heat guard that was supposed to sit underneath and around the stove, dug it out, and placed it correctly.

Finally, the snow melted and began to steam. Hannah pulled one of the thick grey packets from the emergency kit and, using her teeth, ripped it open slightly. Some of the background rations could be boiled in a pot with water, but some were designed to be boiled right in their container bag. One summer, while camping in the back-yard, she had spilled a freshly boiled bag on herself trying to tear it open. Only her T-shirt had saved her stomach from being scalded, and from then on, she had opened the package a little bit before heating it; better to sit by the pot and make sure the bag didn't slip underwater than worry about burning herself with food.

The front of the package said "Country Ham 'N' Eggz" in greasy blue lettering. The inside revealed a sort of crumbly yellow snow with dots of pink in it. It was barely warm, but Hannah ate it, anyway. The dehydrated ham pieces were still crunchy, but it was the best-tasting meal she'd had since she and her family had come to Timmins — better than spaghetti and meatballs, better than fresh bread.

After she was finished, Hannah took out the two collapsible bowls for the dogs and got out one of the portions of dog food. It was slightly sticky with the molasses that her dad put in to keep it from freezing fully. She broke off chunks of it with a small stick. She approached Nook first and put the two bowls in front of her, one with food and one with water, but the lead dog would not eat. She took a few mouthfuls of water, sniffed at the food bowl, then went back to looking up the trail.

"Come on, Nook, it's going to be a long day," said Hannah, but Nook laid her head on her paws and merely looked at her. Hannah added some hot water to the empty grey pouch of her breakfast and swirled it around, then added it to the dog food, and Nook was more interested. She sniffed the bowl and took a small mouthful, but when she raised her head all the pieces dropped out again.

"Fine," said Hannah, "whatever." She took the bowl and offered it to Rudy, but the same thing happened. The big husky looked almost confused, sniffing the bowl and then looking at her. He didn't eat anything, either.

Bogey and Sencha had no reservations. Bogey, sitting nearby, had loops of drool hanging out of his mouth, and as soon as Hannah offered the bowl to them, he gulped down the food, then licked the discarded pouch clean, standing on one edge of it to keep it from moving until Hannah took it away. Sencha's brown and white flanks heaved up and down as she ate from the bowl, her head bobbing in enthusiastic counterpoint.

After the dogs had eaten, Hannah packed up her camp. All told, she was pretty proud of herself. The dogs were fed — *the smart ones, anyway*, she thought — and they were ready to go to Jeb's now. From Jeb's: the phone call, then the snowmobile and the rescue. She wondered what her mom would tell her dad. Would she say that Hannah had been right and she wrong, about going for help? *Because she should*, Hannah thought as she packed the stove back into the pot. Her mom was wrong, her parents were always wrong, but they never admitted it.

The sky was still an ugly, flat grey. There was no wind, and the air lay heavy around them. Sounds carried very far, each one magnified. A tree branch groaning under the weight of ice sounded as if it were right behind her, and the angry chittering of a squirrel deep in the forest seemed directed right at her.

This time she called Sencha first. The Dal came over and Hannah took her collar before delving into the sled to find her harness. There was no arguing this time. Hannah knew she had to get the harness on and keep it on, or else Sencha would always think that wearing it was an option.

The harness slipped over Sencha's smooth, square head and easily onto her back. Hannah lifted each front leg firmly and pulled the harness on. Sencha's harness was royal blue, Bogey's purple. The two sled dogs had on their usual red harnesses that they worked in, though Hannah could barely see them through the thick ruff and double coat of the huskies.

She put Sencha next to Nook, who ignored both of them. Sencha moved a little closer after Hannah got her neckline on and Nook backed away, looking off to the side.

Next, Hannah put Bogey's harness back on and hooked him up, as well. He seemed, if not eager, at least happy to be with the gang. With all the dogs hooked up, Hannah hoped he would remember what to do and settle in. If not, it was going to be a long walk to Jeb's house. She felt a small queasy turn in her gut at that thought.

"Line out," she called. Nook and Rudy stood and drew the line out until it was off the ground. Bogey stood where he was a foot or so back, and Sencha moved out sideways, looking back over her shoulder at Hannah. It was ugly, but it was good enough to get them where they needed to go. She pulled up the snowhook.

"Hup*hup!*" she called out, using two different tones of voice, like other mushers did. It was like saying, "Ready, set, go!" only using the same word. Nook and Rudy began to run, then Bogey, and finally Sencha — half being dragged, half rabbiting off to the side, her tail curved up and her head high. The gangline seesawed a bit as Sencha fought the straight line and tried to go sideways, but Nook put her head down and the two lead dogs' necklines stretched taut as they argued about which way to go. Hannah could see the gangline being pulled into a wide Z as the sled dogs silently tried to get the errant Dalmatian to pull correctly.

After a few metres, Nook pulled suddenly toward Sencha. The Dalmatian, no longer being held on the trail, plowed off into the deep snow for a few strides and struggled to get back onto the trail. The sled slowed down, then bumped into the back of the wheel dogs. Sencha gained the trail again and swerved into the middle of it — where she met the shoulder of Nook, who bumped her *hard*, as if to say, *Smarten up!*

"Let's go, Nook, get up! Get up, Sencha, let's go!" called Hannah. The Dalmatian ignored her and tried to bump Nook back, but Nook moved at the very last second and Sencha swiped into thin air, stumbling again.

And so it went for a few minutes, with Sencha trying to get the upper hand and Nook explaining in plain actions that no, that was not the way to behave. When Sencha bumped Nook, the husky either ignored her or pushed her off course enough to make her flounder. Finally Sencha tripped up and fell, dragging in the traces for a few heartbeats. Just as Hannah's foot began to press on the brake, the plucky Dal gained traction and began running again. For a while she ran very close to Nook, and Hannah could see them trading shoulder rubs in quick succession. But each time there was contact, the Dal's tail went lower and lower, until finally she spread out about a hand's width away from Nook, put her head down, and ran.

"Get up, Nook, good girl, good girl!" sang Hannah. The lead dog looked back for a second without breaking stride, and Hannah could have sworn the old girl grinned at her.

Then they were running, and the white world shushed by as they sped on.

CHAPTER EIGHT

It all went right for long enough for Hannah to relax. She let Nook set the pace — a fast lope that was about the same as Hannah's stride when she was doing the long-distance run at school. The air was still, and the clouds hung like magnets stuck to the sky. The sled pulled straight. Hannah began to feel the sled like a memory; she remembered riding it when she was younger with her dad, with her mom. Remembered how the sled was one thing, but also it was many things, many individual pieces of thin wood lashed together with rope and even sinew, for Pierre had made their sled the old way, the way his father had done. The sled creaked and bent and bowed under the pressures of winter: the dogs pulling, and the snow pushing up, and the ice pieces reaching in to hook the underbelly of the basket and scrape the brushbow. But it held, the pieces leaning on each other. For a few minutes Hannah was both the driver and the sled, feeling the trail through her feet on the long runners, her soles pressing down in the small dimples set on the top of the runners to provide traction for the driver. She was both in her memories and present. It was a very lulling feeling.

Then the line started to slacken as Bogey slowed down again.

"Get up, Bogey, get up!" she called, and the brown Lab took three, four more strides, pulling, then he shied sideways heavily, the sled nearly tipping over as his big body pulled everything askew.

Hannah yelled and tried to stamp on the brake, but the sled had lurched sideways and she was thrown into the handlebars. The breath went out of her for a moment. The sled tilted dangerously and she thought, *Things happen very fast out here*, and chastised herself for not paying attention as the sled slowly, slowly tilted back and settled on the runners, creaking and groaning like the trees around them under the weight of snow. They stopped.

Bogey ignored them all, his flanks heaving as he barfed up everything he had just eaten and then moved a few feet away from it, still dry-heaving. She quickly realized her error as the rank smell of half-digested meat sifted through the dead air around them, realized why Nook and Rudy had not eaten. They were better at this than her, and she felt a flush of shame creep up her neck as she remembered thinking badly of them. They had not eaten because running was hard, and on a full stomach it made one sick, so they would rather go hungry than end up like Bogey was now.

"Stupid, stupid!" she muttered to herself as she walked forward and unclipped the Lab's neckline and tugline. He wandered off, still heaving and hacking, looking miserable as only a Labrador retriever could, with the skin under his eyes sagging and his thick, otter-like tail flat against his crouching body. He moved off a little more and hunched over again, this time letting loose a stream of diarrhea.

Hannah looked at Sencha. The Dalmatian did not seem to be affected, but Hannah let her off anyway, to do her business and just in case she was feeling sick. Hannah herself was feeling sick, too, and the smell of barf and stool made her stomach turn tightly. Her stomach definitely felt … wrong somehow, as though it were trying to digest a lump of coal. She wiped sweat off her forehead and used her shirt to mop up the sweat under her arms. She got out the water dish and filled it for Bogey, and he drank.

She looked at the low clouds. She was getting a headache, so it was going to snow any minute now, she guessed. She called Sencha over; the Dalmatian trotted over expectantly, and Hannah reached over and hooked her up to the sled. Bogey's tail was wagging again, a sure sign he was feeling better. When he was back in his place in the lineup, Hannah pushed off. It was time to get going.

They rounded a slight corner where the trail skirted one of the many marshes in the area, and the first flakes began to hit her face, thick and splattering. The dogs puffed, but their breath did not make clouds because it had suddenly gotten so warm. Hannah was sweating heavily under all her layers, and she kept her toque off even after they started running again, letting the cool air hit her hair and face unimpeded. It felt good.

The snow started to come down more heavily, in the space of a few seconds going from nothing to making it nearly impossible to see. She squinted and realized she had forgotten to bring her goggles — a modified pair of ski goggles that covered her face and allowed her to keep her eyes open in driving wind and snow. Thankfully, she was not going far.

The eerie silence deepened as the snow crowded close together, blocking out sound. Hannah did not know the trail very well, but she did know that where it split into many small tracks, she needed to take the far right-hand one and follow that. It was a long, slow uphill climb that she knew led to the back of Jeb's house.

The trail became wider and more packed down as they headed up the hill, and the dogs spread out a little. Even Sencha pulled — though it was more because everyone else slowed down than because she wanted to work.

They pulled into the area around the back of Jeb's house that was maybe twice the size of their own yard — half an acre that in the summer they played badminton and soccer on. In Jeb's yard there were old cars and a leaning, dilapidated shed. An ice hut stood on steel runners, ready to be pulled out onto the lake that skirted the left side of the cabin.

This was Jeb's house, but while she'd been away with the Army, Peter and his father had lived here. Hannah could see the broken and rusted frame of the old dirt bike she and Peter had used when she was ten years old now half-buried in the snow. That was the summer that Jeb had returned and taken her house back, and after that they hadn't visited as often. Hannah's dad had said that Jeb needed time alone to get back to herself, because she'd had a tough time while she was deployed. Sometimes he would go into the cabin to talk to her and tell Peter and Hannah to stay outside.

Hannah stopped the sled between the shed and the house, about halfway across the yard. There was a low hum coming from the front of the house, like a large mosquito buzzing. The track she followed swept around in a large arc to join back up with itself; snowmobiles did not turn very tightly. She unmoored the snowhook and set it firmly, stepping on the back plate to drive it securely into the snow. For a minute she debated letting Sencha and Bogey off to run around, but there would be time for that later. Right now, Hannah wanted to make her phone call to the pharmacy and make sure she would be able to get a ride back to the cabin before dark. She walked up the steps and knocked on the splintered wood of the back door.

That's it, she thought, *the adventure is over.* The excitement of it was leaving her body, and she felt her headache ebb away as the snow fell with more and more vehemence, until she could barely see the dogs and the sled. She heard movement inside the cabin, but no one came to the door. Hannah knocked again, louder, and the sounds stilled.

"Hi," she called. "It's me, Hannah Williams."

Still no one came to the door, and suddenly Hannah was sick of it all, tired and getting cold, and her stomach ache was back. Probably Peter was ignoring her for a joke, but it wasn't freaking funny. She pounded at the door with her gloved fist as loudly as she could and yelled, "Hey! I need help. My mom is sick. Open up!"

Then Sencha began to bark furiously at something and Hannah turned to see Peter coming around the side of the house in his snowshoes, his arms full of wood, wood-chips all over his thick wool sweater because he hadn't done his coat up.

Behind her the door opened, and things got very bad very quickly.

CHAPTER NINE

Hannah turned to see who had finally opened the door and immediately felt a hot, stinging sensation in her chest. Then she was lying on her back in the snow, unable to breathe.

She had never had the breath knocked out of her before, but a small piece of her understood that was what had happened. She struggled, instinctively placing her hands against her chest as if to help expand her lungs. Her eyesight dimmed as though she were looking through a playground tunnel. Her breath tasted like rust, and the snow pelted down into her open mouth as she gasped for air.

Slowly, agonizingly, her breath came more easily. With it came her hearing, and finally her eyes began to see more than just the darkened circle of her own chest and the snow in which she lay.

Above her on the small porch stood Jeb. Her hair was tied back in a tight bun, and in her right hand she held a rifle with a brown wooden stock.

She was pointing the rifle at Hannah, squinting into the whirling snow.

"Get down! Get down! Get down!" screamed Jeb. Hannah flipped over onto her stomach and pressed her face into the snow, breathing in the smell of snow and woodchips and trying not to suffocate on the terror that clogged her throat.

All the dogs were barking by now, and as Hannah turned her head ever so slightly, she could see Sencha lunging against her collar and gangline, trying to get to her.

"Jeb!" she heard a voice yell. "It's Hannah, Jeb. It's Hannah … George's daughter! It's okay." It was Peter.

"This isn't backup, this isn't scheduled," Jeb said to Peter. Out of the corner of her eye, Hannah saw Peter carefully place an armful of wood on the ground.

"You're at home, Jeb, home in Canada. It's Hannah. She's here. That's her." He pointed at Hannah.

Jeb's voice was hard and angry. "I don't know this individual. I don't know you, either. You'd better take cover from this sandstorm, son."

"Jeb, you're home," Peter said. Through her terror Hannah heard the calmness in Peter's voice; he sounded like a principal announcing a fire drill or a gym teacher instructing students to climb the ropes for the yearly fitness test.

Hannah knew that during Jeb's time in the Army she had spent a long time away from Canada, deployed in Afghanistan. Whenever Hannah had asked where, her father had merely said, "She's in the desert, and it's not pretty." That was all he would say. Jeb had been home now for almost two years, but from what Hannah could make out, she rarely left her house.

Hannah lay there, hardly breathing. The cuffs of her coat were soaking up the snow, and it was melting into her gloves. She felt it trickling down the backs of her hands, but she was too scared to move. Except in the movies, she had never before seen someone point a gun at another human — let alone at her — and this was not like the movies. She had seen her father and Scott fire guns when they hunted in the fall, had seen them kill partridges — the flurry of the bird's takeoff cut off by the sharp crack of the rifle, then the bird suddenly falling like it had forgotten everything it knew about flying. Lying face down in the snow, unable to breathe, the dogs barking and lunging in the background, and Peter's weirdly calm voice — this wasn't like the movies at all.

"Jeb, you don't need a gun," she heard him say.

"Who are you?"

"You know who I am, Jeb. It's your nephew, Peter."

"I … I don't think I do. No, I do know you — Peter. Peter. What are you doing?"

"I was getting some wood."

"Where is this sandstorm coming from? I'm getting close to black on water, here."

"It's snow, Aunt Jenny. You're home now. It's snow."

Jeb said nothing back, but Hannah could hear her shifting on the small porch, her boots knocking against the beat-up wood and scraping against the snow that dotted it.

"I can get you water, Jeb," said Peter in the same *it's all okay* voice. "I'll get us water from the well, okay?"

There were a few moments of silence. Hannah couldn't see anything and didn't dare turn her head. The hairs on the back of her neck felt like barbed wire, stiff and unyielding.

Then came the sound of Peter moving toward the cabin. The dogs were still barking.

"Hannah, the stupid dogs," said Peter in the same voice, all flat and equal stresses on each sound he was making, "Ha-nah-the-stu-pid-dogs," as casual as if he were talking about the weather.

Hannah slowly raised her head. "Sencha," she said, "*enough*." She tried to say it like her mother, in that tone that brooked no argument. The Dal gave two or three more barks, then fell silent.

"I don't see your kit, soldier," Jeb said to Peter. Her voice had gone back to one that Hannah didn't recognize, hard and adult with no comprehension of the person in front of her. It was as though she were pushing what was inside her head outward into the world, to make the world inside her head the real one.

"I don't see your kit," she repeated. "Where's your sidearm?"

"It's in the cabin, Jeb," said Peter. "Maybe ... maybe you could go get it for me?"

"I'm going to call this in, soldier, that's what I'm doing. I don't know the regs on this, and my CO isn't around. I'll call this in, you watch the squirter," she said, and Hannah saw Peter look over like Jeb had pointed at her.

"Okay," he said.

There was the sound of boots on the porch, and then the door slammed shut.

Hannah's mouth was open. She realized she was panting. She was panting, and so, when she felt an arm under hers, jerking it upward, she slammed her mouth closed and bit her tongue, hard.

"Get up," said Peter in an angry whisper. "Get up and get going!"

"What's wrong? What's wrong with her?"

"Shut up and go," he hissed, pushing Hannah forward roughly, "before she comes back and decides to shoot you or one of those bloody dogs."

CHAPTER TEN

Going to die, Hannah thought, *going to die, going to die.*
The whole world was silent under their stumbling feet, the
snow stinging and blinding. It was like being buried alive,
but in whiteness, and claustrophobia gripped at Hannah,
making her want to scream.

But if she screamed, it might bring Jeb back out —
Jeb with the gun, Jeb who could shoot the gun, shoot her
or shoot the dogs or shoot Peter. So she didn't scream.
Instead, a whimpering sound came out with each short
breath, *ummh ummh ummh*, as she followed Peter's snowshoe tracks and his flailing arms. He was already almost
out of sight, as his snowshoes kept him from sinking into
the snow. He had run right past the dogs, ignoring them,
and she started to follow, but then her feet stopped like
they weren't her own and she was turning, grabbing Nook,
thanking everything in the world in that moment that
she had not let Sencha or Bogey off, that they were all
still ganged. She bent low over Nook's head and hissed,

"Get up, Nook, *get up, GO!*" and pushed the husky past her, around the wide snowmobile track that looped back to the main trail. The dogs picked up her fear and pulled hard, their bodies bunching up into an upside-down U and then pushing forward powerfully — but the snow-hook held the sled fast and they couldn't go anywhere, straining and barking. Hannah stumbled to the back of the sled, grabbed the snowhook, and pulled it up, nearly falling as the pulling dogs suddenly gained traction and the sled shot forward.

The snowhook ripped out of her hand, falling to the ground and trailing after them, and she grabbed wildly for the handlebars, twisting her wrist and fighting for a grip on the ash wood. One foot, then two on the runners — the sled creaked and groaned under the torque, but even that was muffled under the constant onslaught of snow.

She reached Peter and flew by him. His jacket was still open and he had his head down now, running awkwardly through the snowstorm. The team rounded the first corner into a more open area; the trees were several feet away on either side. The snow began to smack hard into her face, driven into her eyes by her speed and by the wind. They spun round the corner, back onto the track they had come in on, then shot down the hill to the main trail, Nook turning the team so quickly that the sled almost slid off the track.

Hannah fought the urge to keep going. It was in the dogs, she could feel it. It was in her: panic and anger. Everything in her body screamed *run!,* but she wouldn't run — she couldn't leave Peter. The snowhook, not in its usual holder, bounced up and hit the back of her leg, point first, ripping a hole in her thick pants and making her wince. She tried to reach down and grab it, step on the brake, and keep the sled upright all at the same time.

"Whoa whoa *whooooaaaaa*," she cried.

The sled slowed, and she pressed the brake harder, still wrestling with the urge to let up, to go until they were far away from all this mess, back at her family's cabin, in front of the fire, listening to Kelli talk about mushrooms and wood elves while her mom showed her how to mend holes in socks. But she couldn't go back, and the cold wash of concern about her mom stiffened Hannah's leg, and the sled came to a stop.

Tentatively, she got off the runners and checked the back of her leg, which was stinging and throbbing. It looked like the snowhook had not gone through anything besides her clothing. Still, she would need to close that hole soon. She could already feel the winter air seeping in, and it was only barely cold enough to make her breath fog.

She looked up as Peter came huffing up, his coat still open and his face closed and grim. He slowed as he neared the sled, stopping well away from it, then bent over with his hands on his knees, gasping.

"Is she going to come here?" asked Hannah, straining to look behind him through the snow.

"No," said Peter between gasps. "She stays at the house."

Hannah hardly thought that the dingy, smoke-infused one-room cabin qualified as a "house." The wood stove there leaked, unlike the one Hannah's family had. Every year the Williamses cleared the creosote and nesting birds out of the chimney and re-lined the glass door with special thick rope so that it didn't suck in air from the front. Jeb's stove was old and had no glass door, and the handle was homemade, thick metal welded directly onto the metal door. It got so hot that you had to put on oven mitts to open it, and all the oven mitts in Jeb's house had long, streaky burn marks where they stayed in contact with burning logs or the side of the stove. The top two feet of the cabin were coated in a black, sooty ring, and it stank of cigarette smoke and green kindling.

Peter stood up and came a bit nearer, taking off his mitts and wiping his face of sweat and snow. Even the sound of his breathing was muted as the snow continued to fall. Suddenly, the press of all that precipitation began to weigh on Hannah. The silence was like an accusing stare; the sweat trickling down her back reminded her of the sensation of snow melting down the backs of her hands as she'd lain face down in the snow like a coward. Was that what Peter was thinking as he stared at her, still standing away from her? Why did the satellite phone have to be in Jeb's cabin? It was all so stupid and unfair. And what was wrong with Jeb? Hannah could not understand what had happened. She had never seen an adult act that way, not even the homeless people by the Beer Store at the end of their street in Toronto. Jeb had taken all the rules and thrown them out, and now Hannah didn't know what to do.

"She won't follow us," repeated Peter. "She'll stay in the cabin and try to call people to report us. The guys on the radio, they know what to do when she's like this."

"She's freaking me out!" yelled Hannah, not meaning to shout.

"Shut up!" Peter shouted back. He took a quick step toward her and shoved her, his palm pushing against the centre of her chest, and she fell back into the snow again. The fall didn't knock the breath out of her as the butt of the rifle had, but it was in the same spot and it hurt, it hurt a lot. Hannah sagged back to the ground, curled on her side with the snow pattering down. Then she was crying, and she cursed the crying, but she couldn't stop. The tears were useless — just wasted water, wasted time.

Peter stood above her for a few moments, then moved a few feet over to the side of the trail and looked back toward the house. Blurrily, Hannah could see him clenching his hands into fists and unclenching them. He stared up the hill a long time doing that, then finally threw them up in the air in a strange angry gesture and swore loudly.

It was not a word that Hannah had ever heard him use before, and it shocked her so much she stopped crying. Peter was sixteen, and he was on the local hockey team, so she imagined he swore all the time; the boys on the hockey team at her school swore even more than the football guys. Some of the girls on her volleyball team swore when they were rotated out too soon or they missed a block or they didn't play at the start of a game. But they seemed like kids trying things on compared to Peter just now. When Peter swore, it meant something.

As soon as she stopped crying, Hannah felt stupid about it. She turned her face away from Peter even though he wasn't looking at her and wiped the tears away with her gloved hand. The dogs whined, but they all seemed okay. Nook and Sencha were standing, and Rudy, too, but Bogey sat. Sencha, when she saw Hannah look at her, began wagging her tail rapidly.

Peter turned and looked at her. "Look ... I." He paused. "Are you okay?"

"Yeah."

"Then get up. I know where we can go."

"What do you mean?" asked Hannah.

Peter dipped his head back toward Jeb's cabin. "When she's like this, it's better that I go away for a bit. It'll be okay. It's the storm and stuff; the storm makes her like this. She can't see with the snow and she thinks she's back ... there."

"Back in the war?"

"Yeah. It happens."

"She had a gun!"

Peter started off down the trail. "Don't be an idiot. There weren't any bullets."

He said it with such *duh* in his voice that Hannah couldn't think of a single thing to say. Then a word appeared, and she grabbed hold of it and yelled it at his retreating back for all she was worth.

"Jackass!"

CHAPTER ELEVEN

"Jackass," Hannah muttered again to herself as she struggled to turn the dogs around. They were pointing in the opposite direction to where Peter was heading.

"Hey, give me some help!" she called, but he continued to ignore her and disappeared into the blowing snow, his snowshoes leaving wide, spongy-looking prints.

It took some doing, but she got everyone turned, including the heavy sled. Nook and Rudy were used to being hauled around, so they moved without any trouble, but Bogey was like a lump, looking at her with his sad eyes and not understanding what she wanted until she basically lifted him — one side, then the other — into position. Sencha, who had a ticklish belly, jumped sideways out of the reach of Hannah's hands every time she went to move her. Hannah spent more time untangling the line than actually getting the Dalmatian into position. The sled itself was half on its side after taking that sharp corner, and it was heavy with the packs, making it, too, almost impossible to move. She gritted her teeth and heaved and pulled, and finally the ragged line was pointing the other way.

Her watch said 11:00 a.m., but it didn't feel like it. It felt like a year had passed since she had slipped out the door, since she had decided not to hook up Sencha, since she had boiled the snow to make her breakfast and felt so proud of herself.

None of it mattered, anyway. None of those feelings or memories mattered right now, because Peter was leading them and he had disappeared down the trail. She needed to catch up.

"Huphup*hup*," she called, and the sled started out.

She caught up with him more quickly than she thought she would. Peter had stopped in place on the trail and was staring off to one side, into the trees, at … nothing that she could see.

He heard the sled coming up behind and moved off the trail, stepping onto the unbroken part of the snow and almost falling over as only half of one snowshoe broke through the ice that lay underneath. His arms windmilled for a moment and he swore again, but got his balance back.

"Stay away," he said loudly.

"What were you looking at?" she asked.

"Nothing," said Peter. He looked angry as he brushed the snow off his shoulders where it lay heavy and melting, leaving a darker trail of wet cloth in a ribbon down the front of him.

"Where are we going?" she asked.

He scowled at her. "A place," he said.

"Well, does it have a phone?"

"No." He peered at her, edging toward the back of the sled but staying on the unbroken snow, far from the gangline. "What are you doing here, anyway?" he asked.

Hannah hesitated. She told him that her mother's insulin vials had all been broken, although she didn't say that *she* was the one who had broken them. She also didn't tell him that she'd snuck on the sled without telling anyone. Standing in front of him, she felt suddenly that her story sounded lame, just *blah blah blah insulin, and I need a phone*. She wanted to make it sound more … interesting to listen to, but she was so tired, and her gut was on fire now, twisting and banging at her insides one minute, a dead weight the next. Her headache had never left either, and she was getting cold from the all-over sweat that had dried and the hole in her pant leg, and her eyes were itchy from the dried tears that sat in the corners of her eyes. She had never been so uncomfortable in her life.

Her story seemed to do nothing but make Peter madder. He moved his head from side to side and then up and down the same way Scott did whenever he was saying bad things, right before Hannah's dad would gesture toward her and Kelli and say, "Scotty boy, the girls are in earshot." And his eyes got narrow, like he was questioning her. She felt herself flash hotly at the thought that he might not believe her.

He probably thinks I did everything wrong, thought Hannah, *because he's sixteen and he thinks he's all that.*

Then Hannah was distracted by movement, as all four dogs suddenly swung their heads to look back up the trail behind them, noses twitching. Even Sencha lifted her head and opened her mouth so she could get more scent through her mouth.

Faintly, through the snow, they could hear something, a muffled grunting that Hannah realized was someone shouting.

"Is that Jeb?" she asked.

"Maybe," said Peter. "She may have come back out to keep an eye on us. Or maybe it's over and she's looking for me."

Then there was a short, sharp sound that was muffled but had enough force to tear through the empty air between the snow and prick against their eardrums. *A gunshot.*

All the dogs were spooked — Nook and Rudy shivered in place, Bogey sat upright, suddenly tense, and Sencha, unused to loud noises, skittered sideways, whining — and they all looked back at Hannah.

"She must have found the bullets," said Peter. For the first time, his wide grey eyes looked scared. Not angry or annoyed, but scared. The nakedness of his reaction shocked Hannah. "We hid them," he continued, still looking back up the trail toward the cabin. "We hid them … but she must have found them."

The two teenagers stood there, unable to move in the teeming snow — their footprints were already disappearing under it.

Hannah stood locked in place, a small part of her brain still trying to figure out how the sound of the gunshot had travelled through all the snow. *Kelli would have appreciated working that out*, she thought. Another part of her recognized that she was in shock.

"We have to go, we have to *go*," said Peter finally.

"Okay, all right," Hannah said. "Get in." She motioned to the basket. It would be tight, but he could lie on top of the bags, and it would only be until they reached … wherever it was that Peter was aiming them toward.

"No," he said. He took a step back.

Behind them, the shouts grew louder, sliding through the snowflakes more urgently. Jeb had found their trail despite the heavy snow. The hair on Hannah's neck stood up again. She waited for the tinny sound of the gun, wondered if getting shot felt very painful, wondered how long it would take to die.

"Let me drive," Peter said.

Hannah thought about how Peter stayed well away from the sled and never looked directly at any of the dogs, and she suddenly realized something: he was afraid of dogs.

"They don't listen to people who are afraid of dogs," she snapped, angry that he hadn't just admitted to it. "Get in the basket, Peter. Just get in."

The shouting behind them became more distinct; they could make out words in Jeb's *not-there* tone of voice. Hannah shivered. Nook whined and began to line out.

"Get in the basket or I'm leaving without you!"

Peter got in the basket with an awkward lurch, his snowshoes hanging off one side. Hannah didn't care. She called to the dogs — the words were barely out of her mouth when they all began to pull. She had grasped the handlebars, anticipating having to push the sled to start because of the extra weight, but the four dogs were powerful; even Sencha was straining against the gangline. The sled shot forward. Hannah took a few stumbling steps, then ran almost at full tilt to catch up. When she jumped on the runners the sled didn't even creak, despite her lopsided balancing act. The dogs pulled strongly and smoothly. The force of the lurching sled bowed Peter's legs, which were trailing his heavy snowshoes, and he struggled to get them off his feet as they raced away.

The sled was much more weighted down now, so Hannah could feel every creak and groan of the frame. Under her feet, every clump of hardened snow, every chunk of broken ice snatched at the underside of the frame or lurched it sideways or upward, making the hide webbing stretch and groan.

The dogs ran and ran. The trail, hidden under a heavy canopy of trees, did not have nearly as much debris on it as Hannah's driveway or the road to the cabin had. These trees had not been weakened by years of wind or pollution, so they stood tall and strong. What fallen trees there were, the dogs skirted around.

Peter finally got his snowshoes off and leaned over the side, looking back. This caused the sled to skid on one runner, making it harder to pull. Hannah yelled at him to sit in the middle of the basket, and Peter slumped back down.

At first, Hannah was so tense that she didn't even dare look behind them, but eventually the stiff feeling in her neck ebbed away, and she started to see the trail in front of her as more than just an escape route. Nook slowed without prompting to a pace a little faster than a jog, and the four dogs loped along, their legs scissoring in economical motions that cut through the snowy cloth of the trail. They were entering a part of the forest where there were more deciduous trees than coniferous ones — maple and cherry and poplar, the thin poplar trunks looking like impossibly tall stalks of grey grass in the distance. To the left and right, the ground was smooth and ran into little hollows and hillocks, free of the big marshmallow bumps of boulders that jutted out around her family's cabin.

They topped a small hill, and below them, she could see more of the same kind of landscape. She noticed bits of yellow plastic at the bottoms of many of the maple trees: plastic-covered tin buckets hanging from spigots driven into the trees. They had entered a sugar bush, where the owner was collecting tree sap, which would be boiled down into maple syrup.

"Stop!" said Peter.

"What? Are we here?" Hannah looked around but saw nothing, just the trail stretching out, the green arms of far-off conifers and the thinner fingers of the birch and maple and poplar trees skinned in ice.

"Just stop!"

Finally, they did. Rudy and Nook immediately lay down, their tongues lolling. Bogey also lay down, but with his hind feet splayed out behind him like a frog as he tried to get as much of his belly as possible onto the cool snow. Sencha remained standing, small whines escaping her mouth more from habit than anything, Hannah thought.

Peter had scrambled out of the basket as soon as they halted, not looking at her, and he moved off the path again. The snow was changing fast, no longer small, light flakes, but thick, heavy blobs with a cold, stinging wetness to them. It pelted them, the trees, the dogs. Peter was staring off into the trees again — looking at what, Hannah had no idea.

"I think it's going to storm again," she said. "Are we close?"

"No," said Peter. He kept on staring around at the trees. Bogey began to whine, a surprisingly tinny sound coming from such a big, husky-looking dog.

"Well, what are we supposed to do?" she snapped.

"I don't *know!*" shouted Peter. He bent his head and turned away from her even more. His shoulders twitched under his big heavy parka and Hannah thought, *Now he's crying, too!*

"We went the wrong way," he said finally. His voice was phlegmy and low. "I … there's a big sugar shack I go to when she … when she goes off like that. But you turned the wrong way, okay? I didn't realize you turned the wrong way."

"Well, do you know where we are?"

"No," he said. "Not really."

"What? What do you mean, not really? Come on!"

Peter made an arc with one gloved hand back toward the way they came. "I'm only allowed to ATV those trails, not this one."

"Why?"

"There's some older guys … this is the trail to Timmins. Some of the bush guys aren't very nice. They don't know me, not without my dad."

"Is everyone up here crazy?" she asked.

"Shut up!"

Hannah looked ahead on the trail. It was starting to become hazy in the distance as the warm air of the half snow hit the cold air above the snowpack.

"How far away is it?"

"How far away is what?" he asked, as though talking to her was the worst thing he could be doing with his time.

She rolled her eyes. "Timmins."

He glared at her. "I don't know. Farther than *you* can handle, anyway."

"How far?"

"Too far to go with stupid dogs, that's for sure."

"Jerk!"

"Just shut up," he said again.

"Well, stop being a complete jerk!" she snapped back. Her voice rose into the snow but was smothered almost immediately, making her even more annoyed.

Peter carefully pulled his mitt off and gave her the middle finger.

They yelled at each other then for a long time, calling each other names and throwing things — mostly snow. Once Peter stepped toward her with his palms out, like he was going to shove her again, but she stepped forward, too, and he went back to calling her names. He called her a coward and other, worse things that only made her madder, and she threw words back at him until they were standing face to face just yelling swear words at each other, swear words that didn't even make sense.

Hannah had no idea how long they had been doing this (or how much longer they would have continued) when the sky suddenly lit up a shocking, blinding white, and there was an ear-splitting *boom*: thunder.

They both jumped, startled. It was as though Hannah had been looking through a telescope at nothing but Peter's angry eyes, but now she was seeing his stupid thick glasses and his stupid grey eyes and his stupid flat face with pimples all over his neck. The world popped back into focus and she felt the snow — no, it was freezing rain now — sliding down her neck and into her collar, wetting her hair. They could keep hating each other later; they had bigger problems right now.

CHAPTER TWELVE

They had to get out of the rain, Hannah knew. If the same weather cycle carried on — she realized with surprise that a part of her had been tracking it — that meant it would rain, and then it would get cold again. Very cold. And everything would freeze.

They could go back to Jeb's. She thought about that for a while, felt the weight of it in her mind, the longing for it all to be simple and easy: a fire going in the cabin and Jeb okay again, Jeb calling the right people and then going to get Kelli and their mom, and finally everyone together and *warm* and fed.

Peter walked over to the side of the trail, and Hannah came and stood next to him. He pointed toward the forest.

"Okay. I think there's a hut a ways over there," he said. "Well, it's more a lean-to. It's small, but there's stuff in it."

"Stuff?"

"Matches, a sleeping bag. We could stay there. Maybe. Sometimes she's okay again right away."

"But not all the time?"

"No," he said after a pause. "Sometimes it's hard for her for a while."

Hannah looked across at the snow that by now was almost up to the bottoms of the sap pails. In the summer, the spigots were at the level of her waist, which meant the snow was at least three feet deep.

"We can't take the sled on that," she said, remembering how much effort it had taken to get across the yard when her mom had fallen.

"We'll go on snowshoes."

"What about the dogs?"

He didn't even look at them. "Leave them."

"I'm not leaving them!" she said.

"Well, let them go, then. They'll find someplace. They'll go back to Jeb's or something."

Hannah imagined Bogey trying to do anything without a human being around and almost laughed. Bogey had three priorities: get wet, chase balls, and lick the hands and faces of humans. If she took him off the gangline, he would just hover and get in the way.

"They won't leave." Even if she could drive them off, did she want them going back to Jeb's?

"Well, they can't come with us. It might not even be big enough to fit us." Peter paused and looked at her, wiping the rain off the front of his glasses. "They're just stupid dogs, Hannah."

"They got you away from Jeb, didn't they?" she replied, and Peter's hands clenched as he turned away.

Hannah tried to think more, but the rain was starting

to get into her collar, and it was getting her down. She put her hood up, which immediately made her wet face and neck steam.

"I'm going to Timmins," she said. "I'll take the trails."

"Anyway," continued Peter, as if he hadn't been a jerk the entire time they'd been together, "you don't have the stuff we'd need to go all the way to Timmins."

Hannah felt herself puff up. "Like what?"

"Matches, tinder, a knife, an axe, a sleeping bag —"

"Got 'em," she interrupted. She pointed at the sled. "I've got all that."

"Food?"

"Yes," she said. Food was a little more of a problem, since it was mostly boil-in-a-bag stuff that didn't seem to fully stave off hunger. Even as she thought this, she felt her stomach roar back to life, even around the stomach ache she still had. She'd probably end up getting in trouble for using up all the food, too.

"You have a tent? And two sleeping bags?" said Peter. His voice was still mean. *He wants me to be wrong*, she thought.

"There's a tent," she said.

"A winter tent?"

"Duh," she said, pointing at their surroundings.

"But no sleeping bag for me?"

"I wasn't planning on your crazy freaking aunt waving a gun at us!"

Peter grabbed Hannah's jacket, yanking her close and making her hood fall half over her face so that she could see only the bottom part of his face, his mouth with short, even teeth as he said, "Stop … saying … that word … Hannah." It was almost the same voice that he had used on Jeb in the clearing, as though she needed calming down, or as though he were saying it to calm himself.

She shoved him away from her and he stumbled, but stayed upright.

"We should go to the hut or just turn around and go back to Jeb's," Peter said.

"I'm not going back there," Hannah replied. "You don't know how long the storm or Jeb's … thing will last. I need to get to Timmins for my mom's insulin."

"It's faster to just go back," he argued.

"But how do we know Jeb will be okay?" said Hannah. "If she's not, we'll have to turn around again."

"I could at least get the snowmobile," he said, but even he didn't sound like he wanted to do that.

The rain was coming down harder, and Hannah turned back to the sled. "Do what you want," she said. "I'm making lunch."

"You could at least help," said Peter.

"Help what?"

"Help me get the sleeping bag."

"I thought you were just going back," she taunted.

"Forget it," he said. He walked to the sled and pulled out his snowshoes.

"I'll wait here," she said.

"Whatever." Peter stepped into the bindings. He used the same tone Hannah did with her little sister.

She pulled the snowhook out and set it. She unhooked Sencha, but left Bogey on the gangline with the sled dogs. Unlike Sencha, Bogey was easygoing and adapted pretty quickly, as long as there were other dogs or humans around.

Peter had almost disappeared through the trees by the time Hannah had detached Sencha from the neckline and the gangline and taken off the harness. She left the harness lying across the packs on the sled. Leaving it on would have allowed large packs of snow to get lodged under Sencha's chest and armpits and chafe her. Hannah was pretty proud of herself for remembering that.

It was a small comfort, though. Beyond the rain trickling down her face, her sodden gloves, and the heaviness of the snow sticking to the bottom of her snowshoes as she followed Peter's trail was a feeling of frustration that she couldn't shake. She had planned so carefully and now Peter had ruined it all with his stubbornness and making her feel like she didn't know what to do. She *did* know what to do; she just hadn't been anticipating Jeb, or the rain, or going the wrong way.

She glanced up. The iron-filings clouds had moved away, and the sky above them now was dark, like a big hand pushing down on her. She could not see much of it through the trees, but it looked as though it had lightened a bit in one direction. She hoped it was a break in the weather, and that it was heading their way.

She thought about how far they had come from Jeb's house as Peter's form came trudging back a half hour or so later, hugging a sleeping bag. The dogs had run for a long time, but she had forgotten to check her watch, and she now realized that the trail had grown indistinct as the day grew darker. It was 3:30 p.m. The freezing rain was still coming down, and with it, the darkness of a winter night.

Outside.

CHAPTER THIRTEEN

Knowing they would be sleeping outside sent a jolt of fear and energy through Hannah. The rain was starting to feel even colder, and the air was rank with the rotten, heavy smell of sodden bark and ice. Darkness would be upon them in half an hour or less; they had to set up their camp. There was lots of work to do before Hannah could get herself dry, but she knew she could do it. She was going to be a hero, despite the weather and despite Peter. Wasn't that what heroes did — succeed in spite of their obstacles?

Peter trudged to the sled. Trying to greet him, Bogey began to pull toward him, ducking under the gangline and tangling it. Hannah yelled at him and he doubled back, tangling it even more. Finally, she just unclipped his lines. The big brown Lab went bounding over to Peter, who was crouching, adjusting his snowshoes. Seeing the dog coming toward him, Peter stood quickly and turned away, crossing his arms over himself and showing his back to the dog.

"Get him away!" he shouted. Sencha, noticing the action, trotted over to investigate. Peter turned and twisted awkwardly on his snowshoes, trying to keep the dogs at his back. They thought it was a grand game, as they kept trying to get in front of him to see what he was hiding. They gambolled and tripped over his snowshoes, and soon it was a frothy, snowy mess.

"Hannah, get them off me!" he shouted.

He sounded so frightened that Hannah felt disgusted. *They're just dogs*, she thought.

Sencha — clearly enjoying this game of *what have you got?* — rounded on Peter with determination, wagging her tail furiously and thrusting her nose into his clasped hands.

Peter shouted and kicked at her, striking her chest with the blunt tip of his snowshoe, sending the Dal yelping and sprawling.

"Hey, watch it!" shouted Hannah. She ran over to where Peter was and pushed Bogey away. He went over to the sled dogs and hovered around them, eventually lying down. Hannah grabbed Sencha, hauled her to a tree, and tied her off to it with one of the pieces of rope that had been tying down the packs. Sencha was shivering, she noticed; Dalmatians lacked an undercoat, unlike Labs and huskies. Her fine white hairs were plastered to her body, and her tummy, which had almost no hair at all, was pink from the cold and rain.

Hannah cursed herself. At the cabin there were coats for Sencha that protected her belly and kept her warm, but she hadn't thought to bring any.

"Keep them *away* from me," Peter said. He was looking off the trail at a small copse of young trees that were barely higher than he was.

"I need something to cover Sencha," she said. She held the shivering Dal around the barrel of her torso, hoping to warm her up.

"Well, I don't have anything," he said.

She gritted her teeth. "In the blue bag, get a sweater or something," she said.

"Get it yourself," he replied. "I'm making a fire." He turned and headed for the copse and began to gather twigs from the thin branches that had broken under the weight of ice or feeding deer.

"We don't need a fire, idiot!" she shouted after him. "We need to get the tent up, and we need to get Sencha warm!"

Peter ignored her, his pockets full of twigs as he moved under the larger maples and started to dig up the snow, searching for branches. There was a downed maple, a huge dead tree with the branches of one side sticking up out of the snow like liquorice — they were black from the rain and from weathering. Peter pulled off a few of the underside branches that were still dry and walked back. He crouched down in the snow. "You always make a fire," he said, as if he were standing in front of a classroom. He took out a steel lighter from his inside pocket and made a hollow in the snow between the sled and where Hannah was bent over Sencha. "That's the first thing. You always make a fire."

Hannah gave up and went to the sled. The darkness was dropping rapidly now, and when she lifted the heavy tarp that was lashed over everything in the basket, she could barely distinguish between the blue bag of clothes and the black bag that held the food, the tent, and her sleeping bag. She opened the blue bag and grabbed the first thing that looked big enough — a wool sweater her father's sister had knitted her — and untied some more rope. She returned to the miserable Dal and wrapped the sweater around her, securing it with the rope.

Hannah stood and surveyed her surroundings. She knew that the best place to pitch a tent was close to a rock to keep off the wind, but the closest rocks she had seen on the way there were now lost in the darkness and could not easily be reached.

She realized now that many of the skills she knew — how to collect water, how to signal a plane, how to light a fire without matches — were not helpful for their situation. *They're summer skills*, she thought, and she laughed to herself, thinking how much easier everything would have been if it had been summer, and then she laughed at how ridiculous that thought was. It was pretty funny, for sure, to wish you had been chased by a gun-wielding woman and then gotten stuck out in the forest in the *summer* instead of in the winter.

Summer skills, she thought — all that moving around freely without thinking twice about it. The ground was a friend, the sun was a friend. She thought with sudden intensity about how long the sun was out during the summer. It felt like winter hated the sun, only tolerating it for little bits of time. Winter hated the ground, too; everything took five times as long to do as it did in the summer. Her shoulders and arms were burning from hanging on to the sled and she was starving.

She looked one way down the trail, then the other. They had come gently downhill and were at the bottom of what looked like a shallow depression. Up the trail, the land rose just as gently and disappeared into night and trees.

She decided to set up the tent right there on the edge of the trail, close enough that if a snowmobile did happen to come by, it would see them, but not so close that it would run them over. She shoved the faint hope of rescue aside.

Before setting up the tent, though, she had to feed the dogs. She grabbed a container of food. It was slightly thawed from the higher temperature the rain had brought, though mostly still frozen. This time, she didn't try to warm the food, but just threw some at each dog. There were no complaints. The dogs pounced and grabbed, then settled down to ripping and tearing the pieces of food.

After she'd made sure there wouldn't be any fighting between Bogey and Rudy, the two males — although if anything did happen, she knew Nook would sort it out — she hauled out the tent.

Ten pounds of poles, fabric, and bungee cords. After tamping down the snow to make a flatter, drier surface, she set out the thick waterproof pad that the tent sat on, protected from the snow. Then she pulled out the tent itself — by then she could no longer see it in the darkness, so she had to stop and dig through the supply bag to get the tiny lantern that could throw some light on the area where she was working.

Throughout this, Peter sat on his haunches, trying to start a fire. The smoke sometimes drifted over to her, but more often it just hunkered in place under the control of the rain until the entire area stank.

Hannah rubbed her eyes to try to get the smoke's sting out of them and unrolled the tent and laid out the poles. The tent sat on the pad, and she slid the supple bungee-corded poles through the two long loops on the tent, secured them into eyehooks on one side, then went over to the other side and pulled the tent up to secure the other two hooks. She threw the fly over that. Its thicker material slid easily over the already wet poles. She secured the fly to the tent bottom.

Thankfully, the tent had a large vestibule, like a tiny room before the zippered inner door. This meant they could keep all the gear in one place and nearby if they needed it in the night. It was truly dark now, the clouds still low and threatening. The rain was letting up, at least, but the temperature was dropping very quickly. From where she was stationed at the tree, Sencha whined softly.

Hannah dragged out her sleeping bag and threw it into the tent. Peter, now nursing a small smoking fire that was really more like a badly lit candle, dragged his sleeping bag over and tossed it into the tent, too.

"There's a stove," said Hannah. "It's in the black bag. There's food in there, too."

Peter walked to the sled and, keeping as far away from the dogs as possible, leaned in to look through the bags. He took out the bag that held the stove and fuel and food.

"I don't see the stove."

"That's it, in your hand," she replied.

Peter opened the small black bag in his hands and tipped the contents out over the snow. "Be careful!" Hannah snapped. "It's not a toy."

"How is this a stove?" he asked.

Hannah looked at him. She had assumed he would know what to do with it. But she remembered now that when her family and Peter's had gone camping together when they were both younger, Peter's father had always cooked on a fire and laughed at her dad, who used a camp stove.

"There's some energy bars in the other bag," she said. "Get those instead."

Peter shoved the stove and all its elements back into the bag before standing up. "Where's the water?" he asked, and she gritted her teeth at how, again, he said it as though he didn't expect she would have an answer.

"There's a bottle with the bars and one on the sled."

She turned back to the sled, grabbed the tarp, and unhooked it from the sides. Then she placed it, wet side down, over the snow in the vestibule of the tent. With Peter's help, she dragged the two bags off the sled and into the vestibule. She packed them against the side of the fly to stop the wind, then she untied Sencha and led her into the vestibule. Peter, already inside the tent, stopped unrolling his sleeping bag.

"What are you doing?"

"She has to stay in here or she'll freeze," said Hannah.

"She can't come into the tent." He was unwrapping one of the energy bars and the idea of food caused Hannah's stomach to clench, hard, into her spine almost. She closed her hands into fists until the spasm passed. She hadn't brought any extra blankets, and she'd also forgotten a headlamp. There was a flashlight in the emergency kit, but it was impossible to hold things and do things at the same time.

How would she keep Sencha warm? She groped through the darkness to find her clothing bag, thinking to wrap the Dalmatian in more of her clothes, but then she had an idea: she unzipped the bag and turned it sideways so that Sencha could burrow into it just like she did in Hannah's parents' big bed at home. She coaxed Sencha into the bag of clothes and laid the big woollen sweater over her. It was wet, but not all the way through, and still, it was warm.

Hannah was too tired to eat. She could barely keep her eyes open. The last thing she remembered was struggling to get out of her boots and into her sleeping bag, scrunching her hat down over her head so that it covered her ears, and noticing that there was no difference between the darkness inside her sleeping bag and the darkness of the night.

CHAPTER FOURTEEN

Hannah dreamt she was running, running like the sled dogs, long and easy and full of light, effortless wind. They ran across the greenness of a meadow, and each smell was a tug on her senses: the sharp tang of grass and pine needles, the small, anxious mice and moles hidden at her feet. Then it changed, and the ground became uneven under her feet; instead of springy turf, there were rocks, and she realized she was barefoot, running through raspberry bushes in shorts, and the sharp, spiny bushes scratched and poked her legs until they felt like they were on fire.

She awoke with her legs in agony. Peter was shaking her shoulder.

"Hannah, Hannah. Are you okay?"

"My legs," she gasped, and moaned again, drawing her legs up to her torso and wrapping her arms around them. The grey light of day filtered through the tent. The bush was silent — so silent, Hannah thought through the pain, that it must be snowing again.

Peter looked around the tent and grabbed the water bottle Hannah had put near her head. He shook it, and the water inside sloshed only a little.

"It's full," he said.

"So?" she groaned.

"You need to drink water, Hannah," he replied, uncapping the bottle. "I didn't see you drink anything yesterday. Here."

She took the bottle, put it to her lips, and drank. Immediately, her belly started to rebel; she barely held back from barfing up all the water onto Peter's blue wool pants. She waited for the nausea to pass, then drank a bit more. Her stomach was on fire as well as her legs, and her headache had come back sometime in the night. She lay in her sleeping bag, exhausted, floating in and out, with Peter haranguing her to drink until she fell asleep again with a belly more or less full of water.

"Cidiot," she heard him mutter as she drifted off.

When she awoke, the first thing she saw was Sencha's anxious face. The flap of the vestibule was pulled back, and looking past the Dalmatian's brown and white face, Hannah could see it was snowing. Her cheeks were cold and her whole body ached, but her mind was a little clearer. She was loath to move, as her thick winter sleeping bag filled with goose down had a hood that flipped over her head. That was good, because sometime during the night her toque had slipped off.

Seeing Hannah's eyes open, Sencha begin to whine. Hannah heard crunching sounds, then Peter's body blocked the vestibule opening as he crouched down.

"What time is it?" he asked. No good morning or greeting of any kind. He had his hood pulled up over his toque, and there was a layer of snow on it. One side of his glasses was fogged.

Hannah dragged her hand out of its nice warm spot by her belly and looked at her watch. Her heart jumped.

"Eleven o'clock."

"Are you up yet?"

"Yeah."

"Well, let's go."

He stood and crunched back out of sight. Hannah struggled with the zipper of her sleeping bag, then wormed her way out. She tugged on her boots and jacket, shivering in the steep temperature difference. Sencha pushed past her and burrowed right into the vacant sleeping bag. Hannah reached over and touched the dog's nose. It was cold, which was good; it meant Sencha did not have a fever. Still, the Dal was taking any opportunity she could to be warm, so before leaving the tent, Hannah pulled the top of the sleeping bag over Sencha so that only her brown nose poked out.

Peter was in the same position he'd been in last night while she was erecting the tent, but now he squatted before a small, cheerful fire. On one side of the fire was one of the brand-new cooking pots from the supply pack-sack. The orange enamel was already soot-blackened, and there was something bubbling in it. Hannah's stomach lurched. She was still exhausted and working through her dehydration, so she couldn't tell whether the stomach lurch was good or bad. On the other side of the fire was a pot full of snow he was melting to make water.

The dogs were miserable. Although Bogey's tail wagged, he did not get up from his spot, where he was curled up under the brushbow of the sled with his butt almost touching Rudy's. There was a dusting of snow on all the dogs, and when Nook lifted her head in Hannah's direction, small shards of ice came off her ruff and landed at her feet. Still, her eyes and face were calm.

"Did you feed them?" she asked Peter.

"No." He was stirring the stew pot. He had pulled the supply bag right out of the vestibule and dragged it close to him — and farther from the dogs, she guessed. It was still open and snow was drifting into it, but she was too tired to say anything.

She considered feeding the dogs — the day before had been long and rough — but then she thought about Bogey's unfortunate start yesterday and decided she'd give them two meals at the end of the day, wherever they ended up.

"Hello, Earth to Hannah? Here," said Peter. He was holding out a spoon. In his other gloved hand, he held the steaming pot.

She realized she'd been standing there staring at him like an idiot while she was thinking about the dogs. She grabbed the spoon and they both squatted back down. Peter placed the pot in the snow and stirred, and they watched it melt a hole in the packed-down snow until it was half-buried. The cold from the snow quickly cooled the contents of the pot, and they ate right out of it, spooning the brown liquid — stew, Hannah guessed — into their mouths, dribbling juice down their chins. Peter used the back of his sleeve to wipe away his dribbles.

"What time is it?" he asked her again.

She was already tired of looking at her watch every time he asked, but some part of her did want things to be part of a routine or a schedule, like back home; maybe he felt that way, too. In the city, clocks were an essential part of life. Get up at 6:00, ballet until 7:30, change for school, breakfast, class at 8:30. She liked the orderliness of it, how she could go from day to day in a groove like a sled track on a crisp day. Just like her running dream before it went bad. That was what she liked: the freedom of routine. It allowed her to do different things in her head, like work out the hard math problems, or wonder whether Billy had been talking about her — and if he had, what he'd said — or worry what the more popular girls' clique was saying about her. But the bush was not like that. She had slept until 11:00 and the day didn't care; it just went on.

She had to get that sense of order going again. "Time to figure out what we're going to do," she said. She dropped her spoon into the stew pot and walked back to the tent to get her water bottle. She would start by remembering to stay hydrated. Her legs felt as weak as runny eggs, and her head was like a mouse nest, inside and out — her hair was plastered to one side of her face and her thoughts were sluggish.

She came back and crouched near Peter. She stared at the fire as Peter fed the water pot with more snow.

"How far is it to Timmins?"

"Too far, Hannah."

"Well, how far is that?"

115

Peter shrugged. "Why don't we go back to your place?" he asked.

"There's no power at our place."

"We could use your car. How sick is your mom? I can drive."

"There's no way. It's buried under the snow, and the road isn't even plowed. Haven't you been listening to the radio?"

"No," he said. In his tone, and the way his face pulled down, he made it seem like people who listened to the radio were somehow inferior. "Dad'll call when he gets back, though."

"How come you guys have power?" asked Hannah.

"We have the generator," said Peter. That must have been the source of the humming she had heard when she approached the cabin.

"This is *so stupid*," she said.

"If you hadn't brought those goddamn dogs, if you hadn't yelled and banged on the door, then everything would have been okay," said Peter. "That's what does it — when things surprise her or mess up her routine. She was already stressed out by the storm."

Hannah thought about it. Whenever her dad wanted to see Jeb, he phoned ahead, and it was almost always when Scott was present. She hadn't really noticed before — although she was piecing it together now — how careful everyone was about what they spoke about and how they said things in front of Jeb. The only time Hannah's mom had gone over, she and Jeb had argued over putting a penny in the vase of tulips she'd brought (supposedly to protect the flowers from bacteria). Jeb had suddenly started to shout, and surprisingly, Hannah's mom had quickly acquiesced. With anyone but her husband, when the shouting began, her mom was just getting started.

They sat and watched the water in the pot begin to bubble. Peter took it off the fire and placed it in the snow.

"We could go to Jonny Swede's," he said. "He's nearby."

"How far?"

"I don't know," said Peter. He looked around and squinted up the trail. "We're about halfway, I guess."

"So a full day on the sled?"

"Maybe less. I don't know. I'm not a dogsled *expert* like you are. Most people go on snowmobiles."

"How far is Timmins from his place?"

"I don't know," he said again, "I've never gone to Timmins from his place. Maybe an hour?"

"By car?"

"Yeah," he said, in a tone that said *obviously, idiot.* "We won't need to go to Timmins, Hannah," he added.

"Peter, I need to get insulin for my mom!" Hannah was rapidly calculating in her head. Most of the driving out here was on back roads or secondary highways. An hour by car was probably about nine hours by dogsled. That was two more nights.

"Maybe Jonny Swede has some," said Peter.

"*Insulin*? Only diabetics use insulin." She tried to use her own *obviously, idiot* tone.

Peter shrugged and Hannah glared at him, raging at his careless nonchalance. He didn't even seem to care how sick her mom could get without insulin.

"Does he have a satellite phone?" she asked.

Peter laughed. "He doesn't even have a fridge. He keeps all his stuff in a cold cellar. He dragged this old bus up there to make an outhouse, too. This great big long yellow bus with a shitter in the driver's seat."

"Wow. Gross."

Peter shrugged again. Sometimes it felt like he wrapped himself around this northern place like a blanket, protecting it. Even if *he* thought it was gross that Jonny Swede didn't have a fridge and used a bus for a toilet, he would never say.

"Then why would we go there?"

"He has a snowmobile. He knows my dad."

"Your dad is in Quebec."

"He'll come back when they figure out what's happening here. Plus Jeb probably called in to her case worker."

"Case worker?"

"Yeah, the guy from the Forces who talks to her when she's like this. She always thinks he's her superior officer when she's gone like that," he said, putting a finger to his temple. He poured some of the boiled water into the stew pot, swirled it around, then dumped it out on the trail.

"Who cares who Jeb calls?" said Hannah, annoyed at Peter for making it all about him. As usual.

"Well, if she calls her case worker, he usually calls my other aunt in Temagami, and then she'll come out herself or get in touch with townspeople here and have one of them come out to check on Jeb. Friends of my dad, sometimes. Sometimes a guy from the Legion."

"No one can get to her. The roads are all closed." Peter scowled at her. "You go to Jonny Swede's, then," she continued. "I'm going to Timmins." She looked over at Sencha, who had emerged from the tent and was stretching.

"Well, you can't use the snowmobile, 'cause I am. I'm taking Jonny back to Jeb's. He knows how to take care of her."

"But I need to get to Timmins. We can stop by Jeb's on the way back, after my place."

"We'll see what Jonny says," said Peter.

"Okay."

Peter nodded as though he had expected her to agree — or he didn't care. He covered the fire, put the camping things back into the packsack, and placed it in the sled basket while Hannah broke the tent down. They both folded up the ground sheet that the tent had sat on.

"Do they call him Jonny Swede because he's Swedish?" she asked, packing the ground sheet in the supply bag while Peter poured water from the pot into both of their water bottles.

"No, because he's from *Norway*," said Peter, rolling his eyes. He handed her a full bottle. "Here. Drink."

CHAPTER FIFTEEN

After they'd each finished their bottle of water, Peter refilled them again. He packed away the cooking things while Hannah looked over the dogs and hooked up Sencha's harness.

The sky hovered over the tops of the trees like it was somehow closer than usual, and that feeling was made even worse by the snow that fell and fell and fell. Hannah made an effort to take her mind off the falling snow, lest its constant downward motion creep into her brain, bringing her down, too. Instead, she tried to see it as a good thing: without the snow, the day would have been very dark.

The dogs were a mess. She let Bogey off the gangline to relieve himself. He immediately raced to a nearby tree and watered it for a long time, then busied himself sniffing out the best toilet. Both Nook and Rudy had been trained to relieve themselves while still on the gangline; if they were running, they simply pooped as they ran, and they'd wait for a stop to move off the trail as much as the gangline would allow before urinating where they stood.

But the house dogs were not like that. Bogey, especially, was very picky about his toilet business. No one could watch, and he couldn't do it near anyone else, either. But she could let Bogey off without having to worry about him running away — something she couldn't do with the sled dogs. They had never learned *sit*, *heel*, or *come*, because they had never needed to. Just like Sencha had never had to learn *gee* and *haw*, the right and left of dogsledding.

Hannah picked up Rudy's paw to inspect the tear that she and her father had looked at earlier. It seemed like a year ago that the two of them had crouched, bellies full of lunch, to inspect the doghouses. Rudy's feet were thickly furred; she combed through the fur to see that the cut was still sealed and his feet looked okay. His toenails were shortened from scratching the packed-down area around his kennel; this helped on the trail, as the short nails did not push up against his toes and cause sores to develop.

Hannah snuck a few looks at Peter as she moved on to Nook. He had removed his coat so as to better move his arms. She could make out muscles even through his thick wool sweater, and his torso was wide and thick, but stocky. He was wearing a utility sweater, like hers, but his had a layer of smooth material sewn onto the tops of the shoulders to prevent the wool there from wearing off too quickly.

He was wrapping up everything in quick, economical motions — the pots inside each other, the utensils in the pots, then the pots in a bag tied up neatly. He was doing a good job, but she didn't want to say as much in case he took it the wrong way, like she was confirming that she wasn't as experienced as he was. It was nice to have someone along who had camped before and who knew all kinds of little things from years of experience: where to set up a fire, how to pack for hiking, which socks to wear. She did feel cold and miserable and was barely able to stand, but it could have been much, much worse. If Peter hadn't been there to bully her into drinking water, she didn't know how long it would have taken for her to remember herself.

She went back to attending to the dogs. Nook's feet were clean and problem-free, too, but she did have a heat sore under her left front leg from where her harness swept down her chest and up her back. The area was rubbed raw because, Hannah realized, she had put the wrong harness on Nook. The two sled dogs' harnesses were the same colour, but each was tailored to the individual dog. On the chest piece of Rudy's was the letter *R* then *ND* in marker, faded but still legible. The *R* was for Rudy, and the *ND* meant that he was one of Nook's puppies.

"Hey, Peter, I need to change their harnesses," she said. "Can you hold Nook while I get Rudy?"

Peter was zipping up the supply bag and putting it in the basket. "No."

"They're not going to do anything to you."

"No," he said again. "I'll take down the tent."

"Don't be such a wuss, Peter."

He ignored her, going to the tent and pulling the vestibule back. He righted her bag of clothing and roughly stuffed anything that had spilled out of it back in. She had wanted to change her clothes, but he was packing up already and she had her hands full of dogs, so she let it go and promised herself she'd change when they stopped next. Hopefully, it would be somewhere warmer.

Hannah got some salve and the tie-out line out from the black pack and rubbed it on Nook's heat sore. Then, with the tie-out line, she staked Nook to a tree and removed the harness. Nook shook herself and sat, looking up the trail.

Hannah did the same with Rudy, untying him from the gangline and tying him off to a tree to remove his harness and check for sores. Finally, she switched harnesses so that each dog was wearing the right one. As she worked, Sencha and Bogey watched curiously. Hannah thought about the four of them. Sencha had incredible stamina; they had gotten her from a farm that specialized in making old-fashioned carriages, and all the Dalmatians on the farm ran with horses in parades or in competitions. Bogey's thick body was very powerful — he had once dragged a small tree trunk to Kelli when she couldn't find a suitable stick to throw. But all their lives, the house dogs had depended on the Williamses as their source for everything: food, fun, and rules.

Nook looked at her in a different way than Sencha and Bogey, even than Rudy. Sencha was like Kelli in some ways — a pest and a nuisance, but someone who made life a bit more interesting when she was around. Bogey was omnipresent, trying to be everyone's best friend. Nook, meanwhile, did not want to be her friend at all. But Nook did want to work, and if they could work together — if

Nook could run — then she would do it, and they would get along. It was a pact one made with Nook, one whose weight Hannah could feel. Rudy was similar, but for him, everything went through Nook. He looked at Nook before lifting a paw for Hannah's inspection or before eating. Whatever Nook did, Rudy would do, too, because Nook usually got to run, and that was what Rudy lived for.

With the two sled dogs sorted out and back on the gangline, Hannah turned her attention to the house dogs. Bogey had finished his ablutions, so Hannah started checking him over. As she did so, she thought about her plan of action.

Her ballet teacher was always telling her that she could jump higher if she wanted to. When Hannah disagreed, her teacher said, "That's because you aren't practising it in your head. If you see yourself jumping higher in your head, you'll jump higher here" — and the teacher tapped Hannah's legs.

So that was what she would do. She visualized getting to Jonny Swede's house and his snowmobile and his car, and she visualized him taking her to Timmins. She was visualizing so astutely that only Bogey licking her hand reminded her of where she was.

"Healthy as a horse," she said, slapping his furry flanks. Bogey wagged his tail and licked her hands and tried to get at her face while she hooked him back to the line.

Sencha also came more willingly than usual. As Hannah put the harness on, she ran her hands over the Dal's flanks. Her belly was raw in some areas, so salve went onto those spots. More troubling was that her nose was dry and warm.

Hannah paused and looked over to where Peter was packing the tent down. He had collapsed it, but the tent poles were giving him some trouble. "Need help?" she asked.

"I got it," he snapped.

"Hey, how much do you weigh?"

He stopped wrestling the poles and looked up. "What?"

"How much do you weigh?"

"Why?"

She waved at the sled. "They can only pull so much weight."

"Hundred and forty," he said.

"Pounds?"

"No, feathers. Of course pounds, doofus."

She glared at him across their impromptu campsite. "What are you, five years old? No one says doofus."

"Oh, sorry. Witch," said Peter, and he picked up the poles again.

Hannah looked at the snow on the ground. She fought the urge to start yelling again. Peter was very good at needling her. The snow whispered around her as it fell. The world seemed very small, and that smallness made her feel helpless.

He's just as scared as I am, she thought. She dropped the line in her hand and went over to him. "They have bungee cords in them," she said. "Like this." She took a pole from his hand and pulled it out so that the bungee cord was stretched, then she folded it neatly in half, and then again.

"I've never seen poles like that before," he said.

"Yeah, my dad lives at the sports store when they have sales."

"How does it hold the weight? Like a pulley, right?"

This time it was Hannah's turn to shrug. She was more worried about the dogs. "So that's almost three hundred pounds, then. Three hundred pounds that they have to drag," she said.

He watched her as she continued folding the tent pole. "That's a lot."

"Yeah."

"Can they do it?"

"Yeah, but it'll be tough. Nook and Rudy are okay, but Bogey and Sencha, they don't really do this much —"

"Work?" said Peter. He laughed. "City dogs."

She bent and thrust the neatly folded pole into the tent bag. "Why are you such a jerk about the city? Have you even been to one?"

Peter ducked his head and grabbed another pole. "I'm never going to the city. Too many people, too many cars. Too many immigrants. Not like you," he added, flicking his eyes at her, "but like real immigrants who can't speak English and don't get jobs."

"That's racist!" said Hannah. She had never said the word out loud before, even though they had studied the subject in social sciences at school, and it sounded like it didn't really belong where they were. It was a word that didn't feel relevant to the snow on the maple boughs and the small depression where their fire had been. But at the same time, it felt true.

Peter was stuffing his pole into the bag. "I said not like you. Your mom is fine. Kelli's weird, though."

Hannah launched herself at him. His bent-over head and rounded shoulders received the brunt of her shove, and he landed with a *whomp* in the soft snow of the trail-side. He had been standing in front of a small gully; now he slid back until he was several feet from the trail.

"She's not weird, she's *nine*!" Hannah stood over him, clenching her fists and her teeth.

"Jesus, Hannah!" Peter looked up at her and put his hands to his face. "I'd better not lose these glasses, or you're dead."

She pointed at him. "*You're* an immigrant. *Everyone* is an immigrant."

"I've been here longer than you!" He struggled to get up, but without snowshoes, his feet sank into the soft snow almost to his waist.

"My dad doesn't even like your dad," said Hannah. "He just hangs out with him because he feels sorry for him."

Peter had forded his way back to the trail, and he stood with his hands on his knees, catching his breath. He muttered something low that sounded like, "My dad's an asshole."

"What?" asked Hannah, shocked.

"Nothing," said Peter. "I'm sorry I said you were immigrants."

"We *are* immigrants."

"Well, whatever, I'm sorry."

"Let's just go," said Hannah.

"Fine."

"And stay away from my dogs!" she spat out as she headed back to the line. The sled dogs were lying down snoozing, as though it were an everyday thing to have fights in the middle of the woods in the winter.

Hannah gathered up Sencha and put her harness and collar on, but only attached the tugline. She decided not to use the neckline — the short line that attached the collar to the gangline. That way, Sencha could roam a bit and get used to the team dynamics, instead of being yanked back in line every time she strayed an inch. The bigger dogs could take the rougher handling, but the Dal, though built for stamina, was not built for cold. Hannah would hook up her neckline again after a while.

With all the bags back in the sled and Peter in the basket, they started out. This start was smoother than her first and less panicked than the flight from Jeb's, but still, it was awkward, with half the team pulling and the other half learning. The new snow was deep enough that the sled runners moved almost silently over it, though not so deep as to make it hard for the dogs to reach the ice pack underneath.

Eventually, the running smoothed out and slowed down. During their wild flight the day before, Hannah had stood, crouched tensely on the runners, the whole time — but that was hard on the dogs. Now, she poled, periodically lowering her foot into the snowpack the dogs churned up and pushing, thereby taking her weight off the sled for a moment. This was especially helpful going up hills, while on the downhills, she placed her foot lightly on the wide rubber mat that sat below the sharply pointed brake, using the drag mat to keep the sled at a steady pace, preventing it from speeding up and banging into the backs of Rudy's and Bogey's legs.

The weather and the landscape were grey, and Hannah's thoughts were just like her legs: heavy and irritated. It was cold, but only in the way that cold had become her new constant. Her thick gloves had dried out near the fire that morning, and so had her toque. The hot meal had pushed warmth back into her bones, and poling with her feet every few steps got her warm in a hurry.

The sled rode over the snowpack with a steady *shushing*. The whole world was a dim white ribbon of trail faintly marked with old snowmobile tracks only visible in the dense coniferous forest. Then the sky lit up with sunlight, casting tall shadows across the lengths of the maples. This area of maple bush went on and on; she had never seen anything like it. At home, there were maple trees in the planters outside their school, and there were some carefully manicured maples in the park they went to occasionally, but they were nothing like this. Out here, *she* was the one who felt contained. The trees were just themselves, without any help or hindrance from her.

Each year, the drive up to Timmins was the most boring part of their trip to the cabin, but now memories of it flitted through Hannah's mind as she watched the trees, sentinels in the snow, sweeping by in slow succession. Past the last big town, the road stretched out ahead in a patchwork of sun-faded grey asphalt, a yellow line, and the green sea of tall grass on either side, where the trees were pushed back. But still they were there, the trees. For hundreds of kilometres, there were no towns unless you turned off the highway and drove down a smaller road, and those smaller towns lived among the trees, not separate from them. At one school they passed, the playground was merely some of the same forest with a fence around it.

The green of the trees, which she dismissed so easily when she was riding in the car, came back to her now. After so many hours outside in the snow, she longed for colour. She thought of the waxy green of poplar leaves, the sharp blue-green of spruce trees free of snow cover, the tarnished, dusty green of jack pines that had turned partially red from car exhaust. After a while, even that red disappeared, as the cars travelling the highway became fewer and fewer, and the trees crept closer to the highway's edge.

The memories came and wormed their way in, not chastising or judging her, but rather, venturing in like a curious puppy. She hadn't ever thought memories could be curious, but that was what it felt like — a handshake, or a dog's tongue across the back of a hand. In her memory, summer felt like an impossible blessing.

Out of the corner of her eye, a streak of white shot across the white expanse, under the maples. It was a startling motion, almost alien in the stillness of the winter. Hannah tracked the blur — it suddenly got wider as it made a large circle and started back toward them, with two long ears and black eyes: it was a huge rabbit.

She saw it at the same time that Sencha did. Untethered by a neckline, Sencha bunched up into a brown and white piston and launched herself after the rabbit.

The rabbit changed direction in a way that seemed to defy gravity, going pell-mell one way, suddenly leaping straight up and to its left a good ten feet, landing and reversing direction so quickly that Sencha's straining neck and haunches were still pointed in the wrong direction even as her eyes tried to track it.

It was now behind them, and Sencha was determined to follow it. She jackknifed the gangline, pulling the entire team in a sharp turn to the right as she reached the end of the tugline. The weight of three dogs all going one way against only her going the other way pulled her backward toward them like a slingshot, but she was up again in a second and hustling after the rabbit, which had bounded to the other side of the sled now in a wide arc and was hopping along leisurely parallel to the trail. The rabbit's actions seemed weird to Hannah. *It slowed down right in front of all those dogs?*

Sencha swivelled her head and caught sight of the rabbit on the other side. Once again she lunged after it, this time leaping right over the gangline and pulling the team to the left now. Hannah shouted, and Peter shouted, too, but the Dal ignored them. She wasn't barking or making any other kind of noise, but her whole body said *there is prey*. Nothing in the universe was going to stop her instinct to get to that rabbit.

The entire team was in chaos after that. Rudy and Bogey tried to continue running the trail for a few moments, but Sencha's actions confused them and the yelling scared them. Eventually they just took the path of least resistance, which was to follow Sencha. Sencha, meanwhile, strained and headed down another of the hollows that littered the sides of the trail. This one was fairly steep. The windward side wasn't as deeply snowed in, and the Dal tugged and pulled down it, with the rest of the dogs now haphazardly following, chest-deep in the drift and tugging against each other. The sled jerked sharply and tilted on the edge of the drop.

"Whoa, whoa, *whoa!*" shouted Hannah. She stepped on the brake and dug in its points, but the sled was rising out of the snow on one side, and the brake was useless. She grabbed the snowhook out of its holder, jumped off the sled, and wildly threw it into the snow behind her, hoping it would catch and dig in — but it didn't. It landed on its side and dragged along, bumping over clumps of snow, and she had to leap out of its way as it sped toward her, points first, then disappeared over the lip of the depression.

The sled tilted completely on its side and Peter leapt out, cursing. The bags bulged against their tie-downs and then slid out, not lashed tightly enough to the frame of the sled. The bags and Peter landed hard in the side of another depression, and the sled flipped over completely, landing so close to Bogey that it brushed his tail. The Lab leapt sideways, straight into Rudy, then turned his head to snap at the husky for the unexpected contact. Rudy stumbled and then turned, his lips pulled back to expose long white teeth. He plowed straight into Bogey, going for his throat.

Hannah had seen dogs fight before, but this time there were no adults around, no one else to pull them apart. She stood at the top of the hillock, paralyzed by the noise and by the fear that one of them was going to get seriously hurt down there, at the bottom of the bowl.

Rudy was on top of Bogey for a long time, growling and screaming, tearing at Bogey's face and ears, trying to roll him over. Bogey crouched, digging his paws into the ground and using his powerful legs to keep him upright, protecting his throat and trying to bite at whatever part of Rudy came near. In a flash, the two dogs sprang into the air and arced like fish jumping out of water, snow spraying up with them. And then Bogey was on top, his wide brown muzzle squared off and showing only teeth, the ridge of his back sticking straight up.

Hannah didn't think it was possible for her heart to beat even faster, but she was wrong. Fear came off her in waves. Through the din and the mess and the fear, she saw that Sencha and Nook, still attached to the gangline, were being tugged toward the two roiling dogs. Sencha's back hair was also sticking straight up, and she struggled wildly to get away without success, sprawled halfway up the bowl and very close to Peter's feet. Nook had dug her feet in, but she was still being pulled in as well, and as she got closer, her stance got lower and her lips, too, began to curl back in preparation for entering the fight.

The snarling and barking was so loud that Hannah didn't realize Peter was shouting until she glimpsed him on the other side of the dogs, trapped, with the fight between them. He was holding his hands up in an X against his chest and face and trying to back out of the bowl, but the sides were too steep. With each step back, he slid closer and closer to dozens of sharp teeth, and his shouts soon turned to screams.

CHAPTER SIXTEEN

Hannah slid down the hill feet first. As she slipped, her hand closed on something hard, and she took it with her. She had seen her father break up dog fights before, and once, at a dogsled race, she had seen a whole team fighting another team. It had taken so many people to calm the dogs down that another fight broke out between teams that had been left unattended, and in the end one of the dogs died, getting the gangline wrapped around his neck and choking as he fought.

It was hard to tell, but Hannah thought Rudy and Bogey were getting tired. At first the fight had been all noise and flashes of teeth and ugly stances of muscle, smashing into each other, but as she slid toward them, there was a tiny break in the battle, a growl-less moment before they threw themselves back at each other.

Rudy had gained the upper hand again and was back to trying to roll Bogey, slamming into the Lab's side and biting his shoulder. The teeth of both dogs were red with blood.

Rudy stood atop Bogey and again there was a small, narrow silence for the exhausted heaving of flanks — and Hannah acted. She hefted the hard thing in her hand — the snowhook, she saw — and stumbled and fell toward the two dogs just as they began another round.

"Get off, get off, that's it!" she screamed, hitting Rudy's flank with the flat back of the snowhook. The dogs ignored her, so she hooked the prongs of the snowhook under Rudy's collar and heaved backward, pulling him sideways and off the Lab. Hannah saw Peter turn and, with the help of his hands, scramble up the side of the bowl and out of her view.

In a split second, Bogey was up. His whole mouth dripped blood and phlegm and spit, and his ears were flat against his head, with the crest of his skull puffed up to twice its normal size. Hannah continued yelling and struggling with Rudy, who was rigid under her hands. She didn't know what else to do – he was fighting so hard, and he wasn't even acknowledging her, despite her shouts. Hannah had to get through to him somehow, so she punched him, punched him as hard as she could, in the neck and in the back, screaming, "That's it, that's it!" over and over. At the first punch, Rudy turned and started to snap — at the last second, Hannah saw his eyes register who she was. He turned back to his main antagonist, but she felt a little rigidity go out of him.

Bogey turned his body so that it was parallel to Rudy. He was still growling and showing teeth, his posture imposing, all the hair on his body puffed up. However, Hannah knew that when a dog stood sideways, it was saying, *I don't want to fight anymore*, and she realized in a split second that this was her moment to fix what was happening. Before she even completed the thought, she was standing between the two dogs, kicking backward into Bogey's flanks while still facing Rudy.

"That's enough, that's it!" she said. She grabbed Rudy's muzzle, as she'd seen other mushers do. In her other hand, she held the snowhook over her head, in case he lunged at her. She had seen mushers who in moments like this beat their dogs, and as her fear began to seep away, Hannah lowered the hand that held the snowhook. She did not think that was the right way to do things.

Her fear was seeping away, but in its place rose a terrible anger at what had happened, at how the dogs were not listening to her, Peter was not listening to her, no one listened to her.

She leaned her face right into Rudy's, pushing down with the hand that held his muzzle. "Don't you *ever* do that again," she said. She held his muzzle down and pushed with everything she could. Her deadened legs screamed, but still she pushed, until the sled dog was pushed down onto his elbows, with her nearly on top of him. Behind her, she could hear Bogey moving, and she kicked out backward again, barking, "Go!" at the Lab over her shoulder. Then she returned her face to just above Rudy's.

"Never, never, *never!*" she snarled. Then she waited. She could feel the anger in both her and the dog, like they were having their own silent battle now. Whoever won would be the leader, and she knew that no matter what, it had to be her. Rudy had already been thrown off by

Sencha, and Bogey, not Rudy, had started the fight in fear. But Hannah could not let fear run this team — not the kind of fear that paralyzed or the kind of fear that made them fight. She had to lead them.

Slowly, deliberately, she drained the fear and the anger out of her body until it was gone. She had no idea how long it took, maybe a minute, maybe an hour, but each breath she took became slower. And as her breathing slowed, so did Rudy's. The sled dog tried to take a few looks at Nook, but each time, Hannah pulled him back until he was looking only at her. His muzzle began to drop of its own accord, until in a rush, his body relaxed and she nearly pushed his muzzle through the snowpack, she was still pushing down so hard.

When she took her hand away, her glove was smeared with blood from Rudy's teeth.

Hannah stood up. Behind her, Bogey shook himself, long and hard, then came toward her with his head down. He was panting and wagging his tail, and he shied his head away immediately when Rudy looked at him; he did not want another fight, it was clear. Hannah watched, but Rudy didn't look at Nook again; he looked at her. She had won.

She surveyed the scene of carnage. The silence of the forest was eerie after the explosion of noise from the dog fight. The drifting snow was already covering the trampled-down area. The two blood-covered dogs, Sencha, and Nook were all hopelessly tangled in their lines at the bottom of the depression. The overturned sled teetered on a jutting branch, and the whole area was strewn with bits and pieces of gear: the supply bag, Peter's sleeping bag, the dog food, ropes. Sencha tried to get to a nearby food packet, but her tangled line prevented it, so she sat down instead to scratch her flank, exposing her pink, salve-covered tummy. Hannah saw Peter at the top of the bowl, standing behind a tree.

"You okay?" she called.

He didn't answer, but he sat down in the snow, pulling his hood up so that it covered his eyes and leaning against the tree.

All of this over a rabbit, thought Hannah. Although the truth was, all this had happened because she hadn't been paying attention. No, it went even further back than that: it was because she hadn't used Sencha's neckline. A reckless gamble that they had all paid for. And why had Sencha bolted? Because Hannah hadn't been paying attention, she had been *thinking*. She had blamed it on the dogs and on Peter and the weather and the trees, but she was the one who hadn't been listening.

Once, when she was about eight, she had been at a dog race when a certain sled caught her eye. All the dogs were quiet, pointed in the same direction, not wacky with joy or excitement. The sled was older, the square kind used for heavy loads or long overland trips. A squarish carabiner attached the gangline to two bridles; all the other sleds had only one bridle.

This team was run by two sisters, twins so alike that people could only tell them apart by their different-coloured hats. Hannah drifted toward them, and their dogs watched with mild eyes.

"Why do you have two bridles?" she asked.

The sister in the green hat laughed, and the one in the red hat said, "Because you can't afford to make a mistake in the winter." Then she, too, laughed, and Hannah had wandered off, thinking they were very strange. Why would anyone laugh about making a mistake?

Now she thought she knew why: the sisters had made mistakes but come through them; they were laughing as they thought back to how lucky they had been. Just like Hannah. There were precious few second chances in the winter, and Hannah had just gotten one.

Thinking was for nighttime, she told herself. *Think after dinner. Think when you first wake up; plan and think.* But in the daylight, when the dogs were under her command, when the trail was the only thing between them and getting her mom help, there was no time for thinking. There was seeing and there was doing: seeing what was happening, and doing the next thing that needed doing. That was it. That was all.

The next thing that needed doing was to get everything back together.

CHAPTER SEVENTEEN

Hannah scrambled across to Nook and checked her over. Besides the raw spot from wearing the wrong harness, she was fine. Sencha was also fine, twisting away from Hannah to continue rooting through the snow for the interesting scents she had caught.

Thankfully, neither Rudy nor Bogey was seriously injured. One of Bogey's ears had a few teeth marks in it and a piece of the edge was torn, and Rudy had a few bumps on his chest where Bogey had gotten hold of him, but most of the blood was actually from their own mouths, their gums having gotten cut up when they met mouth-to-mouth during the fight. Hannah washed all their injured areas with snow. Only a couple of the wounds were still bleeding.

Hannah pulled off her gloves, which were soaking wet. One of them had gotten caught in the snowhook, and there was a long tear across the palm. She held her fingers up, flexing them. Her left pinky was white. She hadn't even noticed it was cold. Not good, because it could be the beginning of frostbite. She massaged it until a pink flush started to appear, along with a twinge of pain as her feeling returned. She checked her other hand — it was fine. She looked up to where Peter was still sitting, now with his arms looped around his knees.

"How are your fingers?" she asked. She held up her bare hand. "I had a white one. You all right?"

"Fine," he answered. "Just dandy."

"Okay, well, I need a hand down here."

"With what?"

With what? Is he nuts?

"Uh, with everything."

Peter stood up, promptly delving knee-deep into the snow. "My snowshoes are down there, and I'm not coming to get them. I just got up here."

Hannah heard that same angry tone in his voice that made it sound like everything she said was wrong and stupid. But beneath that now, she could hear it: the fear. Like she and Rudy had felt a few minutes ago. *Don't make me touch the dogs*, it said.

If she could lead the dogs, then she could lead herself — and Peter. Starting now. *Don't think, just act and react to what happens.*

"I'll throw them up to you."

"Then what?"

"Then … then you come around to the trail and pull the sled up."

"With what?"

She looked around at the littered ground. "A piece of rope."

"Yeah, all right," he said. "They're over there, by the pack."

She went and located his snowshoes, under the black packsack and wedged against a rock. They were the old kind, not metal like Hannah's, but made from wood and rawhide and sinew, except for the crampons — the claws that sat under his feet. These were made of sharp, serrated metal and woven into the frame with more webbing. The snowshoes reeked of engine oil or gas, and even after she threw them to Peter, the smell remained.

The packsack had become unzipped in its travels, so she zipped it back up and lugged it to the sled. The sled was turned completely upside down. She inspected all the parts she could see before trying to right it. The white plastic runners that sat on the snow were scratched but intact, and as far as she could tell, none of the sled's main parts had broken. She righted it with some difficulty, then set the packsack inside to stabilize it. Thankfully, her snowshoes were still secured to the side of the sled. She unhooked the gangline from the bridle and tied it around her waist. She didn't think any of the dogs would try to run off, but this way, if they did, she'd know sooner rather than later.

She then set about gathering up all the gear that had fallen out and putting it back in the basket while Peter put his snowshoes on and traced a route through the unbroken snow along the lip of the bowl, back to the hard-packed trail.

Rudy and Bogey lay in the snow, panting. Nook was sitting as far away from them as possible. Only Sencha moved, still sniffing out food packages in the snow. Hannah followed her, unearthing buried packages and saying, "Good girl!" to the Dal whenever she found one. Sencha loved the new game and started locating them quickly. By the time Hannah had gathered what seemed like all of the food packages, Peter was at the lip above the sled.

Hannah saw the snowhook lying near the sled where she had left it. It was fastened to the back of the sled, at the side, by a long twenty-foot line. She picked it up.

"This'll work," she said.

Peter came to the edge and looked down. "Well, be careful where you throw it," he said. "I don't want prongs in my face."

She nodded, aimed at the side of where he stood, and threw. It was like throwing a piece of kindling; the snowhook looked awkward and lumpy as it sailed out of the bowl. But it landed at the top, and that was all that mattered.

"You ready?" Peter called.

"Yeah, ready."

As Peter tugged, Hannah pushed on the brushbow, steadying it so the sled did not tip over as he pulled. The sled slowly turned until it was pointing uphill. Hannah grabbed a few more pieces of gear that had lodged beneath the sled and tossed them into the basket. She could just see Peter as he pulled hand over hand, leaning back to gain traction and using his weight to steady himself. The sled rose slowly out of the bowl, sliding across the trampled snow and out over the lip, out of her line of sight, along with Peter.

She unhooked Sencha and Bogey and untangled the lines. There was very little sound above her, and she wondered what Peter was doing up there on the trail. But that was thinking again — she stopped. She started up the hill, and the dogs followed, ranging around her.

When she reached the top, she stopped a minute to catch her breath. The trees sat silent and the snow drifted down ceaselessly. Peter stood a little way down the trail. He had pulled the supply bag out of the basket and was looking down at it. When he saw her, he lifted his head and pushed back his hood.

"Hannah," he said.

Sencha saw Peter and started off toward him. Peter's face changed abruptly and he quickly turned away from the Dal, showing his back. But now Hannah saw that Peter turning his back was not cowardly, but almost exactly what Bogey had done down in the bowl. Peter was telling Sencha he didn't want to interact with her. However, Sencha was a Dalmatian, and she was not used to humans ignoring her. She was beautiful, and people always wanted to pet her. Whenever people saw her, the first thing they said was, "A Dalmatian!" As soon as Sencha heard that word, she knew that much petting and loving would be coming.

"Sencha, come!" commanded Hannah. The Dal slowed and Hannah said it again, this time using the same tone she had used with Rudy. Sencha turned and came back. Hannah snapped her back onto the gangline, and then Bogey, too. She took one of the short pieces of rope from her pocket and tied the gangline to a mid-size maple close to the trail.

"Stay," she said to the house dogs before going to the sled.

Peter knelt by the packs as she approached. The smell of gas grew stronger. She saw him taking things out of the bag and sorting them into two piles.

Then he pulled out the camp stove, and her mouth tightened. When he had shoved the stove back in the bag, he hadn't been paying attention, and she could see as she got nearer that the fuel canister had broken; the neck of the fuel can was gaping open. So that was where the smell of fuel had been coming from. The can had broken, and fuel had spilled onto his snowshoes during the crash, when the bag had flown open.

She knelt down beside him. He was methodically sorting through the contents of the bag: the first-aid kit, the packages of food. The hatchet and flint and waterproof matches all went into the pile with the first-aid kit. Then there was the spare water bottle and some of the grey ready-to-eat meal packets. They went in the second pile. Some of the food packets went into the first pile, but most were going into the second. She picked up the stove and looked at it. The neck had indeed been punctured, the tines of the stove were bent, and the fuel line had snapped at its base. The stove was flimsy and could easily have been broken in the fall, but the steel on the canister was thick; it could not have been punctured by any of the branches that the sled had landed on. She hadn't seen any rocks jutting out, either.

Her eyes strayed to Peter's snowshoes lying claws-up in the snow, their serrated metal edges like rows of teeth. Peter followed her glance.

"The whole sled fell on them."

Hannah looked at the top of the bag, and sure enough, there were puncture marks through the material. The material was waterproof, but still thin, so the crampons had punctured it like tissue. She lifted the camping stove and shook the canister. It was almost completely empty. They had only used it twice; there should have been lots of fuel left.

She looked back at the piles. "What are you doing?"

"These are fine," he said, pointing to the pile with the first-aid kit and the hatchet. "We can wash them off, and the matches are waterproof, anyway. But these ones …" He pointed at the other pile, where most of the food packets were.

Hannah reached out slowly and picked up a "Ham 'N' Eggz" packet. It was coated in fuel oil, and when she turned it over, she saw puncture marks.

"It's not my fault," said Peter. He sat on his haunches, looking down between his legs at the ground.

"I know," she said.

Then both continued, almost exactly at the same time, "You always pack food at the top."

No, it wasn't Peter's fault. You packed food at the top of the supplies, so it was easy to get to and put up out of the way of predators. Dealing with food was always one of the first things you did when camping, after setting up the tent.

The tent. Hannah scrambled over to the sled. The tent bag was one of the items that she had picked up out of the snow. If it was covered in fuel, they wouldn't be able to use it, and then they'd be in real trouble.

But it was probably okay, because it had been thrown clear of the bag when the sled tipped. A small thing, an important thing. But still, it felt like ever since she had seen that rabbit, she was living in a nightmare.

"I thought rabbits were supposed to be lucky," she said, staring at their ruined supplies.

More than half of their food supply had been punctured in the fall, then poisoned with the stove fuel, making it useless. She had started out with a king's ransom of food, and now there was only enough for one more day for the two of them, plus the leftovers she had grabbed from the fridge and a few energy bars that had been packed in the other bag and thus escaped contamination.

The camping stove and food packets had been inside their own smaller bag within the big black packsack, which might have limited the disaster somewhat. Hannah's extra gloves were still usable, but the last-minute items she had pushed into the pack — including the wool sweater she'd used to keep Sencha warm overnight — were soaked. So, too, was the bag holding the utensils, pots, and stove. For such a small canister, the smell was strong, and Hannah's head began to pound after a while. She drank more water.

"We could probably keep this," said Peter. He held up a packet with only tiny pinpricks in it.

"No," said Hannah. She was using snow and the tiny bottle of camp soap to clean what could be reused. "It's no good."

"You don't have to eat it, I will," said Peter.

She shoved the empty fuel canister in front of his glasses. "See the big red warning label? Poison." She grabbed the packet and tossed it with the others. They tied all the spoiled gear together and hung it from a nearby tree branch so it wouldn't poison any animals, then packed the sled again.

"Isn't there a thing that covers all this stuff?" he asked as Hannah looped pieces of rope over and across the frame.

"Yeah, it's called a sled bag. It fits over the sled and has a zipper so stuff can't fall out."

"Why don't you have one?" he asked.

The rope under her fingers was climbing rope, thick and slightly spongy. It tied easily, and Hannah concentrated on making sure the slipknots she made would allow easy access later, when she wanted to undo them. She didn't say anything.

"You forgot it," he said.

She finished and looked up at him. She thought about the snow goggles, and the sound of her mom's insulin ampoules skittering across the counter like angry spiders. She remembered the sudden look of fear that had crossed her mother's face as they looked down at the broken pieces.

"I didn't think I'd need it," she said.

"Nuh-uh, you forgot it."

Her mother hadn't gotten angry at her for making that mistake, and yet here she was lying about it, doing exactly what she hated other people to do. She sighed, feeling sadness creep past her shame.

"Yeah. I forgot it." She put her hands on the basket and pushed herself up to standing. She remembered the extra blankets, the headlamp, tissues. "I forgot a lot of things."

"Okay." Peter shrugged, took his toque out of his pocket, and put it on. He made a fist, leaned over, and bopped her shoulder. "Let's get to Jonny's place. I'm starving."

CHAPTER EIGHTEEN

They had just gained the first hill leading them out of the maple bush when Hannah spied another trail off to their right, at the bottom of the rocky outcrop they had just topped. Beyond the tantalizing stick-straight section, she saw another layer of forest, and then an empty white space with curved edges. A lake.

"What's that?" she asked, pointing down toward the base of the rocks. "Is that the trail?"

She put her foot on the drag mat and slowed the team to a stop. It had stopped snowing. Now, without the snow's hindrance, it felt like she was seeing every single leaf and branch and bird. She was starting to notice not the *sameness* of the forest, but all the *differences*: the snow load falling off a tree from its own weight, the red berries of a wintergreen bush by a low pond, the barred brown back of an owl ghosting so close to her head that the side of her hood ruffled, flying so silently that the dogs didn't even notice it.

And so, her eye was caught by an impossibly straight

line. Nothing in the bush was straight for too long; it must be something man-made.

Peter got out of the sled, and they stood staring down at it. All four dogs immediately lay down, Bogey and Rudy back to back like they hadn't been trying to maul each other just a few hours earlier.

"The trail splits up ahead," he said. "It splits three ways: to our place, Jonny's, and way back to a trapline they run back there." He looked at her and pointed down at the trail. "That's the one that goes to Jonny's."

Hannah felt excitement for the first time since she'd eaten breakfast. "So we're close?"

Peter squatted, peering at the trail. "I don't really remember," he said. "I think we have to go a ways before we switch back."

"You said we were halfway this morning."

"I don't remember how far it is, Hannah. I've only been there maybe five times with my dad. Usually we take the highway."

Hannah closed her eyes. She was tired. She had no idea what time it was because her watch had broken when the snowhook hit it on the way down to the bowl.

Every time she thought she couldn't feel more tired, another part of her body decided to tell her how tired it was — her elbows, her neck, her hips. *This is the worst kind of thinking*, came a voice in her head. She couldn't afford to give in to this kind of negative thinking at all.

"Do you think we could get down there?" she asked.

Peter looked up at her from where he was squatting. "What, to the other trail?"

"Yeah. Maybe not here," she said, gesturing to the sharp rocks. There was no way they could get down those with the sled. "But farther up."

"Maybe," he said, standing. "I'll keep an eye out."

He got back on the sled, Hannah called the dogs up, and they started. There was no pushing or shoving from Sencha now. The Dal started when the team started, her neckline loose and the gangline taut, so Hannah knew that she was pulling, as well as keeping pace.

They descended the hill, Hannah riding the drag mat lightly, and then the trail flattened out to the usual rolls and wide turns designed for the more cumbersome width and turning radius of snowmobiles.

The sled swayed from side to side, and instead of just looking ahead to the next portion of the trail, Hannah began to closely watch what Nook was doing. The veteran sled dog would often run very close to the side of the trail instead of in the middle, and as she swept past one such spot, Hannah saw that the middle of the trail, which outer dogs Sencha and Rudy ran over, was softer; the right-side runner slid slightly deeper into the snowpack. After they'd passed a section like that, Nook would swing back to the middle, and the sled, already shifting that way from the softer snow, followed easily.

If Nook ran all the dogs through the middle, it would be harder to pull, Hannah realized, so she was making them take turns at doing the hardest work. Sometimes Nook and Bogey, who was behind her, delved through the softer snow, and sometimes the other two did. Just like Canada geese taking turns dealing with the most turbulence at the front of the migration V until a different bird took the lead.

Okay, she thought, *that's enough.* She had allowed herself that tiny thought, but now she yanked her attention back to the task at hand. She tried to see the different types of snow, the small bumps that signalled the presence of rocks or sometimes branches, the blue-coloured snow that hid water beneath it, the shallow depressions of old summer ATV ruts. She identified kinds of snow: the snow that lay like a skin on rocks and was hard to travel over, the fat snow that lay heavy on thinly populated parts of the wilderness that were probably marsh. The snow at the bottom of the bowl where Rudy and Bogey fought had been fat snow, waist-deep and clingy like a cold, deep leaf pile.

There was crisp snow on the sides of the trail that lay deep in the shade of the trees almost all the time, and then there was what she thought of as summer snow in the middle of the trail. It was usually the most packed-down and the easiest to travel over, but it also got the most kinds of weather, so it could be mushy from sun or rain or pitted from uneven freezing. She felt the awesome grandeur of snow: all of it was snow, but each kind was distinct, with its own life cycle.

She began to call out the types in her mind to see if she could anticipate where Nook would go when faced with skinny over-the-rocks snow, with fat snow on the windward side of the trail, with mushy, out-in-the-weather snow, or with a section of ice with a thin layer of snow over it. Hannah got better at it as she went along.

"There!" shouted Peter, pointing.

Hannah had already placed her foot on the drag mat before he'd even said anything, and she realized it was because she'd reacted to him lifting his hand to point. It felt good to be able to do something right. She had watched the dogs and the snow and their surroundings, and when something had changed, she hadn't panicked, but merely acted cautiously.

I can learn this, I can learn, she thought.

The sled stopped. She set the snowhook firmly, and they walked back to where he had pointed. Once again, the dogs lay down immediately to sleep.

At first Hannah saw nothing, but then she noticed a tree that looked like it had been nicked by something — the bumper of a snowmobile or perhaps one of the sleds that they sometimes pulled. Maybe an ATV in the summer had stripped the bark off, although the nick was a little high to have been made by the bumper of a recreational vehicle.

"What?" she said. "That tree?"

"It's a blaze."

"A what?"

"A blaze," he said again, more slowly. "It's how loggers and surveyors mark trails."

She thought about the boundaries of the property at their cabin and how her father sometimes used a chainsaw to clear any obstructions around the edges of the property line. "No, they don't, they use that orange marker tape."

Peter shook his head. "Not the old-timers. They use an axe. Like this." He mimed swinging an axe one-handed —

down, then upward on an angle. "They cut down the underbrush, then they notch a tree when it's young," he continued, placing his hand palm down just above his knee, "and it grows up and the mark gets higher and easier to see when the underbrush grows back." He raised his hand to the level of the mark on the tree they were standing in front of.

"That's still not a trail; it's just a tree," Hannah replied.

Peter grinned at her. "Oh, yeah? Watch this."

He took her arm and moved Hannah so that she stood in front of him.

"See it?" he asked, pointing over her shoulder toward the notched tree.

"No. What am I supposed to be seeing besides trees?"

"The trail." He squinted over her shoulder and angled her so she faced a bit more toward the way they had come.

"There. See it?"

"Like, another tree with a notch? Yeah, I see that. Oh, okay, there's another …" She trailed off and instinctively moved just a hair to the left. Suddenly, it was like the forest had welcomed her in on a secret.

One tree notch; then another a bit farther along to its right; then another to the left; another to the right, on and on. They were all the same kind of axed notch, at the same height, on the same type of tree — medium-size birches scattered among the tamarack and pine. It was a secret, glorious trail.

"Wow." It looked so effortless, as though the trees had always been meant to stand that way, pointing to each other like families going through photo albums, seeing people they knew and places they belonged to.

"Yeah," said Peter. "Those old-timers, they knew what they were doing. See, they used the spruce like a hedge to keep back the undergrowth; spruce trees grow higher and other trees won't grow around them, so they wouldn't lose the blaze. Fifty bucks says Jonny's just using their old blazes from back when they were parcelling out this piece for the government. Sounds like something he'd do."

Hannah stared at the tiny white ribbon of unbroken snow before her, shouldered on either side by the marked trees and the green fringes of spruce boughs. Her wrists ached from holding on to the sled, her legs alternated between numbness and burning from the poling, her feet were sore from wearing heavy boots, and her back stung from staying upright against the constant movement of the sled. Winking just at the end of her sight, wavering in and out at the end of a shallow incline, she saw the white blob of the other trail.

"It'll work. It's wide enough for the sled," said Peter. "It'll save a lot of time."

She nodded. It would work, but she was scared. The snowmobile trail may have been deserted, ungroomed, and slow, but it was clear, it led somewhere, and if worst came to worst, she could turn around and go back. This path, even with the trees marked, was thin, dark, and worst of all, unpacked. She had no idea what lay under the snow, nor even how deep it was. She had no idea if this path was the right one. She had no idea if she'd be able to find it again, if she had to.

Stop thinking, Hannah. Just breathe and go.

"You'll have to carry some stuff," she said. "Me, too."

"Why?"

"They'll have to break trail, and it's too deep for them to do that and carry all our stuff."

He looked around, considering. "Okay, I'll take my sleeping bag."

"And the tent." Next to the sleeping bags, the tent was the heaviest single item that was easy to carry.

"Whatever."

She felt herself flush and wished she hadn't blurted it out, like an order, but it was too late now. She was just scared.

They went back to the sled. Peter stood on the runners while Hannah clipped a line on Nook to lead her and the team in a short, sharp arc, turning the sled to point at the blaze trail. They would not be able to turn once on the trail; then there would only be forward.

They pulled the sled until it was almost at the start of the blaze, with the dogs loosely assembled in front of it. *They're tired now, or content, or maybe both*, thought Hannah, and even Sencha did not mind the jostling and rubbing of trying to squeeze the sled and the dogs sideways on the trail.

Peter had put his snowshoes on. He slung the tent bag over one shoulder and hefted his sleeping bag onto the other.

"I'll break trail," he said, and started out. Hannah set Nook to following him, walking between the blaze marks and further packing down Peter's wide tracks, leaving a trail that the sled would just fit on, with Hannah at the back on the runners, poling.

It was torturous, but it worked. They stuck mostly to the line of tamarack, but twice Nook had to make sharp turns that caught the sled so it wouldn't be able to move without tipping over. Hannah called for a stop and wrestled the sled back into position before *huphup*ing the team again.

Finally, there were no more blaze cuts, and the trail was visible ahead of them. Nook paused, lifting her head.

"What's his name?" asked Peter, who was standing on the trail.

"It's a her. Her name is Nook."

"Nook?" Peter dropped his hands to his knees and awkwardly patted them.

"C'mon, Nook, c'mon girl, here, Nook."

Completely ignoring Peter, Nook angled away from him and again leaned into her traces, this time with a strong heave that Hannah knew meant a short burst of speed was coming.

"Let's go, guys, get up get up!" she called as loudly and enthusiastically as she could. They travelled the last thirty metres in a messy rush, with anything but team spirit. Sencha gained dry land first, as she hated having wet feet, then Nook, then Rudy, and finally Bogey, who lingered, panting, in the last bit of muddy, churned-up earth.

CHAPTER NINETEEN

"We have to keep going," Peter said. He still had the tent and his sleeping bag was sitting at his feet.

Hannah flicked her eyes over at the dogs. "It's too late. The dogs are exhausted, and so am I."

Peter shifted his feet, nudging the bags. "I could go."

"Fine, but it's my tent."

They glared at each other. Hannah knew they were fighting in part because they were so tired; tiredness was as much an enemy as anything else. When you were tired, you made bad decisions. She had to focus on *the next thing, and the next.* Her body told her what was needed; she just had to listen.

"It's late," she said. "It's snowing. I'm starving. So are you. What time do you think it is?"

He looked at her like she was crazy. "You have the watch."

"It broke." She showed him the cracked front. "Anyway, it takes forever to set up camp. Plus …"

"Plus what?"

If she could not be a hero, she could at least be a good leader. Hannah took a deep breath and stood up as squarely as her aching legs would allow.

"Plus, you're better at making a fire than I am."

She'd thought that he would crow at this and say he knew he was right and she was wrong — but he didn't. Instead, he blushed suddenly, red creeping up his neck, and looked pleased.

"I don't think this would be a good place, though," she said. "It's too low." The air, though thick with falling snow, was dank and smelled like stillness and rot.

"No," Peter agreed. "We need to get up a bit." He looked at the sky, straight up into the falling snow, then back down, blinking away the flakes from his eyes.

"I figure late afternoon," he said.

"Okay, then let's get out of this swamp and set up."

Peter nodded. They lashed the packs back onto the sled and set out, both of them trudging on their snowshoes, with Peter in front and Hannah near Nook's shoulder. The dogs pulled without enthusiasm, but Hannah knew that pulling would warm them up and dry them off. It was tough, but it was the best thing to do.

Up out of the marsh the trail went. The snow got crisper as they moved out of the lowlands, and snowshoeing was no longer like walking in corn syrup. The dogs started to dry off — steam was rising from Bogey — and they had their heads low, looking at nothing, following Nook more from instinct than any outward sense. The old husky kept her head level with her shoulders, flicking an ear now and then toward Hannah. It seemed that Nook was listening to the woods, the trail, the team. Hannah tried to do the same.

The trail wound upward still, although so gradually that it didn't prove too hard for the group. The snow did not stop, flying thickly, obscuring everything except the edges of the forest on either side of the trail visible.

Hannah's tiredness was so constant and present that it was like a second her, a ghost trailing behind her that she had to drag along. Her legs had gone from lead to heavy iron. She drank whenever she remembered to, keeping the bottle in her inside pocket so that it didn't freeze.

With no wind, the snow piled up on her shoulders, on Peter's toque, on the backs of the slow-moving dogs, and in the basket of the sled.

Finally, they came around a long, sloping corner, and Hannah had a dislocating sense of déjà vu. To her left was a tall rocky wall, its red-orange metamorphic layers jutting out showily from under its snowy mantle. Rivulets of water ran down the rock face, a weeping wall with a pool of ice at the bottom where the water collected and froze. Above them, the top of the hill looked down on them, and she realized why this place looked so familiar.

"We were up there, right?" she said.

Peter turned, squinted up through the snow, and nodded.

She dropped her hand and they continued silently, Peter stopping now and then to pick up various-size branches. She felt both relief that their plan had worked and disappointment that after all that, they were back where they had been so many hours ago, just thirty feet lower.

They skirted the icy patches and wound around the outcrop, coming closer and closer to the lake until they were following the contours of it, glimpsing the vast whiteness of the lake through the thin scrub that separated them from it. The lake wound in a big W, in close to the rock face and out again. The first V was a mess, with rocks piled up and jutting every which way, but the second V was deeper, recessed deeper into the rock face, and there were trees, as well, that sheltered it from the wind.

"Peter."

He lifted his head and turned. He didn't seem to have been thinking of anything besides putting one foot in front of the other and picking up branches. His arms were stuffed with wood. It was time to stop.

"Here, I think. This is a good spot," she said. He nodded. "Can you make the fire?" she asked.

He nodded again, shifting the wood and feeling in his pocket for matches. Stepping back, he took in the roughly enclosed circle of their temporary home and selected a good spot for the fire: away from the trees, near a medium-size boulder with a sheer face on one side. He stamped down a square patch, then took his snowshoes off and used one to dig out a hollow for the fire.

While he was doing that, Hannah got the tent bag out and placed it between the trees and the firepit, facing the lake. Then she went back to the sled and got out eight portions of dog food and unwrapped them.

She approached the dogs. They were all lying down again, Bogey already asleep, curled on his side with his tail tucked over his feet. Rudy and Nook, who were used to being fed at the end of the day like this, lay on their elbows, waiting patiently. Rudy licked his chops as she approached. Only Sencha stood, tail wagging, whining softly the way she did when she was very hungry.

Hannah stood looking at the team, waiting. Eventually, Nook looked at her, eye to eye, and when she did that, Hannah went over to the husky. Again, she stood there, waiting for Nook to meet her eyes. She looked at the lead dog a long time. At first the husky's brilliant blue eyes looked back at her stolidly, but after a little while, her nose flared and her head dipped, and she looked away. When this happened, Hannah dropped the two portions of dog food in front of her, and Nook immediately lay down and began eating.

Nook would not run away now. The muzzle dip, the flaring of her nose, and the breaking of Hannah's gaze meant that Nook had acquiesced to Hannah as the leader, and from now on, the sled dog would defer to her. Hannah unfastened Nook's tugline and neckline, leaving her free. She would not leave, and neither would Rudy, because Hannah had already had that conversation with him after the fight.

Hannah fed Bogey next, unclipping him from the gangline and dropping his dinner at his feet. The Lab didn't even try to lick her hands, he was so hungry; he dropped down and immediately began tearing at his dinner.

Next was Rudy, and finally Sencha. With each dog she repeated the contest of wills she'd had with Nook. Rudy dipped his head immediately, clearly granting her authority, and his reward was dropped at his feet. Only

Sencha was left. She was still whining, and as Hannah approached her, the Dalmatian began to pace.

Hannah's family had a tendency to quickly give in to Sencha's quirks and manipulations, and holding still was excruciating — Hannah was so tired. But she stood with the food in her hands at waist height while Sencha lifted her paws and put her bum on the ground only to spring up again right away, all the time staring at the food and not at Hannah. Finally, she sat, then lay down on her elbows, still staring at the food. Hannah waited.

Slowly, millimetre by millimetre, Sencha's eyes rose, returning often to Hannah's waist, but eventually, agonizingly, making contact with Hannah's eyes. It was even longer before Sencha showed any submission, but finally she reached out her neck and sniffed, then placed her head on her paws, relaxing her body. It was not perfect, but something in Hannah told her it was enough, so she knelt and put the food in front of Sencha, patting her flanks.

Now that she'd fed the dogs, Hannah turned her attention to putting up the tent. The ground sheet, the poles, the tent, and the vestibule — one thing and then the next.

By the time the tent was up, the dogs had finished eating. Rudy, Nook, and Bogey were curled up, the sled dogs' tails over their noses and Bogey's over his feet, as before. They were all asleep.

From her spot, still lying down, Sencha watched Hannah. When she saw Hannah looking at her, she wagged her tail.

"C'mere, Little Jane Austen," said Hannah. She got her packsack from the sled basket, took out some clean clothes, then laid it sideways as she had the night before. Sencha burrowed in without a backward glance and was asleep in seconds.

Hannah pulled the rest of the sleeping gear into the tent. She pulled off her parka, took her almost-empty water bottle out of the pocket, and gritted her teeth. She needed to clean off the sweat of two days, or risk getting sick from her body being overrun by bacteria or being unable to regulate its own temperature.

She wet her dirty shirt with the water left in the bottle and sponged herself off, trying not to shout when the freezing water hit her skin. It made her teeth ache and her jaw clench, and wherever she sponged, the sore muscles underneath the skin contracted in miserable rebellion. The sensation was like burning, or stinging ants, or the time she'd spilled rubbing alcohol on her shoulder: a white-hot cold.

She dried herself with the small camp towel in the emergency kit and put on the fresh clothes she'd dug out: a sports bra and an undershirt, a long-sleeved undershirt over that, a turtleneck and a sweater, a vest over that, and finally her parka.

She sponged her cold feet and inspected her toes in case they, too, had gone white, but they were fine, as poling all day drove blood to her feet, and for most of the time she'd been awake today, she had been hot, not cold. She put on new socks. She couldn't bring herself to change her pants. It was already hard enough to pee during the day, when she had to spread her parka around her while squatting to keep out the worst of the cold; there was no way she was fully removing them. Half-clean would have to be better than all dirty. Through the tent wall she saw the faint glow of a fire, and she was suddenly ravenous. She stuffed her discarded clothing around the Dalmatian, still out cold, checked her nose to make sure it wasn't warm, then went out.

Her teeth were chattering by the time she got to the fire. Peter stood up when he saw her, the bent camp stove tines peeking through his fingers.

"You think it'll still work?" he said, lifting his hand to indicate the stove.

"Let me see," she said.

He already had a pot of snow melting on the side of the fire. He had built the fire several feet from the sheared-off boulder face, scooping most of the snow so that it built a bank on the other side, toward the lake. The glow of the campfire on the rock illuminated their faces with reddish light. The rock was absorbing the fire's warmth, but soon it would start radiating heat back, which was why Peter had built the fire several feet away from it: they could sit between the fire and the rock, getting warmth from both sides. The snow, still falling, sputtered on the branches in the fire and wetted their ends, but only for a few moments, as the heat of the fire dried them out.

It was a good fire. She had underestimated the importance of the light, for as she was getting changed, twilight had fallen around them in its quick wintry way. The heat drew her in. *Is this what moths feel like?* she wondered. The way she was feeling, she could have cheerfully jumped right into the fire. She settled for leaning in close, feeling the heat coating her face as she studied the stove by firelight.

The tines were bent, but otherwise the stove seemed okay. Peter had gotten another fuel canister out, so she carefully threaded it onto the stove, primed it, and started it up. Peter watched carefully. The stove sputtered from the air in the line, flickered, caught, then held steady. They grinned at each other over the blue, hissing flames.

"I'll get another pot, you grab some dinner," he said. Hannah went to the pack and got out two packages of spaghetti and meatballs. Her hand knocked into something square as she was searching the pack. It was the emergency radio.

She took the backcountry rations and the radio back to the fire and lifted the red plastic radio.

"We can hear the weather," she said.

Peter took the grey food packets from her, grunting. "I have to get more wood before it gets too dark." He opened both and dumped them into a big pot, set it on the camp stove, and adjusted the heat.

"Okay," she said. "I'll watch dinner."

He put his snowshoes on. In the middle of buckling them, he paused. "It was a hare, by the way," he said.

Hannah looked up from stirring. "Huh?"

"You said it was a rabbit. That the dog was chasing. It wasn't — it was a hare."

"What's the difference?"

He stood up, shucking snow off the shoes and putting his mitts back on. "Rabbits don't change colour. And they don't hang out in big open spaces like the

167

sugar bush. They like scrub, small trees, and stuff where they blend in."

"It did look kind of big for a rabbit," she said. She remembered how huge a leap it had taken and the sheer impossibility of it leaping sideways ten feet, then turning on a dime.

"So, they're not the same species?" she asked.

"Not really. Lots of people get them mixed up," he added. He had picked up a short piece of rope and was slinging it around his body to help hold firewood. "Rabbits, they have lots of babies, more than once. Hares have fewer, and they nurse them, too. Rabbits kick out the kits once they've weaned."

Hannah was feeling light-headed; she didn't know if it was the tiredness, or the smell of warming spaghetti, but laughter was bubbling up in her chest. "Well, I guess that answers one question."

He looked at her. "Eh?"

"Why there's no expression about breeding like hares."

Peter rolled his eyes, but in a teasing way. "Duhhh."

She stuck the spoon in her mouth. "Hurry up or I'll eat everything."

Peter adjusted his glasses and started off. "You'd better not."

After he'd moved out of the circle of light and slowly disappeared into the gloom, Hannah turned her attention to the radio. It had a solar panel and also a battery. Since it had been sitting in the dark pack for two days, she would need the battery. She popped the back open, connected the leads to the nine-volt battery cell, and turned the radio on.

The radio, though small, had many functions. Besides the solar panel on top, it had a flashlight on the side and a small speaker on the bottom. It even had a hand crank in case the battery died and there was no sunlight.

There were three settings: AM, FM, and WB. It was already set to WB, the weather band. There were no stations on the weather band, just a constant repetition of the weather in English and then in French for the entire region, from North Bay to Kapuskasing. She turned up the volume until she could clearly hear the forecast. It was odd to hear another human being, even one who sounded slightly robotic, like the broadcast was snippets of different people talking cut together, instead of a live person.

"Today, for Timmins and surrounding area, snow and ice pellets. High minus one, low minus fourteen, with one hundred percent chance of precipitation. Fifteen to twenty centimetres of snow. Visibility zero. Overnight, temperature dropping to minus twenty degrees. For tomorrow, clear in the morning —"

She switched from the weather band to FM and pushed the tuner buttons, trying to find a station.

"So let's make sure we've got what we need with the cold snap moving in. Bundle up, people, I know there's lots of you without power or a generator. Get to a neighbour or, if you're okay, go check on your neighbour, all right? They've got help on the way, but still, it's no time to be alone. Remember, the community centre is open, and so is the gym at —"

She switched off the radio and put it back in the bag, carefully wiping off the snow before she did so. She went back to the fire to stir the spaghetti and her stomach growled. The snow in the pot on the edge of the fire had melted, and she added more to fill it up again. It took a lot of snow to fill the pot with water.

So, the cold was coming and the power was still out. She knew they had been lucky so far, even with the heavy snow.

The other emergency radio was at the cabin, maybe being hand-cranked by her mom right now. Hannah tried not to let her gnawing worries get the better of her. She hoped that her mom was not too worried, that she would understand that Hannah was going for help, so she could stop rationing. She imagined her mom and Kelli going through the daily chores, getting the wood and making the food, doing the shovelling and tidying up. She tried hard to imagine her mom injecting her insulin before dinner, as she usually did. *If it can work with ballet, maybe it can work with other things, too.*

From her spot near the tent, Nook raised her head and looked off into the darkness. Hannah turned to see Peter coming out from the dark with his arms wrapped around a big bundle of wood. He laid the wood beside the fire, careful not to get snow on it, and put a few more sticks on the flames before taking his snowshoes off.

She wrinkled her nose. "Man, those snowshoes stink."

"Yeah, I guess we didn't clean the fuel off them very well." He looked at the webbing of each one, pulling the sinew and gut, and checking the bindings. "The snow will clean the rest off."

She turned off the stove and placed the pot in the snow, and they squatted as they had that morning, stirring the pot to cool its contents and leaning toward the fire for warmth.

Peter removed his gloves and held his hands to the fire for a bit. He studied his pile of branches and selected a smooth one, then broke it into smaller pieces on his knee. Moving between the fire and the rock, he propped his gloves up carefully by the fire, using the sticks to keep them upright. Just as when he'd been packing up, his movements were economical, but she sensed that he was working out the problem as he went: which stick to use, where to place the gloves so they would dry the best.

When the gloves were arranged to his satisfaction, he sat back on his heels and picked up two more short pieces of branch.

"Want me to do yours, too?"

Hannah took her gloves off and handed them over. He looked at the torn palm on the one before propping them up.

"Is there a sewing kit?" he asked.

"Yeah, in the supply pack."

"You should fix that glove."

She looked back at the pot and shrugged. "I have another pair."

"Those ones are fine, they just need to be stitched up. They're good gloves," he said.

It sounds like he'd like to have them, Hannah thought, and she looked at his mitts drying by the fire. They were thick wool, the kind where the tops flipped back to reveal finger gloves. The leather palms were scarred in some places.

"I don't know how." She tasted a spoonful of food. "It's ready, anyhow."

"I can fix it," he said, coming around to the pot. She handed him a spoon and they began to eat.

"You kinda remind me of my sister," Hannah said, her mouth full. The spaghetti was still too hot, but they ate it anyway, shovelling it in and then huffing through their open mouths, trying to cool it down. She burned her tongue and the back of her throat, but she didn't care. It was warm, and it was food. In fact, it was all she could do not to snatch the pot away and eat it all. And judging by the way Peter was spooning up gobs, red sauce dripping off his chin, he felt the same way.

He sat up taller, holding his spoon upright. "Huh?"

"She would have known that stuff about hares and rabbits," she said.

"Yeah, but she learned it from a book."

"So?"

"So, it's different."

"Oh, your way is better?" she said bitterly. *Same old Peter.*

"No, just …" He stopped and made a circular motion with his spoon. Then he took another mouthful.

They ate in silence for a while. The snow began to taper off. The dogs, just within the light of the fire, moved now and then to reposition themselves, but no more than a few inches. Bogey was the closest, and Hannah saw his head slipping off his paws. He began to snore.

"What did the radio say?" asked Peter, spaghetti showing between his teeth as he talked with his mouth full. He wiped his chin with his parka sleeve.

"More snow tonight," she said. Her mouth was full, too. It was funny how talking with their mouths full wasn't a big deal to them, no more than their tacit agreement to wait when one of them stopped and turned off the trail a little to pee. It made things very simple, and Hannah found that despite the cold and the nausea and the pangs of anxiety about her mom, she was relaxing into this routine and familiarity.

"After the snow, it's going to get cold," she continued.

"How cold?"

She dragged her spoon around the mostly empty pot, scraping up the last bits. She felt like she could eat for weeks, but there were only five packets of food left. She carefully licked the spoon clean.

"Cold," she said.

"My sleeping bag is really warm. I'm not worried. It can get to minus thirty and I'll be okay."

"It's not us I'm worried about."

"The sled dogs will be fine," said Peter. "That's why dogs have fur. You worry too much."

"Bogey and Sencha don't live outside."

Peter looked at the dogs, three snow-covered lumps near the sled. "Where's the other one?"

"She's in the tent. Exactly where she was last night." He looked back at her, quick and angry. "Do you want her to freeze?" Hannah snapped.

"She's a dog," he insisted. "They stay warm."

"She has to sleep inside or she'll die, Peter."

He grunted and went to check on their drying gloves. There was nothing she could do about his fear of dogs, but she had to make sure the dogs were properly taken care of without putting too much pressure on him.

Hannah scoured the spaghetti pot with snow and refilled their water bottles from the other. Then she dragged out the emergency kit. The contents had gotten jumbled up from being thrown off the sled, carried through the blaze trail, sat on, and rummaged through. If she'd had any strength at all, she would have gone through it to check that everything was intact, but the warmth of the fire and the spaghetti had turned her will to mush. She just wanted to sit in front of the fire and watch the light, so bright and compelling after two days of greyness and dark.

She located the sewing kit next to a small silver bundle tied with elastics. Emergency blankets. She mentally slapped herself on the forehead. She took out two of the four blankets, along with the sewing kit, and went back to the fire. "Look what I found!"

Peter was putting more wood across the centre of the fire, making the flames leap and sparks fly up to fight the thinning snow momentarily before winking out. He didn't have his glasses on, and when he looked up, squinting to see her, she saw dark circles beneath his eyes. She handed him the sewing kit and one of the folded-up blankets. It was very small, as small as her cellphone, but once unfolded it was big enough to wrap right around a person, covering them from head to toe. The thin plastic layer didn't look like much, but Hannah had used these before in ice fishing huts, and she knew that they worked almost as well as sitting near a fire because they were airtight and waterproof and reflected back almost all of your body heat, trapping it inside the blanket and keeping you warm.

"Nice!" said Peter. They unwrapped the blankets, tossing the wrappers into the fire.

Hannah watched as Peter awkwardly threaded a needle, his blunt fingers too cold to be dexterous. Then he took her ripped glove off its warming pedestal and began to sew neat stitches along the tear.

"You're left-handed."

"Yeah," he said, not looking up. "Sucks."

"I am, too," she said. It was the first thing they had in common since both being afraid of Jeb. The leadership teacher at Hannah's school, Mrs. Dowling, had said that the more people had in common with you, the easier it was to lead them. "It doesn't suck. It means we're smart."

"Maybe. But it makes everything hard. Like this," he said, holding up the glove.

"Why?"

"Because Jeb taught me how to sew, and she's right-handed."

"Oh."

Hannah watched the small needle dip into the thick fabric and out again. Their blankets caught all the heat from the fire, and the rock behind them reflected heat onto the backs of their heads. She took her toque off, running her fingers through her dirty hair. "My mom's left-handed, too."

"Yeah." He said it like he didn't care, but Hannah saw his brow furrow. "I mean, no one is in my family," he continued, still sewing. "No ... my uncle is. I don't know, maybe my mom was, too. Probably."

Peter's mom was dead. Now it was Hannah's turn to say "yeah" in an uncomfortable way. They didn't have much in common, really.

The fire snapped and more sparks flew skyward, climbing higher into the snowless air. She could feel the dropping temperature on the edges of her cheeks and on her bare hands, which held her emergency blanket loosely around her. Beads of sweat appeared on Peter's forehead.

"Whew," he said, pushing the silver foil down to his waist. "I'm sweating up a storm. These blankets are awesome." Hannah's classmates used the word *awesome* with irony whenever they were instructed to do something they didn't want to, like write on the board or pick up gym equipment. But Peter said it like it was something important. The word was a perfect summation of the blanket. "I won't need it tonight," he continued. "If you want, well ... maybe you can use it for the dog ... the Dalmatian ... or whatever."

Hannah picked up the poker — the long, fire-blackened stick Peter had selected to control the size and shape of the fire — and stabbed at it. Another line of sparks flew skyward, a red gangline headed to the stars. She could say many things right now, talk and talk, but it didn't fit here. It didn't fit the cold, because talking was wasting energy. It didn't fit the fire, which kept them warm in its simple way. It didn't fit winter. Talking was another summer skill. "Thanks," she said simply. And she meant it.

Peter nodded, pulled his last stitch tight, and bit through the thread to snap it. Then he slid his hand in and opened and closed it to test the mend. He handed her back the glove. She didn't say thanks again, and he didn't seem to mind. He put the needle away and threw the remaining short end of thread into the fire.

They sat watching the fire for a while. Hannah was full, her belly and body full of warmth and her head full of thoughts. In school, she remembered writing down a list of leadership qualities like they were parts of a game. Out here, only a few parts of all of that were important. Maybe Peter was right, about the difference between learning from books and learning from experience. But that didn't seem quite right; without her course on leadership — learning from books — she wouldn't have understood why she had to take the lead, or how. Then she thought of her father patiently teaching her to identify birch from maple when she was young. It seemed to her that both were important. You learned some stuff in stillness, and some stuff by doing.

Peter wiped more sweat off his forehead and took off his sweater. The armpits of his long-sleeved shirt were wet, and seeing that, Hannah had another idea. She pushed herself up and went to the tent. In the vestibule she could barely see Sencha, because there was little light away from the fire, and because the Dal had burrowed her entire body except for her nose into the bag. She opened her eyes briefly as Hannah gingerly felt around her, but she didn't move, not even when Hannah had to pull something out from under her. She made sure Sencha was well covered again and walked back to the fire.

"Here," she said, holding out a pair of socks and a long undershirt.

"They won't fit me."

"Take them. They're clean, and you need them."

"No thanks."

"Come on," she said. "I'm giving them to you, for free, okay? You can have the gloves, too." She wagged her hands, which were clad in her second pair. "These ones fit me better."

"They won't fit," he repeated, reaching out nonetheless to take the items. He fingered the expensive wicking fabric of the undershirt. It was dark blue and made from merino wool, lighter than regular wool and warmer, too.

"The socks are tube socks, so they'll be okay. And the shirt is my dad's."

Peter looked unhappy with his hands full of gifts. He put his glasses in his pants pocket and took off his old undershirt, then put the new one on and smoothed it down. He looked less unhappy. "Why do you have one of your dad's shirts?"

She looked at him and shrugged. "I don't know. You never know, right?"

His face cleared and he laughed. "Right. You never know."

The cold night seemed to recede a bit, and Hannah relaxed. They were going to be okay. They might not be friends, but at least they had things in common now. And that was all she really needed until they got to Jonny Swede's and she got the snowmobile. After that, she didn't really care.

CHAPTER TWENTY

Hannah woke to find a sheen of frost on her sleeping bag, despite the fact they were inside a tent — this was the result of the moisture from her and Peter's breathing. At the first sign of movement, Sencha whined from the vestibule, crinkling Peter's emergency blanket, which Hannah had placed around her before going to bed. Her own emergency blanket had fallen off sometime during the night. Hannah sat up, gasping at the cold, and opened the zipper of her sleeping bag. Sencha shot inside it. Peter, waking to the movement, drew back in alarm, but the Dal wasn't interested in anything but Hannah's warm sleeping bag. She crawled in and lay down with a series of groans and huffs, shivering dramatically.

Hannah went outside and Peter scrambled after her, donning his toque and shuddering as he closed his jacket tightly.

"By the Jesus, it's cold," he said between chattering teeth. "Minus fifteen, at least."

They stamped their feet and slapped their arms to get blood flowing into their hands and feet. The fire had gone out long ago, but they covered it carefully with snow before setting up the heat shield and the stove and warming up breakfast. Hannah took out two energy bars, as well. There were three bars and three packets left, but they wouldn't need them once they got to Jonny's, so she took the third energy bar and broke it up, feeding half to Sencha and half to Bogey. The sled dogs looked the same as they always did, long and efficient, but the house dogs were changing; their flanks were leaner, and the muscles on their back legs were visible even when they were just standing there without moving. Bogey's shoulders had additional bulk on them, and Sencha's chest reminded Hannah of a horse's — deep and padded and wide. Despite eating breakfast, Hannah was starving, and she said so.

"Don't worry, Jonny'll make us pancakes," said Peter. "He loves making pancakes. And his own syrup, special. And breakfast sausages, too."

"Good, and just in time, too," said Hannah. She pointed back behind them. "Looks like a big storm is coming in."

She shivered, not from the cold, but from anticipation. She enjoyed a few minutes of daydreaming about sliding into Timmins, getting the insulin, then getting an escort back, maybe even with an OPP officer, or maybe — she let herself dream big — an RCMP officer, because it was an emergency. She might even make it into the papers. Her parents would let her go to the sports camp for sure after that. They couldn't say no.

Then she told herself that she couldn't be weak now, so close to the end. She roused the dogs, and they stood and stretched and shook. Shards of ice fell off Bogey's ruff, and his muzzle had a white fringe, but he was not shivering. In fact, he kept looking back as he made off to do his business, waiting until she turned away before going.

Hannah devised a makeshift coat for Sencha using one of her shirts. It seemed to help, but she was still concerned about the short-haired dog's belly, which was bare, so she tied extra material there and wrapped lead lines around Sencha's torso to keep it in place.

Plumes of steam rose from their faces into the morning air. It was cold. It was very cold. So cold that stopping for even a minute as they packed up meant that the cold went from knocking on the door of their lungs to stepping right inside the veranda of their parkas, the pantry of their leggings, the mudroom of their boots. The cold air stepped in and stayed until they forced it out with movement, whooshing warm air back into the house of their clothes by sheer effort. Hannah put a scarf over her face, because breathing through her nose made her nose hair freeze and her sinuses hurt. For the first time since they had fled Jeb's cabin, the sun was out, but its weak light didn't even warm their faces. All it did was highlight their breath, showcasing how cold it was.

Finally ready, they pulled away from their trampled little campsite. It was sure to be back the way they'd found it within a few hours, after the wind scoured the lake.

After they left the lake, the wilderness clasped them again, offering tree branches like old friends, and Hannah reached out as they slid past, giving them a high five. The branches creaked and shuddered, dumping the enormous amount of snow that had held them down so low, then springing up and rousing the whole tree until a mini avalanche of snow cascaded to the ground.

The trail was so obscured with snow now that only its bevelled edges and the absence of trees indicated that it was a trail at all. Sometimes Peter walked, and sometimes he rode in the sled while Hannah walked. They were letting the dogs rest a bit as they now had to break trail as well as pull.

By the time she glimpsed the dark blob of Jonny Swede's house, Hannah was plenty warm from alternately snowshoeing and poling. As they rounded the last corner, she felt sweat trickling down her back, and she grabbed her water bottle from the inside of her jacket. Peter drank, too. He caught her eye and lifted his water bottle. His mood had lightened as they had gotten nearer. He said, "Pancakes!" again and started toward the cabin at a half jog on his snowshoes.

Jonny Swede's place was nothing like what Hannah had thought it would be. She had expected a shack, something even more dilapidated than Jeb's cabin, with rough, streaky, unpainted boarding on the outside, a warped tin roof, an ill-fitting door. The guy had an old bus for an outhouse, right?

But it wasn't like that. It was small and neat and, even from the back, organized. The aluminum chimney top looked so clean against the sky that she wondered if Jonny polished it. As they approached, she stared at the paraphernalia hanging on the back of the cabin. Secured by long iron nails hammered on the back wall under the wide overhang of the roof was every piece of junk she could think of: long-handled hoes and seeders; shovels of all types; tires in pairs and alone, all in neat rows according to size. There were three old handsaws, one as long as her gangline, all bundled together and perched on thick pitted nails, at arm's reach. There were big pliers, too, and tracks for snowmobiles, their black rubber links held together with metal grommets and bearings.

The snowmobile! Hannah's heartbeat sped up, and her breath steamed out in short puffs, matching the dogs' panting breaths. In the winter, a snowmobile could travel as fast as a regular vehicle, if not faster. Regular vehicles had to make their way on old logging roads to get to the secondary roads. From there, they had to wind onto the highway, which was itself an old logging road. Even though it was paved now and had two lanes, it wasn't an easy road; it meandered and dipped and cornered its way back to town. But the snowmobile trails had been made for one reason: getting to Timmins.

"Hey, Jonny Swede!" called Peter as he broke through the ring of trees around the tiny backyard behind the cabin. On the far left-hand side, incredibly, there really was an old bus, now half-buried in snow. The front part, with the driver's seat, had been kept almost exactly as it was, including the long bus doors that hinged in the centre as well as on the side. She could see through the door that the steering wheel had been removed, but the seat remained, now facing the doors. Hannah imagined looking out the glass doors as she sat on the privy, with a view onto the back of the house and the forest. The other half of the bus had been made over into a big yellow lean-to with bus windows still intact, letting in light. One metal side had been cut and peeled outward and propped on thick posts made of tree trunks. On the bench at the back of the lean-to sat a neat row of engines and parts.

She stopped the sled and tied the snub line, looping it around a tree, then followed Peter.

She was right behind him as they rounded the corner of the house, slogging through the unbroken snow. Peter was still calling. The front yard, larger than the back, had a wide driveway leading off to the road, which she could see from the porch. She stood on the deck, stamping the snow off her snowshoes. The driveway was not cleared.

"He's half-deaf," said Peter, and he began to pound on the door. It was peculiar-looking, wide and low and made from thick wood. It had two metal bars across it, like on metal emergency exit doors. The bars reached only halfway across the door, but they were fastened together in the middle by a large padlock.

The shiny chimney. The half-buried outhouse. Hannah touched Peter's shoulder and he stopped pounding on the door. She pointed up. "No smoke. No tracks." She lifted the padlock and let it fall. It clanged metallically against the bars, then stilled.

"Shit. Shit!" he said.

Jonny wasn't there.

Not only was Jonny Swede's place not what Hannah had expected, it was also downright frustrating. In addition to the padlocked door, every window was fastened tightly with thick wooden storm shutters nailed shut over top of it. The tool shed in the front was locked. The woodshed also had a locked door on it.

"Who locks their woodshed?" she said after they'd trooped out to it, hoping to find a key to the cabin.

"Paranoid asshole," muttered Peter. "Jesus, he doesn't even have anything *worth* stealing." He was swearing more and more as they found each entrance impassable and felt each hope crushed.

The only window that wasn't shuttered was up in the crawlspace at the top of the cabin, and they had no way to reach it.

It was while they were looking up at the small window that Hannah tripped over something buried in the snow. They dug frantically for five minutes, shoving the tips of their snowshoes down like shovels and dragging up huge clumps of the heavy, white snow. Finding a tarp, they used their hands and feet to free it from the layers of snow and ice that had accumulated during the storm. The snowmobile!

"If there's enough gas, we'll go right to Jeb's after we go to Timmins," said Hannah as they dug. "Or maybe he has extra gas here. My mom will pay for it."

She didn't think long about what to do with the dogs. It would be faster if Peter stayed behind with them. They could break one of the shutters, maybe, and they could all stay inside. It would be warm there until she came back with help and the police.

Peter was wrestling with a trapped corner, and he pulled upward viciously. "I'm not going to Timmins. I'm taking the sled and going back to Jeb's. You can use the satellite phone there. They'll send someone out. Your mom is probably fine, anyway." He pulled again and the tarp ripped free, tearing on one side and leaving long, fluttering pieces of plastic.

"We're not going back!" said Hannah.

"Whatever. You don't even know how to use a snow-mobile."

"I do so! And it's not like you know how to drive a sled!"

"Move." Peter pushed her aside and straddled the machine, placing his feet on the long runners on either side. He pulled the gas tank up and looked inside, pulled the throttle to make sure it worked. Then he leaned over, looking on either side of the engine, and turned the gas line to ON. He reached for the ignition switch. "Oh, come on. *Come on!*" His gloved hand formed into a fist and he pounded at the centre of the snowmobile, between the gas tank and the steering post.

"No no no no *NO!*" he shouted. He was hitting something in particular, and beneath his striking fist, Hannah saw it: the keyhole where the ignition key went.

It was empty.

The snowmobile was useless. The boarded-up house was useless, and the locked sheds, the empty lean-to, the stupid yellow bus. All of it was useless to them.

Hannah tried to stay positive, swivelling around to find something, anything they could use. But there was nothing. Just the naked forest, the white snow smothering everything, the grey sky pushing down.

She could see the dogsled and the dogs from where they were. Nook, Rudy, and Bogey were lying down, but Sencha was standing. Over the makeshift coat, her blue sled harness stood out from the monochrome of winter. When Hannah's gaze drifted to her, Sencha's tail wagged and she sat, watching.

Waiting.

Ready.

"Peter," she said. He was still punching the snow-mobile. "Peter!"

"What!" he snarled.

"We'll keep going, okay? We'll keep going to Timmins." She could look past his stubbornness. And it was better to have two people together than two people alone. Anyway, she doubted they could break through those shutters.

"Hannah, we are not … going … to Timmins."

"Why not? We're almost there, aren't we?"

"I don't know," he said. "Maybe, maybe not. But we're not going there. We're going back."

"Back? We can't go back. Jeb —"

"We're going back!" he said, pushing himself out of the seat and climbing off the snowmobile.

They couldn't go back. It was two days out, and they were only one day from Timmins, she was sure of it. "Peter, we can't! If we don't go to Timmins, my mom could die!"

"Jeb has bullets!" he shouted back. "She's sick, and she's alone. Do you know what she could do to herself? She gets so scared, she once thought some snowmen at the park were the enemy … *she wanted a gun so she could shoot at them!* And nobody cares, nobody's there to help her because my dad is too chickenshit to deal and the Army abandoned her. It's just me and her. No. We're going back. You can use the satellite phone. Or not, I don't care." He groped around for his discarded snowshoes.

He sounded so sure. As though he had already decided. As though it was always going to be this way, even if Jonny Swede had been there to help them. She remembered how reluctant he'd been to take the shirt and the gloves from her. It was because he had been planning to do this, to thwart her plans and do exactly as he wanted.

She looked at him accusingly. "All this time, you were planning to just go back. You *lied*."

"Yeah, well so did you."

"You knew I needed to get to Timmins!"

"You tried to act like you'd just let Jonny decide what was best, but the whole time you were planning to wheedle and nag him into doing what you wanted, weren't you? Because you knew he'd side with me, with family."

Hannah felt hot shame rush to her face. Peter was right; she had been planning to do just that. "My mom needs help! And he's not your real family."

"He *is* family," snapped Peter. "Just because he's not blood-related doesn't mean he's not family. He helps us because he wants to, not because he can get something out of it. He's not like your goddamn family. He would have taken my side and you know it, so you were planning all along to screw me over and get what you wanted. You lied to *me*."

Peter's face was swathed in frost as he shouted, little pieces of it sticking to his scraggly facial hair and fogging his glasses. Off to their right, chickadees chirped in the bush, flitting around an empty bird feeder.

"Yeah?" she shouted back. "Well, I don't need you, and I didn't need this stupid machine, either," she said, pushing ineffectually at the handlebar of the snowmobile, which she was still leaning on. "I'll get there on my own, and you can freeze and die walking back because you'll probably get lost since you're too *stupid* to even know where you are!"

"I'm tired of you bossing me around and giving me free stuff like I'm some charity. Screw you, Hannah. *My mom could die, Peter*," he mimicked. "Yeah, right. You wouldn't know hard times if they slapped you in the face." He threw the tarp haphazardly over the snowmobile and put his snowshoes back on.

She stood back, her fists clenched and her mood ugly. "You don't have to slag off my mom just because you don't have one!"

He'd finished putting his snowshoes on, and he stood up and looked at her. His eyes were dark and his lips white, his face twisted. "You're just a snotty little city girl. Go to hell," he said, starting back toward the sled, lifting his snowshoes high to clear the snow.

She stared after him, so numb with shock and disappointment — they had worked so hard, and it had seemed so natural that they'd do what she thought best. Wasn't she the leader? — that she could only watch as each of his snowshoes lifted, dripping snow, canted, then hit the snow again as he drove it angrily through the snowpack.

Eight, nine, ten steps, and then his right foot came up, dripped, canted, came down — but it did not hit flat. Instead, it bulged in the middle as the snowshoe hit something hard and solid, and Peter yelled, then leaned sideways, losing his balance. He fell on his side in the snow and grabbed his right leg with both hands.

Hannah fumbled with her snowshoes and stumbled over to where he lay. He had taken a glove off and was rocking back and forth, holding his leg. Beside him, the long spiky handle of an old hand plow stuck out of the snow, the shearing pin sticking up at an angle. His snowshoe dangled from his foot, and there was a jagged rip in the side of his pants, from his ankle to his knee. She could see that his foot had gone right through the sinew and lashing of the snowshoe, and the shearing pin had acted as a knife along one side of it and up Peter's leg. The smell of fuel lingered, and she realized that, although they had cleaned the shoes as best they could, the spilled fuel had eaten through the webbing of his snowshoes. The resistant force of the plow coupled with his angry stomping had broken the webbing. His snowshoes were useless now.

"You idiot," she said.

She looked up the length of his woollen pants and saw that his leg was bleeding; the blood was darkening the blue wool to black in a slow stain near his knee that curled over itself like a hook.

CHAPTER TWENTY-ONE

Peter rocked back and forth, still trying to hold his leg, but every time he touched it, he winced and moved his hand away. He was swearing, his face contorted in pain.

Hannah looked up. They were about twenty feet from the dogs. She took off her gloves and knelt down. "Let me see," she said. He tried to clasp his leg again. She pushed his hand away and peeled back the torn fabric.

For a moment she fought the urge to gag. A long, shallow gash had opened the back of Peter's leg, right below his knee, from his ankle up. The flap of skin hanging off it was twice as long as Hannah's hand, and the wound was partially hidden by his socks, now soaked in blood.

She turned away and walked to the side of the shuttered house, gasping. It was suddenly hard to see as the sun came out, reflecting off the snow crystals and making her eyes water. Once again, she cursed herself for forgetting her goggles. She stared at the dark, stout poplar trunks until her eyes adjusted and she'd stopped crying, and by then she had a plan.

She couldn't close the skin with a needle and thread because Peter had used the last of the thread fixing her glove — and she had no idea how to do that, anyway. Instead, she could use strips of clothing and whatever was in the first-aid kit to bind the wound until they could get help. She went back to Peter.

"What is it? Is it bad?" Peter said. He stopped his rocking motion, but his voice betrayed the agony he was in. He was still on his side with one arm underneath him, and the deep snow prevented him from twisting to see his leg.

"It's going to be okay," Hannah said.

There was a lot of blood. The smell was like blackflies in her nose, sharp and biting. She tried not to worry too much about how much blood he was losing, though it was probably more than was good for him. She pulled the torn flaps of his blood-soaked pants wide and used snow to clear off what she could. Peter clenched his teeth and hissed and swore.

"Stay here, and don't touch it," she said. He continued rocking as she went to the sled, pulled out the emergency kit and, from it, the first-aid box.

When she returned to his side, he'd propped himself up, one hand packing down the snow beneath him. He was staring at his leg in disbelief.

"Jesus," he said.

"Hey, lie down." She put the first-aid kit down next to him.

"Jesus, look at it," he said, his voice tight. His movements had brought a fresh gush of blood out of the wound, and it dripped down onto the snow under his leg.

"Stop moving, okay? I need to wrap it."

She stood up, removed her coat, and laid it open on the snow. She placed the first-aid kit on its still-warm surface. She would need freedom of movement to bandage the wound.

"Rest, ice, compression, elevate," Hannah recited. She had learned this in gym class. She said it out loud to calm herself and to let Peter know what was happening. Had she been in his place, she'd have felt better if the person helping her spoke as though they knew exactly what to do.

Peter nodded, and Hannah felt a small measure of relief. She went back to studying the ragged gash on his leg while taking out gauze, ointment, and sterile pads.

The wound could not be elevated, and she didn't think that ice was the best idea since they were outdoors, but she could apply compression. The first problem was what to do about his clothing: should she keep it on against the cold, or remove it? Pulling back the flaps of the cut pants as wide as they would go, she considered. She could remove his pants — but she rejected that idea almost immediately. He had no spare pants, and it would be too much exposure of skin in the winter. She decided that the blood-speckled pants, even wet, would be warmer than nothing. She went back to the sled, grabbed some spare clothing, and used it to pad around the wound so that any blood would soak into the clothing, not his pants.

His boot was another thing: there was nothing to do but try to get it off.

"Go back, we have to go back. We have to go *back*, Hannah," he said, and she could hear sheer panic in his voice; it sounded just like hers had after they'd run from Jeb. His body was reacting to the fear with the urge to *do* something.

"Just lie still," she said.

He lay down, his teeth chattering, his glasses pushing across his nose from the awkward position. She took them off his face.

"Put these in your pocket, okay? You won't need them for a bit."

"Just hurry up so we can goddamn well get back."

"Stop swearing," she said. "It's not helping us, and it's just using up energy."

He grunted, clenched his arms around himself in a bear hug, and started rocking again. Every now and then he would lift his head to try to see what she was doing.

Hannah grabbed a gauze pad and the disinfectant and started cleaning the wound, in her mind trying to figure out how to say the obvious to him: there was no way to turn around now, what with the empty trail, the flooded shortcut, and the storm behind them. She also had no idea how much farther it was to Timmins, but she figured it was at least another day, especially if Peter had to ride in the sled, with the dogs breaking trail. She also had no idea how bad Peter's injury was, but it looked really bad. And they had only enough food for that day.

The panic pushed through her arm and she accidentally pushed Peter's wound hard with the gauze. Peter groaned and twitched his leg away. Frustration and fear spread through Hannah's body, and she began to cry. Thinking of the wastefulness of her tears — now she'd have to drink more, which meant getting a stomach ache from the barely unfrozen water — made her feel even worse, and the tears just kept coming.

She couldn't keep up. She couldn't keep up with everything that was happening, not even with the mantra of *the next thing, and then the next* that had gotten her as far as this without succumbing to panic, claustrophobia, or despair. Not in the face of the broken promise of pancakes, the empty house, the hateful words, Peter's bloodied leg. Each breath he took brought more blood, and Hannah's gorge rose each time she caught herself staring at the red drops falling from the mangled flesh, like she and Kelli taking little jumps off the low cliffside at Jeb's swimming hole in the summer.

Things kept happening and she couldn't keep up, and now there was a terrible, unbridgeable gap between her mental picture of them mushing into Timmins — or toward any house with lights on and people and warmth inside — and the reality of this bloodied boy on the bloodied snow, and her bloodied hands, which she could barely feel because she'd had her gloves off for so long.

In desperation, she kept cleaning Peter's leg, sponging as neatly and gently as she could. The disinfectant itself did not hurt, but the flesh had not been cut cleanly, and it was ragged, with little pieces of skin that flopped over when she sponged them. Twice she had to stop herself from retching. Her crying was almost a good thing, as it kept her eyes a bit bleary so she couldn't see the wound clearly.

Eventually her tears began to dwindle, and as they did, Hannah noticed a little kernel of thought inside her mind. It had a weird feeling to it; she kept running over it like running a tongue over a new tooth, or fingers over a new scarf that was so soft it clung to your fingers a bit like little soft hooks. Again and again, Hannah went through what had happened to Peter (the fight and his anger, the wound, the blood and cold), then the terrible gap between that and what she hoped for and had imagined so clearly, which was the town, and people, someone to help her, someone to help her mother. Each time, that gap made it impossible for her to connect things up; she couldn't visualize a way to move from the first thing to the second the way she could other things, like coming to Jonny Swede's in the first place or jumping higher in ballet. But each time she failed, she took a sidelong look at the little kernel, which felt like it was … waiting.

It was sort of like the times she'd gone ice fishing on the lake with her family, before she'd grown too old to like such things. They would all sit in the little hut or, if it was a sunny day, outside in a circle on the ice, and although there was a sense of cold and dislocation — sitting motionless outside in the winter, for *fun*? — there was also a sense of ease, of knowledge that *waiting* was the correct thing to do. That was what the kernel felt like, and when she tried, she found she could sort of move the kernel, so she placed it right in the gap, between the events of the morning and the lights of the town. And it fit. It slipped between the two things so that she could imagine going from the cold, bloody fight all the way to the town, and it somehow fit, even if it didn't make sense. And now her drying eyes could once again make out the sled and the four dogs, waiting. Waiting for her.

She looked toward them. "All right. I have my job, you have yours. Line out!" she called, and they uncurled themselves and stood and stretched, tails wagging slowly. She'd finished bandaging Peter's wound, and now she propped him up so that he was sitting. "I'll be right back," she said. She went over to the pack, dug out one of the remaining emergency blankets, and unfolded it before returning to help Peter remove his ruined snowshoe.

"Can you walk?" she asked.

"Yeah," he said, thrusting his wounded leg under him and trying to stand. He got halfway up, but once he put weight on the injured leg, he pitched forward into the snow, yelling in pain. "Come on, come on!" he gasped. At the centre of the wound, where the cut was the deepest, Hannah saw a fleck of blood seeping through the gauze and bandages. If he moved too much, he would just bleed through them, and she didn't have enough bandages to change the dressing more than once.

"Hang on," she said. She trooped back to the sled and rearranged it so that one pack lay across the bed instead of lengthwise, tied it down tightly with the pack line, then laid out the unfolded emergency blanket on the basket of the sled.

The sled was still snubbed to a tree; she took the snub line off and attached it to the carabiner at the back of the gangline, so that the dogs were now tied to the tree and the sled was free. She grabbed the bridle and pulled and heaved the sled over the unbroken snow to where Peter was, then she pulled and heaved some more to turn it around so it was facing the dogs. She took off Peter's other snowshoe and tied it to the back of the sled. Together they eased him into the basket in the middle of the blanket and pulled the sides up over him. His teeth were chattering.

"Are you cold?"

"No."

She went back to the tree and untied the snub line, led the dogs through the now-broken snow, and hooked them up, pointing back toward the trail they had come in on. Then she checked each dog over. Peter was holding his leg and trying to get comfortable. The emergency blanket made crinkly sounds as he shifted on the wooden slats. Finally, he settled half lying down, half sitting, with his right leg propped out straight over the packs and his good leg bent, the knee pointing up.

"We're going back, right?"

"No, we're going to Timmins. It's closer."

"I knew we'd just end up doing what you wanted," he said. He shook his head and crossed his arms tightly. "I'm going to die out here and it'll be your fault."

Hannah was working salve into Rudy's foot. *If you don't want me to treat you like a stupid jerk, stop acting like one*, she thought. But she wouldn't say it out loud, because then she'd be exactly what he said she was: a mouthy cidiot.

She realized that she did owe him an explanation so that he wasn't in the dark about why they were doing this.

"I think … I think the most important thing to do is to get you to a hospital."

"Jeb can fix this," he protested. "She did stuff like this in the field." His face was set in a scowl, but she couldn't tell if it was from pain, fear, or anger — maybe it was all three.

"That thing was rusted, Peter. The plow."

"So?"

"Have you ever had a tetanus shot?"

"I don't know. Maybe."

She finished up with Rudy's paw. "You can get really, really sick from tetanus."

"You're just saying that. You just want to get to Timmins."

She moved on to Nook. Nook turned her head and Hannah tried to scritch it the way her father did, the way Nook liked. She was rewarded by Nook leaning in to her hands.

Getting help for her mother was still important. But something else was there now: a deep dissatisfaction with almost everything she had done about it. Maybe she *was* just stubborn, maybe she *did* just want everyone to do what she wanted. Maybe. Now that she had found a way to change things as they were to how she wanted them to be, she felt a weird sense of gratitude. Now she had a chance to earn the skills and experience of this trip — to earn them with her team, and with Peter.

"The truth is," she said, "our dads are probably already on their way back by now. Someone will probably be able to help my mom before we even get to Timmins. Or maybe Jeb will go check on her. Maybe the power will come back on. I don't know. But what I know for sure is you need help right away."

"I thought you said she was dying."

"It's not really like that. It's a progressive disease."

"I know what diabetes is. Your body can't control the level of sugar in your blood. You can go blind or lose a limb. Your organs can fail. I know you can die from it. But I know it's not likely."

His words were so stark and simple that Hannah was taken aback, even though he didn't say them cruelly. He was just listing things.

"It's just ..." Hannah mentally ran over the fixed gangline of her thoughts one more time. Later she could look back on all that she'd done and wonder or freak out about it, but for now, there was only the task ahead ... and to do that task, she would need to be honest.

"I did it," she said. "I was the one who broke her insulin vials. I broke them, and then I left her and Kelli trapped by the storm, because *I* wanted to be a hero."

Peter waited quietly in the sled while she finished inspecting the dogs. She reapplied salve on Nook and Sencha's heat sores. Nook's was healing well, but Sencha's was still red, as her belly constantly had churned-up snow plastered to it. Hannah decided to keep the Dal in her makeshift coat, as it covered her belly and would give the sore a chance to heal.

"I was going to get my tetanus shot," Peter said suddenly. "For Air Cadets."

"What's that?"

"It's like the military but for teenagers. Only my dad said I couldn't be in it this year. He doesn't think it's real enough — he hates the Cadets because they're not really in the Armed Forces. Like *he* is," Peter finished sarcastically.

"Isn't he?"

"No, he's not. He plays at the Army just like he says I do. The Reserves," scoffed Peter. "Do you know what they do? They shovel sand into bags for floods and hand out water at marathons. They don't even have guns."

Hannah started on the rigging, making sure none of the lines was frayed and that each one was securely tied to the gangline, as well as checking that the gangline was strong and securely attached to the sled.

"As soon as I turn eighteen, I'm joining the real Army," Peter blurted after a moment. "He can play soldier all he wants. But I'll be the real deal, like Jeb. We'll make a difference, not like the Reserves people. We'll go places, save people. Not just be glorified sandbaggers."

Hannah quickly stepped onto the runners at the back, hurrying because they needed to get going, but also to hide her shock from Peter; she had heard longing in his voice.

He wanted to be a hero, too.

CHAPTER TWENTY-TWO

Peter stopped talking after his outburst, burrowing into the emergency blanket and leaning his head back with his eyes closed.

Hannah got the dogs up, and they started back along the trail they'd come in on, but this time, they turned left instead of right. She looked longingly the way they had come — not because she wanted to go there, but because the trail was so much easier. Their two sets of snowshoes, four dogs, and a sled had packed the trail down nicely. Ahead of them now, the unbroken skein of snow was almost chest-high on Nook. As soon as they were on that thick powder, Hannah dropped off the runners and began walking. She wasn't worried about the dogs getting ahead now. Nook would stop at her command, but it was unlikely Hannah would have to do that, as the snow and Peter's added weight slowed the team down to her own walking pace.

She tried getting ahead of the dogs to break the trail for them, but the snow was too deep for her to walk over it with any speed; she only ended up making herself tired and the dogs confused.

She watched the trail and named the types of snow. They were in the deep bush now, among spruce and pine, with the odd maple or birch. On either side of the trail, the bush was unbroken, dense with the bowed heads of small trees and large bushes. *Rabbit territory*, she thought, *not hare territory*.

She halted the sled. Peter struggled to sit up, grimacing. She opened the supply bag, handed him a water bottle, and took out the radio before starting up the sled again.

"*Well, Trapper Tom stopped by again this morning, and he says a huge storm is coming, because the last time it snowed, the snow was sticking to the fence posts. I kid you not, folks, this is what Trapper Tom is telling me. I go with what Environment Canada tells me. But hey, guess what? They're saying the same thing, just without the fence posts.*

"*I know you folks in town are better off now, and thanks to Gerald for giving me a lift in to work on his snowmobile. They're getting to things as soon as they can, but it's a mess out there. Remember to keep the young ones inside and away from the roads. Having all these power lines down can be dangerous.*"

Hannah turned the radio off again and passed it to Peter. The sun was still marking black shadows on the trees, but they were tiny slivers now, as the sun was almost directly above them, sitting on her left shoulder. She looked behind her. This morning, the storm had seemed imminent, but now she saw nothing but blue sky. The sun's rays were much warmer, too. She took off her toque, letting fresh air get to her greasy, matted hair. A little while later, she undid her jacket, and finally she removed her gloves, because her hands were sweating. She wiggled her hot fingers as she walked. They felt funny without the extra encasing of the gloves, suddenly weightless and free.

She went back to watching the trail and the dogs. They were moving more easily now, still struggling with the height of the snow but moving together naturally as a unit. She watched how three of the dogs shortened their strides, trying to match the Dalmatian's gait as she plowed through the snow. The line slackened, tightened, slackened again as they figured out the best way to attack the ungroomed top of the trail. Sencha in particular was struggling; she was the shortest dog with the deepest chest, and she looked like she was swimming rather than walking.

Finally Hannah called, "Whoaa," and the sled stopped.

"What is it?" asked Peter.

"Gotta change dogs. And here —" she pulled out their last two energy bars and gave him one. They hadn't eaten since breakfast, and it was at least noon now. She debated giving him both, but she needed to be able to walk and pole and pull as necessary. It would be foolhardy to leave herself hungry and unable to do things with Peter injured.

"The Dalmatian is too short," he said as he pocketed the energy bar.

"Yeah. I'll switch her out."

"Use the other husky one," he said, pointing at Rudy. This was the first time Peter had really paid attention to the dogs. "He's strong," he continued, "and then you'd have weak, strong" — he pointed to Nook, Rudy — "and behind them, strong, weak." He pointed to Bogey and Sencha in turn.

"That won't work," she said immediately, making a face. She sounded just like a know-it-all idiot. "I mean, it *would* work, but Nook is old. Rudy will pull too hard for her because he loves to pull, but she'll try to keep up. Bogey is …"

"He's the nice one," said Peter.

"Yeah. The nice brown face," she said. "He'll listen to Nook and not pull too hard. And then I'll put Sencha behind Bogey, because he'll break a wider trail than Nook — won't you, you brown tank?" Bogey's tongue, already half out of his mouth as he panted away his excess heat, slurped her hand.

"Yeah," Peter said after a moment. "That's cool, too." He shrugged and leaned back again, closing his eyes.

As Hannah redistributed the team, she checked all the dogs again and took off Sencha's makeshift coat, which was wet from the snow and hot — the Dal was plenty warm now.

Hannah risked a glance back as they turned a corner. Behind her the sled tracks stretched out all the way back until they disappeared around the last corner. The furrows where the dogs' paws had dug up the snow caught the afternoon sunlight. She spied another set of animal tracks off at the side of the trail, also glinting. They were deep and heavy and closely set. The dogs paid them no mind, their heads down and shoulders forward, panting.

They topped a small rise and went around another corner. Hannah saw they had been slowly climbing for a while and were on a sort of plateau now. The pines thinned out, and she saw tall poplar and maple trees and, below them, the ever-present thatch of small branches and trees that her father called scrub. There were large bare patches that tumbled and jutted like a bowl of marshmallows, though the granite boulders visible beneath the snow were decidedly not soft. The sound of the trail beneath the runners was thin and she knew they were running over rock.

The plateau started to slope downward again, and soon they were back in the dark arms of the forest. The trail swept down around yet another corner and through a heavily wooded area. The snowpack petered out until they were running over mostly ice; the snow had all been trapped in the pine boughs above.

"Easy," called Hannah. "Easy, Nook." They slowed to navigate the icy patch. The shade and placement of the trees made it seem as though they were underground, so dark was the trail and so still the air. She was concentrating on keeping her feet from sliding when she poled so that the sled didn't skitter sideways on the ice, so when Sencha barked, short and tense, Hannah didn't register it right away. The dogs slowed suddenly and Hannah had to quickly step on the brake to keep the sled from hitting the backs of Rudy's legs.

"Nook! Get up!" she shouted, but the dog didn't, instead placing her paws slightly wider and lifting her tail and head the way she did to signal to the team to slow down. Then one of the dark blobs by the side of the trail moved, and Hannah realized there was something else there with them. The sharp corner had hidden both parties from each other's sight until they were almost on top of each other.

Hannah's heart slammed into her chest as the hulking mass lurched upright in front of them. Black. Shaggy. It was a moose. It still had one side of its antlers, a huge scooped bowl tipped with hooked tines. It was massive, bigger than any animal she had ever seen in the wild. Its upper body was at least as big as their car and as wide, and when it stood up, it was easily twice as tall as her. How did it hold up those antlers? They were huge, and she knew they were made of bone, so they must be incredibly heavy.

The moose turned his shaggy head to look at them, the breath coming out of its nostrils in loud blowing noises. There was no steam because it was so warm, but Hannah knew it was clearly warning them.

Nook stood stock still. Her teeth were bared and her shoulders were straining against the traces of her harness; only Hannah's foot digging into the brake was keeping the sled from vaulting forward. Carefully, still watching the moose, Hannah eased the snowhook out of its pocket and placed it on the snowpack, stepping carefully on the back rod to set it deeply. Although it was on a long rope, if she did lose control or fall off the sled, the snowhook would eventually stop the sled and root it, even if it tipped.

The other dogs were not behaving, either. Sencha looked at Nook and began to jump against the traces, yipping. Bogey's hair stood fully erect all along his back and neck, though he wasn't making a noise. And Rudy barked excitedly, a high-pitched sound. The moose stretched out his massive, thick neck and lowered it, points first, toward the dogs. Its huffing began to get louder and shorter.

"It's going to run them, Hannah!" said Peter, then he coughed. "It doesn't see you. Walk toward it. Wave your arms."

"I can't," she said. "I'm standing on the brake."

"Shit. Well, wave your arms. Shout!"

She saw the square plastic object still in his arms. "Turn the radio on!"

He fumbled with the buttons as she waved her arms, turning the radio on to static. He cranked up the volume and held the radio above his head, yelling. "G'won now, get!"

The static hissed and the movement of Hannah's arms caught the moose's eye. He raised his head in alarm, tilting back the massive antler rack until his throat showed — *His neck is as long as I am tall*, Hannah thought. Then he turned in a heaving rush of snow, his impossibly long legs growing even longer as he broke back into the forest. His antlers *clack, clack, clack*ed against branches as he sped away.

The dogs fell silent as soon as the moose turned away. Even Sencha did not try to chase it. Instead, all four dogs stood there, their flanks heaving from tension, watching to make sure the threat had gone for good.

Hannah watched the moose disappear into the undergrowth. It was only a few heartbeats before it was obscured by the treeline, its dark flanks merging with the dark trunks. Only the distant sound of its heavy tread could be heard, as well as the faint complaint of antler-whacked tree branches now and then.

"I can't believe he moved so *fast*," she said. Even to her own ears, her voice was awed and breathless.

Peter nodded. "They can really move when they want to. I guess we caught him napping." He laughed, coughing at the end of it. As he brought his hand up to cover his mouth, flakes of snow landed on his fisted glove.

"Great," he said. "It's snowing."

The snow was a good sign because that meant it was getting colder, and it would be easier for the dogs to run. The warmth played havoc with the snowpack, making it become impassable. Finally, Hannah stopped, her legs aching and her back a steel rod of soreness. If she was this tired, she could only imagine how exhausted the dogs were.

"Why are we stopping?" asked Peter.

She didn't answer him but went over to the dogs, concentrating on assessing their condition; if the dogs failed, they would be in deep trouble. They would have to walk, either Timmins or back to Jonny Swede's, hoping to break in.

"Hannah, are the dogs okay?"

"Tired," she said, moving to the next one.

Rudy's paw was fine. Nook, who'd lain down as soon as the sled stopped, didn't even get up when Hannah looked her over. She could feel a slight trembling in Nook's legs and back she ran her hands over the lead dog's body. She was tired. Hannah smoothed down the old dog's ruff and left her to sleep.

Bogey's underbelly was starting to lose hair from rubbing against the harness, but otherwise, he was fine. She slapped his flanks the way he liked, and he licked her hand, his tail wagging. Many of her friends had dogs, too, but they were all special small breeds like Papillons and Schipperkes. Bogey was the dog everyone had: large and square and easygoing, obsessive about his ball. But he was solid, and had strength to spare, and did not complain; Hannah would take ten Bogeys over any of those other breeds.

Sencha's belly was still red, but at least it didn't seem to be getting worse. She applied more salve. Unlike the double-coated dogs, whose thick fur hid their frame, Sencha's body readily showed the changes wrought by four days of pulling: her legs were corded with muscle and even her neck had thickened, making her small, equine head look slightly silly. Hannah chuckled as she ran her hands over Sencha's flanks. A Dalmatian would *not* take kindly to being made fun of.

When Hannah had finished her dog detail, she unhooked them all, got out the camp stove, and set it up. After cursory explorations, each of the dogs lay down and went to sleep. Hannah took out her dirty clothing from yesterday and the makeshift dog coat. She covered Sencha with it, then helped Peter off the sled. He winced each time his leg bumped something.

"Do you have anything for pain?" he asked.

"Yes," she answered immediately. "Let me get it." Why hadn't she gotten some right away, back at Jonny Swede's? Because she'd been *thinking* again.

She brought the Tylenol and the last two packets of food over to the tamped-down spot where Peter lay, nursing the stove flame. Together they checked his bandages. There was some blood spotting through from the worst part of the wound, where the shearing pin had dug especially deep, but the bandages had held up.

"How does it feel?" she asked.

"How do you think? Hurts like hell."

"The Tylenol will help. I should have given you some earlier."

"Yeah, you should have," he said, coughing. "And I have a massive headache, too."

She didn't reply, just opened the bags of food and handed him the fork to stir them.

Now, while they were waiting for food, was the time to think, to plan. With a glance up at the snowless sky, she took out all the gear they had and spread it out on the tent ground sheet.

She sorted everything into piles. The batteries, the flashlight, which they had yet to use, the radio, and a can opener went in the one pile. A small handheld mirror, the now fairly useless sewing kit, and the first-aid kit went in another. A small, rubber-banded wad of money, water purification tablets, playing cards, and a roll of duct tape went in another. The sleeping bags and tent in yet another. The supply bag was almost empty now; it just held crayons and a whistle and some toothbrushes and toothpaste. She stuck her hand in and felt around, then drew out the covered tin she had grabbed from the fridge at the last minute. When she opened it, she felt her chest expand and let out a whoop of joy.

"Kimchi!"

"What?" said Peter. He was still stirring the melted snow water with the food packages in it. The sun had disappeared completely now, and the wind had risen, flickering the stove flame slightly.

"Food!" She made sure nothing was going to fall off the ground sheet, then headed to the fire. She opened the tin and showed him.

"It's a kimchi stew. Korean food. I thought it was spaghetti."

"It looks like sauerkraut or something. It smells disgusting."

She grinned. "I know, right? It's hot."

"How can it be hot when it's been sitting in the sled for four days?"

"No, spicy."

"Oh, really?" said Peter. His dull eyes lightened a bit. "I love spicy food. And I'm going to need it, I think."

"What do you mean?"

He gestured at his leg. "Shock. I've seen it. My uncle got a chainsaw bite once. He was fine, then halfway out to the truck, he just sort of keeled over." His voice was measured and even. "Spicy food might wake me up. I'm really tired. And it's getting colder."

"You need to sleep. We need to get to Timmins."

"Yeah." He gestured to the kimchi. "Well, get it in ya, then."

"It's better hot," she said. "Here, I'll clean up."

She handed him the tin and he wedged it into the pot. Hannah repacked all the items in the supply bag. The wind gusted now, slipping under the edges of the ground sheet and lifting it.

Hannah looked over her shoulder and there it was again, the same storm she'd seen that morning funnelling toward them in great grey furrows. This was not going to be a regular storm, she could tell. These clouds were different, not the fat, snow-bearing slate-grey clouds of two days ago. These clouds roiled. They separated and merged again, mutating thus across the skyline, forming darker, uglier patches.

A storm like that would not be over in an hour. A storm like that could last for days.

She began to pack more quickly, still keenly aware of the packages beneath her fingers, the cold plastic of the radio, the lightened weight of the first-aid kit, which she kept near the top.

She called the dogs and hooked them to the line before walking over to the fire. She took out her fork as she made her way back to where Peter sat, still stirring the pot.

"Okay, let's eat."

"It's not ready yet."

"We have to eat fast and get going."

"Well, you'll be eating it half-frozen, then."

"Fine. But hurry up."

He made a face as if to say, *How exactly can I hurry this?* and kept stirring.

Hannah looked up at the sky again, then at the packed sled and the dogs. She felt tendrils of urgency gathering in her belly, mimicking the clouds above, making her feel slightly sick to her stomach. She took out her spoon and tried not to hover as Peter stirred the pot — their last meal.

"Does Jeb know you want to join the Army?"

"Yeah."

"What does she think?"

"Depends. Sometimes she thinks it's the best way for me to get out of here, like it was for her. Other times she says I should do anything but that."

"I think you could be something else, too."

"Nuh-unh." He tipped one of the bags toward him and tasted its contents, frowning. "God, this isn't ham and eggs, this is sawdust and cardboard."

The wind gusted, yanking on the flame of their stove. Hannah watched it, hearing the hollow roar of the fuel as it sucked in more air than needed. "I think you'd be a good doctor," she said.

She could tell he thought she was making fun of him. "A doctor, eh?" he said. He pulled the packets out of the water, then the tin of kimchi, setting them all carefully in the snow before turning off the stove.

"Yes, really." She reached out and folded up the heat shield, which was already cool to the touch, as was the stove. She dumped out the pot, took all the gear to the sled, and put it away neatly. When she came back, Peter handed her one of the packets of food. She got the cardboard and sawdust.

She looked at the open tin of kimchi, which was steaming. She hadn't seen red in so long that it was almost alarming to look at the bits of hot red pepper.

"Let's eat this first," said Peter.

"Be careful, it's really spicy."

"Jeb and I used to put hot sauce on cornflakes," he said. "I love spicy food."

"Hot sauce on breakfast? That's disgusting."

He shrugged and they ate the kimchi in silence. The heat of the spices travelled right down her throat and into her belly, and she grabbed her bottle and choked down some water.

"Whew!" said Peter, grinning. "That is spicy!"

She took a few more mouthfuls, then handed him the tin and started on her packet. There was no seasoning except for salt, and there was way too much of that. *Salt and sugar*, she thought — that was what she was craving almost all the time. She wondered if that was what it felt like to have diabetes; did you crave sweet and starchy foods all the time, because you had to limit eating them? Her mom rarely talked about the disease that she had to manage daily. What must it be like to have a health problem for the rest of your life? To have to rely on medications? To have to test your own blood all the time to see how much medication you had to take? She needed to get that insulin. She thought about how long she and Peter had been away and closed her eyes, trying not to think about how worried her mom must be by now.

Hannah opened her eyes, looking up when she realized that Peter had been saying something. He was looking at her as she spun her spoon around her half-eaten meal.

"Pardon?" she said.

"I said I can't be a doctor. I flunked science." He looked away, his face bright red, but she couldn't tell if it was from embarrassment or the spicy food.

"So? I hate math, but I still want to be an engineer."

They ate, sucking in mouthfuls of cold, windy air to cool the food down.

"There's a big difference between me and you," said Peter.

"Maybe. I want to help people, too."

"As an engineer? What are you going to do, build a better mousetrap?" He chuckled at himself. "You're fourteen. You don't know what you want."

"I know what I want," argued Hannah. "I want to create buildings that don't scare people, that make people want to go into them."

"That doesn't even make sense."

"Hospitals," she said with her mouth full.

"What?"

"Hospitals. They always look scary, right? I could build a hospital that's inviting and calms people down." She paused. "I like it when you look at something and it's like looking at a mirror, not a wall. That's what I'm good at, too, putting together things that don't usually go together. You're good at observing things, and you keep a lot of information in your head. So that's good for being a doctor."

"Yeah, plus I already know how to sew," he said, rolling his eyes. "Brain surgeon, for sure."

"You put things together, too, is what I mean. In your head. You think," she said, "you analyze just as much as I do. Doctors do all that, put things together. Like about my mom. You just said all this stuff about diabetes —"

"I get it, Hannah," he interrupted. "How about I don't want to be a doctor?"

"Why?" She hesitated, then said, "Being a doctor is cool."

She waited for him to say something like, *What are you, five?* But he didn't; he said nothing, but ate faster until his packet was empty. He took her empty packet and his, filled them with snow, and emptied them, then Hannah added them to the small refuse bag they carried. She tied everything down to the sled and placed the emergency blanket in the basket.

She came back as Peter was struggling to his feet, but she said nothing. She merely swung her shoulder under his arm and helped him up. He was gasping as he lowered himself back onto the sled.

The wind was rising more and more, not content just to slip among their things, but pawing at them now with baby bear paws, thick and padded and immensely strong. It had started to shift, at first coming from behind, but now moving into their faces. They were running right into it.

"More Tylenol," Peter said as he lowered himself into the basket. He arranged the tatters of his pants over the bandage and sat back, grabbing the sides of the sled.

"There's only a few left," she said.

"Just give me some," he said, and she saw that his knuckles were tight on the wood frame. He hadn't even looked at the dogs when they walked very close to him.

She came around to the side of the sled and knelt down. The sled was perpendicular to the trail, pulled there to make emptying it out easier.

"I can't give you more right now."

"Hannah, it hurts."

"Do you see behind me?"

He looked over her shoulder and saw what she no longer wanted to look at, but could see clearly in her mind, anyway: the angry face of a winter storm.

"That's what the radio guy was talking about. We have to beat that, Peter."

He looked from the storm to her face. His glasses sat crookedly on his nose, and she realized they no longer fit because his face had lost some of its padding, making the glasses slide farther down. He rubbed his red-rimmed eyes. "This is bullshit."

"I know. I'm scared, too."

She called up the dogs and they lined out. She walked to the head of the gangline and started breaking trail for the team. The wind died down, and for a while it was just the thick, heavy snow falling and the jagged rent of the approaching storm in the sky above the empty tree trunks, but it started up again as they approached a section where the trees thinned. She could see the storm had swung around so they were facing it full-on now. It crept across the sky, dark enough that it covered the whole section of sky in front of them like it was night. Around the edges of the massive system, a sickly green light leaked, changed on its course from the sun by the suffocating storm clouds.

They came out of the trees head-on into a wind that almost blew Hannah off her feet. The snow sang past her ears, keening and slicing, stinging her eyes. She swore that she would never again go outside without a pair of goggles in her pocket. The darkness was falling fast, and she could barely see three feet in front of her through the snow and lapsing light, but there was a large open area — another lake? — in front of them. For a moment, the snow arced away in the wind and fell against their backs instead of their faces, and she saw the snow in front of her being driven far past her feet and then down, straight down, a good ten feet …

Hannah yelled and windmilled her arms, almost falling back onto Nook's head. The darkness of the storm ebbed, and for a moment the scene ahead of them was suddenly lit with a weak, greenish wash of sunlight.

They were at the lip of a pit. Down and down it went, cascading in layered tiers ten feet apart to a wide-bottomed pit ten times that depth. They had missed the snowmobile trail turning to the left to run parallel with the edge and had almost fallen into the pit.

Hannah grabbed Nook's collar, even though the husky had not moved. The wind shifted, and like a million frozen hornets, the snow tore at her face again. She brought her scarf up over her nose and turned, leading Nook carefully away from the edge and back to where the trail curved along the side.

Once she had relocated the trail, she struggled back to where Peter lay huddled under the emergency blanket. The wind whipped the foil, cracking and ripping it and making it sound like a broken wind chime.

"What's wrong?" he shouted over the howling of the storm. The snow was driving so hard that it was piling up on the front of the blanket, sliding off in clumps each time he moved.

It was no longer a storm, she realized. It was a blizzard.

"There's a pit or something," she shouted back.

He sat up straighter and looked to his right into the dark-grey air where the snow disappeared from sight.

"The quarry?"

"I don't know, maybe. It's huge."

"Yeah, it's the quarry. That's good, we're almost there! It's just the quarry, then the lake, then Timmins! We can make it!"

The wind was making her eyes tear up, and it felt like the temperature was still dropping. She could feel her eyelashes gluing together at the outside edges as her tears froze almost immediately.

There was no way they could stop now; the top of the lip was like a ski ramp for the wind; it whistled up the side of the quarry and blasted past them, almost lifting her off her feet. Then, from behind them, blizzard gales would swipe, full-grown grizzly bear swipes, lashing and buffeting them. At any moment, they could get caught leaning the wrong way and go tumbling off the side.

"Get under the blanket, including your head, and try not to move!" She had to shout so loudly that her voice was getting hoarse. Peter nodded and slid down until his head and wounded leg were the only things not lying flat. He pulled the emergency blanket right over his head and left only a small opening for his mouth.

Hannah groped her way to the black packsack and rummaged blindly in it until she felt a piece of rope. All the dogs were standing with their backs hunched against the wind, tails tucked and heads close to the ground. She struggled to the front of the sled again, tied the rope to Nook's collar, and started off.

CHAPTER TWENTY-THREE

One foot, then the other. Keeping the pit and the blizzard winds on her right, Hannah followed the trail around the rim of the quarry, rocked by the competing winds coming in from underneath and from the side and hemmed in by the thick undergrowth on the left.

She glanced back now and then to make sure everyone was okay. What she had thought of as darkness was, she saw now, just the sheer size of the storm. The dogs squinted against the wind so hard their eyes were almost shut, and they walked in a drunken zigzag, trying to keep up with the heaving of the sled as it rocked back and forth, buffeted by the wind.

The gusts were so strong now that the younger trees were almost completely bowed over. The trail they were following got thinner and thinner, until finally they were standing in front of a wind-bent wall of bush. Hannah cast her eyes around, lifting her scarf as high as it would go and shading her forehead with her mitt, trying to see through the snow.

The trail must go somewhere. It can't just stop.

She swept her eyes along the bush, looking for where the trail cut into it, but there was nothing but trees and shrubs and the occasional rock. She looked back down at her feet, then behind them a few metres, and she saw the tiniest of ridges on the edge of the lip, disappearing fast under the driving snow. She went back and looked more closely.

It was a trail that led down — down into the pit, the tiny edge following the pit wall on an angle.

The trail would have been tricky enough in broad daylight, with fresh dogs who knew what they were doing; but with an injured passenger in a blizzard on the edge of night, with her and the dogs dead tired and inexperienced, it was impossible.

She would have to lead the dogs down to make sure they didn't miss the trail or capsize the sled. But someone needed to ride the brake as they descended, or the sled would run them all over.

Impossible.

But it can't be impossible, can it? she thought. *Because we're going to do it.* She thought of ways to make it work. She could cut a gee pole — a long pole lashed to the sled so she could walk in front of it, steering and acting as a brake. That wouldn't work, though; the sled was too heavy and would be on an angle. She could unhook the dogs and pull the empty sled down, then go back and get Peter, but the snow and the wind made it impossible to see anything. She was scared that if she left something or someone alone, they'd get lost. No, it was better to keep everyone together. After a few more minutes of brainstorming, Hannah had a plan.

The path down was not straight, but canted, so if she didn't steer or brake the sled, it would begin to slide downhill sideways, eventually capsizing, or worse, falling off the ledge. She went back and untied Peter's remaining snowshoe from the back of the sled, then wedged it between the basket and the brushbow, with the curved end pointed toward the dogs.

"Use it on this side," she said to Peter, pointing to his left-hand side. "Push down." She still had to shout to be heard over the wind.

Peter nodded, understanding what she wanted: an additional brake that dug into the hill, keeping them from tipping over. He moved the snowshoe to the far left of the space and grabbed on with two hands, using his good leg for leverage against the brushbow.

Hannah went to the front of the sled and bent over Nook's head.

"Easy, Nook, easy and slow," she said, rubbing the husky's flanks.

Back behind the sled, she took off her snowshoes and slung them over her back, got the brake ready, and shouted, "Hup*hup, eeeeeasy* now!"

The sled moved forward over the lip of the quarry and down the steep slope to the next tier. Peter dug his snowshoe into the side of the bank, using it like a rudder to keep them more or less straight, and down they went.

Hannah kept one foot on the drag mat and the other on the brake, using the drag mat to steer and the brake to slow them down.

The sled tilted and slid, and the dogs hustled to the uphill side of the trail to compensate, straining almost perpendicular to the trail. The wind rushed in again and blew them all toward the wall of the pit, and Hannah's foot slipped off the brake for a moment. The sled shot forward. The gangline slackened suddenly and the dogs stumbled. The sled slid hard toward the side of the ledge.

"Hurry, *huphup*!" shouted Hannah, getting back on the brake. The dogs responded, pulling hard, and with their force, Hannah's drag mat steering, and Peter's leverage, they evened the sled out onto the trail.

It was only a hundred feet, but it felt like a hundred miles. The ledge loomed whenever the sled skidded too far, and Hannah's heart slammed in her throat. If they went over it, they were all done. She could see Peter's shoulder straining to keep the snowshoe brake in place against the incline, and the dogs scrambled and heaved and panted, digging through the snowbanks that the blizzard was piling up.

Finally, they were down to the next ledge and the trail flattened out again. Hannah couldn't tell where they were in the quarry, but the ledge afforded them some relief from the wind.

She reached out a hand to her right, the pit side of the shelf. Her mitt was caught immediately by the up-rushing wind, which lifted her entire arm over her head, and she drew it back, her heart thudding. It was like they were in a bubble, and outside the bubble, the wind and the cold and the snow — winter — wanted to end them.

She stopped the team, grabbed the snowhook, and stumbled off the runners. There was nowhere to tie off to, just the smooth, endless expanse of the shelf running away from them. She set the snowhook as close to the pit wall as she could; if the sled somehow got caught in the wind and was dragged over the side, the snowhook would stop it from falling all the way to the bottom.

She hoped.

Peter sat up, rubbing his right shoulder with his left hand.

"What are we doing?" he shouted. They didn't have to scream anymore, as they had at the top of the quarry, but he did still have to raise his voice to be heard, and if she went more than four feet away from him, she would lose sight of him in the swirling, stinging snow.

"We have to stop," she yelled back. "We almost fell off the edge, I can't see anything, and the dogs are exhausted."

"We're so close!"

"I know."

"We could keep going," he said. He sounded angry. "I don't want to stop!"

He half rose from his seat, grimacing and starting to sound off some more, when the wind suddenly shifted. It was like Hannah had touched one of those static electricity generators they had at science fairs; beneath all the layers of clothing, she felt the hair on her arms lift as the space around them turned into a momentary vacuum, sucking everything upward, and then the blizzard was upon them, knocking Hannah off her feet, the dogs sideways against the quarry wall, and Peter back against the basket.

She struggled upright, hanging on to the bucking sled's sides. The dogs were pressed in a single line against the side of the shelf. Sencha was keening, trying to get behind Nook, and Bogey's eyes were wide with terror. Rudy and Nook pressed as close to the wall as possible, their paws splayed, their heads bowed as they metaphorically gritted their teeth.

"We're stopping!" she yelled. Peter, gasping and holding his leg, agreed.

"Don't get out," she continued, "I need you to hold down the sled, okay? I need the weight. Don't move."

He nodded, and she crawled forward to get out the tent.

Setting it up was almost impossible. Four times, she put the poles in place and tried to spring them up to form the tent roof, and each time, the wind ripped one section or another from its mooring, or it pulled up the tent pegs, or it blinded her with snow. Each time, the tent ended up flapping in the wind like a handkerchief hung out the window of a car going at high speed.

Finally, the wind shifted. Again, it felt as though someone had turned on a vacuum over top of them, sucking up all the air. She had better luck then and eventually got the tent up and the fly over it. She pulled the two packsacks out and stuffed them into the vestibule, packing them up against the tent wall to keep out the wind and anchor the tent, however weakly.

Hannah could no longer feel her fingers, and her nose alternated between stinging and numb. The wind pushed and pulled at her clothing like teeth, snapping on the flapping hood that kept getting blown off her head. Her legs felt like lead again, lead bars that she had to lift and drag around. Her neck was sore from the constant shifting to keep it straight in the conflicting winds, and her arms burned from setting the poles upright over and over while she'd tried and failed to get the tent up.

Then she saw the dogs. They were as doing as badly as she was, if not worse. Sencha was the most pitiful; still tied to the gangline, she roamed the three feet available to her, trying to burrow in behind the other dogs and shivering violently. The three double-coated dogs were lying down, folded into themselves as tightly as Christmas presents wrapped at the store, but still Hannah saw the edge of the wind skimming across their bodies, lifting their coats so cleanly that she could see the pink skin beneath.

That was not good. The sled dogs could combat almost any temperature and be fine, but they couldn't fight the wind. The wind lifting their coats allowed the cold to get in, and if that happened, the huskies were no better off than the short-haired Dal was. They could all get hypothermia and die.

The wind whacked Hannah's hood against the back of her head again. There was nothing on the shelf but the tent and the sled and them. The slats of the sled would not be an effective windbreak for the dogs, and they couldn't get behind the tent because she'd put it right up against the rock wall. Besides, the wind was constantly shifting and knifing at them from different directions.

"Peter," she called, "get out. I have to do something with the sled."

Peter slowly hauled himself out. Wincing, he limped to the tent.

She crawled to the sled and released the snowhook, leaving it out on the snow for the moment. Then she tipped the sled over so that the runners pointed out toward the black nothingness of the pit and jammed the top of it up against the tent. It wasn't a great windbreak, but it was better than nothing. Then she scrambled inside the tent.

Peter lay on his back. In one hand was the water bottle, in the other the flashlight.

"I feel like crap," he said. She took the flashlight, got out more Tylenol and handed it to him, then handed back the flashlight.

"Thank you," he said. He took the pills and drank some water and lay down again.

"Are you hungry?" she asked.

"Yes. No. I don't know."

"You need to eat something."

"I know. Gimme a minute. I had a heck of a time getting in here."

The side of the tent bulged around the outline of the dog sled up against it as the wind tore at them.

"Peter, I have to bring the dogs into the tent with us," she said. "It's too windy."

"Yeah." His voice reminded Hannah of the insulin vials: cold, rigid, and thin.

"I'll put up a barrier, okay? They won't touch you."

"I'm tired."

"Me, too. I'm sorry."

"Me, too." He handed her the flashlight and she put it in her pocket.

She pulled her sleeping bag out of its stuff sack and lay it out lengthwise, very close to Peter, leaving a small space on the other side between it and the tent wall. Then she crawled to the vestibule and looked at the two packsacks she had wedged there. They took up almost the entire space. She went through the blue one, making sure there was nothing in it but clothing, and took out two pairs of socks and her last pair of mittens.

The snow was piling up against the sled and the side of the tent. Hannah dragged the bag to the end of the sled and wedged it as well as she could up against the tent where the least amount of snow had drifted. The wind plucked at the handles of the packsack, at her hair, at anything that was loose.

She crawled back over to the dogs. Sencha was whining continuously now, her eyes and nose crusted with wind-blown little icicles. Hannah unhooked her from the gangline and the Dal leapt into her arms, trying to crawl into her coat. She grabbed Sencha's collar firmly and took her into the tent, lifting the side of the sleeping bag so she could crawl in.

She played her flashlight quickly over Peter to make sure the dog wasn't going to bother him. His eyes were closed and he looked asleep, but she saw glistening tracks down the sides of his face.

She moved the flashlight away quickly, went back to unhook Bogey, and then she brought him into the tent. The big Lab trampled right to the only open spot available, the space between her sleeping bag and the tent wall, and lay down.

Next Hannah unhooked both the sled dogs, rolled up the gangline around her fist, and crawled back with her other hand on Nook's collar. She had left the vestibule open, and it flapped in the fresh onslaught of the wind, making Rudy nervous. He swung his head from side to side, watching it. Hannah threw the gangline inside, then reached up and pulled the vestibule zipper halfway down. She kept hold of Nook's collar and began to push the lead husky in.

Nook's butt hit the ground and she began resisting. She twisted her head away from Hannah, bending her head down to sniff the snow.

Something tugged at Hannah: that kernel of thought she had found at Jonny Swede's. This time, it wasn't a place-holder between two things, but it had that same quiet, grounded feeling of waiting. Now, though, it was wrapped around something — a memory.

Nook had twisted her head away and bent it downward. Hannah had seen that move before, from Sencha. *I don't understand this, I am nervous.* Nook wasn't showing rebelliousness, but nervousness.

Hannah loosened her pressure on Nook's collar, and immediately the husky relaxed. She had to find a way to communicate that being in the vestibule was better than being outside in the blizzard.

The kernel tugged again. Hannah stared at the tent, willing whatever memory it was to come forward, but it didn't. *I am in the middle of a blizzard and I do not have time to wait!* she yelled inside her head.

The wind howled, filling itself with snow and throwing it at her. The tent was dark and silent. She gritted her teeth, closed her eyes, and slowly pushed her breath out in a steady stream. At the end of the breath, she opened her eyes again. The vestibule was the same yellow as the plastic they used to cover the doors of the kennels in the winter. It flapped again in a quick upward motion, like when Nook poked her head out of her kennel in the mornings when someone came outside for the first time.

Kennel.

None of the sled dogs knew obedience commands like sit, stay, come, heel. But they knew gee, haw, line out … and they knew "kennel up" meant to go into the doghouse, whether it was their own, or the beige plastic crate for the vet, or the specially designed dog truck with two rows of dog boxes for transporting them to races.

Was that right? She ran through her thoughts and felt the kernel there.

Yes.

"Nook, kennel," she said.

Nook nosed forward, then paused.

"Kennel up, Nook, let's go." Hannah used the everyday musher voice that said everything was fine.

The husky nosed forward again, looked back, then went into the vestibule. Hannah turned to the remaining sled dog.

"Rudy, kennel up."

The poor wheel dog looked around in confusion; sled dogs each had their own kennel, or else they slept outside. Now it seemed Nook was in the only kennel there. She could almost see him thinking, *Where do I go?*

She grabbed his collar and backed into the tent, calling, "Kennel up, Rudy, let's go, kennel," and slowly he was coaxed into the shelter. Nook had claimed the most protected spot, between the supply pack and the shelf wall, but Rudy didn't seem to care. He lay down by the vestibule entrance, and after Hannah zipped it down, he curled up with his nose sticking out so that he didn't miss anything.

CHAPTER TWENTY-FOUR

Hannah woke up sweating and cramped, with her head crammed under a very heavy pillow and her legs jammed up against something soft but unyielding. She tried to lift her head free of the pillow, but couldn't. Instead, it became heavier, pushing down on her head, suffocating her.

She ducked her head down, sliding it out from underneath the pillow, and tried to sit up, gasping. She had awful vertigo. It was dark, and the air was warm and moist — was she in some sort of low cave? Her head banged on something hard as she sat up, making her yelp with pain and surprise. Then her sleeping bag rustled and Sencha's brown nose came into view. She had been lying across one of Hannah's legs, and now that she had moved, the feeling came back painfully. Hannah lay back, trying to bring her knee up to her chest as she rubbed it. The Dalmatian immediately flopped down again, half on top of her, grumbling.

Hannah's eyes adjusted to the dark, and the vertigo ebbed away, no doubt helped by the pins and needles in her foot and calf. Her mind whirled with thoughts: Tent. Dogs. Peter. Snow. Jeb. Flooded trail. Dog fight. Bus outhouse. Sawdust for dinner.

What she had thought was a pillow was actually snow load; the tent had half collapsed under the weight of it. Bogey had been forced to move and was wedged into a tiny space on the door side of the tent.

Hannah's rubbing elbow bumped against Peter in his sleeping bag.

"What the …" he said sleepily. "Why is it so hot in here?"

It *was* hot. There were four dogs and two humans, and they were half-buried in the snow; their tent had become a hot, humid, uncomfortable winter dwelling.

"The dogs," she said, still grimacing.

"Dogs?" he said, still groggy. She was close enough that she could smell his breath, and it was terrible. Her own was probably just as gross. She turned her head and inched down in the sleeping bag.

The pain in her leg had dulled to an irritating throb, and she pulled out the two pairs of socks she had rescued from the packsack before lugging it outside. "Here," she said, tossing a pair at Peter. She pulled up her long underwear and pulled off her own socks, checking her feet. She used the tops of the dirty socks to dry them, carefully sponging between her toes to wick away the moisture. She checked them for the telltale white spots that meant frostbite, but they looked fine. *There are advantages to having a Dalmatian foot warmer*, she thought.

She put the new socks on and turned to Peter. He was awake now, warily watching the dogs.

"It stinks in here," he said.

"It's probably you," she said. "Let's see your leg."

He unzipped his sleeping bag and rolled it back, exposing the wounded leg. They had slit his long johns up to his knee so that they didn't press on the wound, but would still provide some warmth to the back of his leg. She carefully moved the fabric out of the way. The dressing on the wound had a patch of dried blood on it, and some spots here and there. She would have to change the bandage. She rolled off his sock.

Peter looked down, grimacing.

"Does it hurt?" she asked.

"Yes. Stop asking."

"I have to ask. Does it hurt more, or less than before?"

He pulled off his toque and pushed back his tangled hair. It was so greasy now that it stood straight up, flopping over in big mounds at the top.

"About the same. Maybe less — but I need more Tylenol. And I'm starving."

"Starving is good."

"I know that, bossy britches," he said. "That's why I'm telling you."

"That isn't good, though," she said. Below the wound, his foot was a chalky white. All the blood was pooling near the wound, and not enough was getting down to his foot. She moved down so that his foot was between her knees. She looked up at him.

"This is probably going to hurt."

He bared his teeth and blew out a short breath through his nose. "Wouldn't be fun if it didn't, eh?"

She picked up his foot and began to rub it, using as gentle a motion as she could. Peter shifted and wiped sweat off his face, hissing as the blood began to move into his foot. She knew he must be in real pain since he didn't even swear, just grunted and hissed as the blood began to circulate and the white skin began to colour.

She massaged his foot for a long time, moving her fingers in small, gentle circles, paying extra attention to his toes. It took a long time for his baby toe to start getting some colour, but eventually it did. When there were no more white patches anywhere that she could see, she was relieved.

"Is it okay?" he asked.

"Yeah, no frostbite."

"Whew."

She put his foot down. "I'll grab the first-aid kit and let the dogs out."

He nodded, pulling off his other sock, and began to inspect his foot.

Hannah told the dogs to stay, unzipped the tent and the vestibule, and clamoured out.

She squinted as she emerged into the sunlight. The blizzard had passed; the sky was bright blue, with only the pale early morning sun marring it. The sunlight hit the quarry's sloped sides and flat planes and turned the pit into a giant mirror, bouncing light back and forth across the face of the snowpack so brightly that after a few seconds, even squinting, Hannah saw black spots in front of her eyes. She ducked back into the tent.

"Holy crap, it's bright out there," she said.

"Thank God," said Peter. He had finished changing his socks and was putting his grimy woollen pants on.

"I can barely see."

He tapped his glasses. "Tinted. Not a problem for me."

She resisted the urge to stick her tongue out at him.

"The Inuit make snow goggles from leather," he said.

"Yeah, let me just pull my trusty polar bear hide out of my pocket, genius," she said.

"I'm just telling you there are other things you can do, smartass."

She looked around the tent, surveying their rumpled sleeping bags and stuff sacks, her discarded socks and scarf. She yanked her toque down low, then wrapped the scarf around the top of her head, over her face, and down to her neck, tucking the ends in and leaving just the barest slit for her eyes.

"How's that?" she asked.

"Good. Now I don't have to stare at that pimple on your chin anymore."

She turned and went back out to the vestibule. At the door, she couldn't resist turning back to the dimness of the tent. "You've had a piece of dried snot on your cheek since yesterday morning," she said, then turned and called the dogs out into the sunlight.

Now that she was no longer blinded by the light and the reflection off the quarry floor, she could see that the blizzard winds had swept most of the snow off the trail they were on, rushing it past the top lip and down into the quarry.

The dogs wandered around while Hannah trudged over to right the sled. They hadn't had any meat the night before and must be starving. They needed to be fed before anything else, so that the food was digested enough to allow them to pull. It might delay their departure, but they needed to eat.

The sled was almost totally buried, with only the top runner and a hand width of the basket sticking out of the snowdrift. Hannah had to dig for a long time until she could tip the sled back upright. She opened the container of dog food. There were still more than a dozen portions left. She could give the dogs twice, even three times their normal amount and still be okay for a few days. But for now, they just needed enough to keep going. Maybe tonight they would get extra. She pulled out four portions and opened them and distributed them among the dogs, Nook first.

While the dogs ate, she ducked back into the tent and opened the supply pack to get out the first-aid kit.

"About time," said Peter. He had stuffed the sleeping bags into their stuff sacks. They were getting to be very efficient. On the other hand, besides the sleeping bags and the packsack in the vestibule, there was nothing else to pack but their water bottles.

Hannah wondered where Peter had put the dirty socks. Her scalp itched, and she scratched it through her toque. What she wouldn't have given for a bath or a shower right now.

Peter had managed to get his pants on and put a sock on his good foot. He sat waiting with the ends of his bandage unwrapped. Hannah opened the first-aid kit and took out the last of the gauze and bandages. Together, they peeled back the old bandage, exposing the skin to the air and making Peter hiss again. This time he was sitting up and could clearly see what was happening.

Hannah pulled away the bandages and placed them to the side. The skin looked angry and swollen, puffy at the bottom where the shearing pin had initially dug in, and again in the middle from when his weight had shifted, driving the pin more deeply into the muscle. Peter leaned over to get a better look, and his foot flexed. Hannah saw the muscle move in the wound and her gut roiled.

"Damn it, that hurts," he said.

"The muscle is cut."

"Looks like it. Flexing hurts a lot." He examined the wound. "Should we let it air out a bit?"

"I don't know."

He lifted his eyebrows, making his glasses bob up. "Is it possible?"

"Shut up," she said, but she was starting to understand that Peter's way of talking was different than hers, and that he was teasing her because he was worried. He wasn't trying to make her angry, so she'd said *shut up* without any heat, the same way she would have said it to Kelli, like she knew that he never *would* shut up, but still.

She used parts of the old bandage to wipe up what she could, then applied antibacterial ointment from the first-aid kit. Peter wiped his hands with snow and then helped to spread ointment over the wound, biting his tongue or gasping whenever he hit a tender spot. Hannah bound it up with the last of their bandages.

"Can we pull the sock over it today?" she asked.

"I guess we can try. It's starting to itch already," he said. "Driving me crazy."

They rolled the sock up carefully, letting the elastic hold the bandages close against his skin.

She watched him roll his long johns back down, and his pant leg, and then she handed him an energy bar.

"I have one," he said, patting his pocket.

"I know. I found these yesterday. Two extra."

"Sweet," he said, tearing it open and eating it in three bites.

"Wait here and I'll bring the sled," she said.

"Knock it off, Hannah, I'm feeling better this morning. I can help."

She gestured to her steel and plastic snowshoes. "You don't have any snowshoes."

She turned away from his frustrated face and went out to pull the sled over to the tent opening.

"Get the other bag," he said, pulling the battered emergency blanket from his pocket. "I'll put this stuff in. Do we need water?"

She shook her bottle. "I have more than half a bottle."

"Me, too."

"We'll wait, then," she said. She wanted to get going while the sun was out and it wasn't snowing for once.

"I can do the tent while you do the dogs," said Peter.

"Make sure it's all packed up tight. It's tough to get it all into the bag."

"It won't matter, anyway," he responded. "We only have to get past the lake now, and it's really close. Timmins is right after that."

She pointed up to the top of the quarry. "And we almost fell over that yesterday because we got trapped in a blizzard. Who knows what could happen."

"Fine," he snapped, then nodded more firmly. "Yeah. Okay, I got it."

He handed her the rolled-up gangline, then tossed the rest of the gear out of the tent and began to take it down, limping heavily and coughing every now and then.

Hannah attached the gangline to the sled bridle and hooked up the dogs before setting the snowhook to keep them secure. All the dogs had slept in their harnesses, and she went over them carefully, checking Rudy's paw and reapplying salve to Sencha's belly. Nook's harness sore had healed, but as Hannah ran her palms over the husky's flanks, she could again feel the old girl trembling. Hannah knelt in front of the husky, pulling her ruff around until they were eye to eye. Nook kept trying to look down or around, anywhere but at Hannah, and each time she looked up the white slope of the quarry trail to where it disappeared over the lip, her trembling increased. But her nose was cold, her feet were fine, and when Hannah parted her thick fur to check her skin, it was a nice healthy pink, not wet or splotchy. *Nook is probably just happy to get out of the confines of the tent*, thought Hannah.

She patted the lead dog's sides and stood up. Peter had the tent down and was stuffing the poles into the bag, being careful not to ram them in, in case they ripped the still-wet tent walls.

"You'll have to dry this tent when you can," he said.

Hannah barely heard him; she was looking at the empty space where the tent had been. At one end was the imprint of the sled where she had dug it out, then a small, empty space, then the quarry wall.

"Where's the bag?" she asked.

"Which bag?"

"The blue packsack with all the clothing in it. Gloves. Batteries. The flashlight. The radio. The ground sheet for the tent." She stumbled, not wearing snowshoes, over the open ground to the place where she had wedged it, scurrying her hands through the small mounds of snow to see if it had been buried. But it was gone, blown away by the nighttime winds.

There was a bitter taste in her mouth of bile. She felt sick. What if it had been the supply bag she'd left outside? Then they would have lost everything, the first-aid kit and the food and the stove and the fuel and the matches — everything. Still, as it was, they'd lost the ability to find out what kind of weather was coming, their alternative light source, and their clean clothes. She was lucky she had taken out the new socks when she had. They had only the clothes they were now wearing left.

She peered over the edge of the shelf down to the next one, but saw nothing, just row after snowed-in row. Kneeling in the snow, she pounded at her legs in frustration.

"Hey, stop that," said Peter from over by the sled.

"Stupid, stupid, stupid! I should have known better than to leave it outside!"

"What else could you do, leave the dogs outside?"

"I should have stuck it under the sled. I should have known."

Peter continued putting their gear into the sled. "It was a *blizzard*. I should have known to keep my snowshoes secure instead of having them loose, and look what happened. The crampons could have cut the dogs, and then where would we be?"

But it didn't matter what he said, because the only thing she could control was her own actions, and she couldn't bear to think that every single action she'd taken since leaving Kelli and her mom had been wrong. She took a shaky breath, moving away in her head from the idea that they had almost lost everything as she stood up and drew away from the edge.

"We still have the important bag." She looked up. "And for once, it's not snowing."

"And we're close," added Peter. "We can get there. We can get there today."

She nodded. "Nook, line out! Rudy, Bogey, line out!"

The dogs stood, lining out. Peter limped over and hauled himself into the sled. Hannah took her place, calling to the dogs to start. The sled rose slowly and jaggedly, taking them up and out of the quarry and then onto the trail that led to Timmins.

CHAPTER TWENTY-FIVE

The sled tilted from side to side. Hannah had her head down, pushing and poling hard to get them up the side of the quarry, over the lip, and back into the bush, when she felt the sled pull more on the right than on the left. She looked up. Something was wrong; Nook's head was raised, and so was her tail. The other three dogs were still pulling, but Nook's lines were slack. The big dog looked from side to side as though she were taking in the scenery instead of leading a dogsled team.

They were still on the hill, and the sled slid back a bit when Hannah stepped off the runners. The dogs hunched their shoulders and dug in to keep it still. She spared a moment to laugh: there were lots of ways to stop the sled from going *forward*, but none for stopping it going backward. She kept her hand on the side of the sled and then on the gangline as she walked to the front.

"Nook, what's up?" she said. "Let's go, Nook, come on girl, get up."

The husky turned back to the trail and began to pull again, and the team followed, Hannah pushing and poling again once the sled slid by. Near the top, she tripped and fell, breathing heavily from the exertion. The sled crested the ridge and stopped dead. Hannah got up and shuffled over the edge as well. "How did you get them to stop?" she asked.

Peter turned in the basket, the emergency blanket crinkling. "I didn't. She just stopped by herself."

Hannah looked down the line to where Nook was lying down, looking off into the bush again. Hannah walked forward and knelt down beside the dog, frowning. Nook laid her head on her paws and sighed. Hannah checked the husky again: teeth and ears, her feet and legs, her chest, the fit of her harness. Everything was fine. The lead dog kept her eyes open, watching Hannah. She wasn't interested in food, and she didn't move even when Hannah let her off the gangline completely. She stayed in the line, lying still.

"What's wrong with her?" asked Peter.

"I don't know," said Hannah, shaking her head. "She ate fine this morning."

"Maybe she has an upset stomach."

"Maybe," said Hannah. She watched Nook carefully; the husky's eyes looked everywhere but at the trail. The other dogs looked around, too, but none of them avoided looking at the trail. And when they did, they showed no signs of alarm. So it wasn't an animal. And it wasn't an injury.

What else could it be?

"Maybe she's tired," said Peter.

"She runs all day, every day, with Pierre," said Hannah. "She pulls heavier loads than this, and for longer runs." She placed her hand gently under Nook's belly to get her to stand. The old husky stood willingly, but again her eyes swept along the bush, at the other dogs, quickly over Hannah. When she did look up the trail, the trembling began again.

Hannah looked over her shoulder and down the trail. A little way along, it dipped out of sight. It was nothing alarming, just another corner that they couldn't see around. After a while, Hannah had stopped trying to guess which way the trail was going to lead, because it was too tiring to be so alert all the time. She had trusted that Nook would lead them through safely.

Hannah felt a flash of comprehension. Nook had led the team through blizzards, fights, floods, gunshots, and animal encounters, all the while teaching two new dogs how to pull and run and not complain, learning how to work with a new driver, and putting up with a human who feared her. She wasn't physically tired; she was *mentally* tired.

"I think she needs a break," said Hannah.

"We can't stop now, we're way too close."

"No, I mean she needs like a brain break. A break from leading the team."

"She's a dog pulling a sled. It's not a hard job."

She shook her head. "It is a hard job. Dealing with you and me, the two house dogs, a new trail, the weather, the wrong harness, the animals ..."

Peter lifted his blanket and rearranged his leg.

"Okay, just unhook her, then."

"And then what?"

"And then, I don't know, she'll run along beside?"

Hannah considered. They were all tired, maybe with the exception of Rudy, who also ran all day, every day. Like most sled dogs, he knew how to take advantage of rest times, and unlike Nook, he had no responsibilities except following the dog ahead of him and pulling hard. But running the team without Nook? Nook was the one they all depended on; other dogs ran alongside *her*, not the other way around.

Hannah swallowed the cold air. She knew she needed both sled dogs. They listened and followed and calmed things down; they gave the house dogs focus. She would keep Nook in the gangline — just not at the front as its leader.

She bent down and unhooked Nook's neckline and tugline, then walked a bit down the trail and called the husky to her. Nook came willingly, turning her body sideways on the trail. For a few minutes, Hannah did nothing but pet her and rub her body, saying soothing things and massaging her through the harness. Then she walked back to the sled with Nook following. The husky went right past the other three dogs, ignoring them, and started back down the trail the way they had come. Hannah picked up the back of her harness and pulled her back.

Immediately, the husky lowered her head and began pulling against Hannah, slow and steady. Hannah called her to stop, easing up and dropping the harness.

Nook could still pull, which meant Hannah's team was intact. There was just one problem: she had no lead dog.

A lead dog was not trained overnight. That much Hannah knew. While the other dogs ran because everyone else was running, the lead dog was the one who decided how fast, how far, and where. She chose the route, responded to the commands of the musher, and set the pace. She was usually the boss of the team, too, the de facto leader who set the rules for the pack: who could sniff whom, who ate where, who peed where. She disciplined the wayward dogs, the way Nook had done with Sencha when Sencha first resisted running with the team.

Now who would fill all of those roles?

Hannah walked around the sled, observing the dogs and noticing what each one was doing. Sencha watched her eagerly, moving a bit in the traces to follow her left, right, forward as Hannah circled. That was not good; even though Sencha was eager to please, the energetic Dal was better being told what to do and following those instructions. She would have been good at disciplining, as she liked to be the boss of every situation, but neither Rudy nor Bogey was prone to making mistakes or mischief.

Off in the distance, the snapping bark of a poplar tree popping in the cold made Sencha jump and look around, completely losing focus on Hannah as she twisted wildly, trying to find the source of the sound.

Well, that settled it. Sencha would not be the lead dog.

Hannah circled the sled again, watching Bogey and Rudy. Rudy felt duller than Bogey somehow, almost passive, even though she knew that of all the dogs, Rudy knew the job the best and had the most stamina. Rudy would be a passable lead dog, but he wouldn't be the best at making decisions, because he had always followed.

Bogey turned his wide brown head to watch her, but then he looked back up the trail. Bogey would be the best of the bunch. He wasn't ever startled off the trail by popping up, and he was beginning to get the itch — not just to run and pull, but also to quest out where they were going. He was big and strong and he led by example. He didn't back down in a fight, but he wasn't mean or a bully.

She would leave Sencha where she was: at the front, beside the lead dog. Supported by Sencha's enthusiasm to just *do* things and Rudy's work ethic as the wheel dog, Bogey would have the best chance of leading. Nook would run behind Bogey, still on the team, but without all the responsibilities.

So she unhooked Bogey's neckline and snapped him into the lead, moving Nook back into the gangline, but now beside Rudy. Then she lined out her new team. Bogey looked up the trail, his head up, sniffing the air. She checked one more time to make sure that the packs were as secure as she could make them. Then she stepped on the runners and yelled, "Get up!"

And chaos happened. Nook lifted her head but didn't move. Rudy heaved once, saw that no one else was doing it, and quit. Sencha rabbited into the side of Bogey, confused by the change in leadership, and her spooked cry startled the Lab, who shied sideways, then began to back up, tail down. In the space of three heartbeats, the whole gangline was a tangled mess.

Dogs, Hannah reminded herself as she hauled the recalcitrant Dalmatian back into line and coaxed Bogey forward to a lined-out position so she could untangle them, *are not humans*. So, while in her mind Bogey was the best fit, he obviously couldn't read her mind or discuss being the lead dog with her. He would need some help.

She thought about it. The Lab was unsure of how to start, but Hannah was fairly confident that once he got going, he would be okay; just the act of running itself solved many problems, she was beginning to understand. When in doubt, you did something physical, just like her personal mantra, *the next thing*.

Until now, the sound of Hannah's voice, coupled with the jerk of the harness as Nook pulled him forward, was what got Bogey going. She would try replicating that. She went back to the packsack, grabbed a lead, and snapped it to Bogey's collar. She lined out ahead of the Lab and yelled, "Get up!" This time she started to run. Her timing was off and there was another muddle, and she had to stop and untangle everyone. Twice more she lined them out and started the team as though she were the lead dog. Each time, they got a bit smoother, but they'd also eventually cue wrong off each other, and in their confusion, get hopelessly tangled up. In a way, it was a small miracle they had gotten through all they had so far without something like this happening. Nook, Hannah was learning, was despite her age a very, very valuable dog.

Yelling wouldn't solve anything. This many days into the running, Hannah could predict what would happen: Sencha would cower and become stubborn, Rudy would ignore it and continue to do what the pack leader said, and Bogey would shut down and refuse to do anything. So Hannah wrestled with her frustration and with the nagging fear they were losing too much time on the trail, and she lined out the team and tried again.

Three more starts — each one minutely better than the last. Hannah was hot and tired, but didn't dare take her coat off in case they got going. On the second-to-last try, she turned to see Bogey put his head down as he pulled — just before they got hopelessly tangled up again — and she knew it was a good sign. It meant he was relaxing and just doing the work. They had only gotten tangled because she had stopped and turned, breaking his concentration.

She gave herself a few moments to catch her breath. Kneeling down by Bogey's side, Hannah grabbed his jowls playfully and rubbed his ears. He licked her face, not overly concerned that he was failing miserably as their new lead dog. She put her forehead to his. "You're going to do it this time, Bogey. We have to get going, okay? The faster we get there, the faster you get to lie down by a fire somewhere with a big disgusting bone." She stood up and ruffled Bogey's head one more time. He shook himself, and she lined out the dogs, but this time, instead of standing in front of Bogey, she stood beside him.

"Okay, let's go, get up!" she cried again, and they all began to pull. She laboured beside the Labrador for a few moments, and then, as she slowed, called out, "On by! On by!" as though she were a mere distraction, and they should just ignore her and keep going. Bogey hesitated.

"Get up, Bogey! Get up!" The Lab swung his head back toward the trail, and the line straightened. He glanced once more at her, then pulled back to the centre of the trail and kept running. Sencha went by, then Rudy. Their heads were lifted, but they followed their lead dog. Nook's head was low, her body relaxed, just pulling.

"Good boy, Bogey! Hike! Hike!" Hannah began running again and caught the bow handle as it went by, jumping with one foot onto the runners and poling hard with the other to keep the sled feeling light and easy to pull. Rudy's tail dropped, then Sencha's, and the sled shushed on.

"I think he's got it this time," said Peter.

"Good guys, good guys!" she hollered. "Let's go!"

The sled moved a little slower, and she knew she would have to rest a bit more often, but she let those worries lie dormant. They were moving in the right direction, and once again, it seemed everything was possible. Her empty stomach, the aches and pains, Peter's surliness — all of that faded.

"Did you see that?" she shouted at the trees. "We're doing it! Woooo-hoooo!" she shouted. "Good guys, good guys! Get up!"

They ran. The bush was thinner here; the quarry had been located up high in the side of a large rocky hill. These were old, old mountains now worn down to nubs, their tops clear of snow and a steady ochre that warmed to the winter sun. The team rushed over the cobbled skeleton of the Canadian Shield, leaving the thicker, darker bush a gloomy cloud below them. She saw more hares, their white bodies startlingly big, explode to the left and right. She saw them before the dogs this time because she was actively looking for them. She watched the trail and the dogs and the hares; if the hares were blindside to the dogs, she said nothing, but if they were somewhere she thought the dogs might see them, she would call out, "On by! On by!" again.

Neither Sencha nor Bogey really knew what that command meant, but Bogey took his cue from her encouraging *let's run* voice, and Sencha reacted to that now, instead of to her instincts. Even if she paused, her predator's nose or ears or eyes taking over for a moment, she would be pulled along in the traces and recover.

As the sled flexed and bounded forward, Hannah looked at Bogey. His head was rising — so were the other dogs' heads, even Nook's. Unease grew in her belly, and she flipped down the drag mat, pressing lightly to let the dogs know she was listening.

The trail had been following a series of small hills with short plateaus, but now it turned, and they ran downhill alongside an unnaturally wide swath of snow. On their left, the bush continued, an endless thicket of poplar and willow and smaller leggy conifers — forest that had been cut down, but was growing back now. Hannah's father called it scrub bush.

On their right, yellow plastic poles stuck up out of the cleared ground, and in other places, there were long metals rods taller than Hannah painted blue with CAUTION symbols painted on them.

But that wasn't what was disturbing the dogs. What interested them was about a hundred metres ahead, loping in the same direction they were. Hannah felt as though the world had moved sideways a step. A dog? Out here? Strange instincts rose in her mind. She could use that dog — catch it and use it.

Then the dog turned its head to look behind it, and Hannah's instincts were drowned out by another, even older instinct; it didn't come from her thoughts, but originated in her whole body, twisting her wrists outward and locking her elbows and making her stamp hard on the drag mat.

It was not a dog. It was a wolf. And now it was less than ten metres away.

The wolf was almost twice the size of Rudy, both in height and girth. Nothing about those yellow eyes that stared at them said *dog*. That was the first thing Hannah noticed — or, rather, felt through her whole body. The wolf's muzzle was long and tapered, and its legs were also long and thin next to the thickness of its fur, which puffed out in the cold, making it look almost sheep-like. Outside of this forest, it may have looked gangly, or awkward. But it didn't look like that here. Here, it looked like what it was: the apex predator, top of the food chain.

She abandoned the drag mat and punched down on the two-pronged brake. It dug into the snow and stopped the sled without ceremony; Peter lurched forward and Hannah slammed her belly into the bow of the sled, losing her breath for a moment.

All four dogs knew that this was no dog, and certainly no friend. The gangline slackened just a little bit as they faced the wolf, drawing together into an even smaller, tighter pack. Bogey, the closest to the wolf, had his ears flat to his head, and the lips of his wide brown muzzle were stretched back as far as they would go to reveal all of his teeth and most of his gums. Beside him, Sencha stood stock-still in a half crouch. The hair along her entire back was raised. She moved at such a glacial pace that there was almost a minute between her lifting her paw and taking a step forward.

The wolf swung its muzzle up, catching their scents and exposing its throat. Rudy exploded, screaming and howling, his inhales hooked with hate and the instinct to kill or be killed. Only Nook was silent, her body mirroring the wolf's in an easy, half-relaxed stance. Interested. Deciding. The wolf dropped its head and took a few steps toward them. With that, Nook changed, bringing her body down into a slight crouch like Sencha, and baring her teeth like Bogey.

The wolf's gaze flickered over to Hannah. *It doesn't look like it's scared*, she thought as the wolf stared at her, unblinking. *It looks like … like it's measuring the odds.*

Beside Nook, Rudy was throwing himself into his harness, trying to get at the wolf. Each jump forward caused the sled to lurch and thrust the brake up painfully into Hannah's foot. She was already at the limit of her strength; if all the dogs threw their weight into their harnesses like that, she wouldn't be able to hold it back.

Hannah took one arm off the bow of the sled and began shouting hoarsely, the cold air and her dry mouth causing her voice to crack. She waved her arm like a maniac, trying to look threatening, but was completely ignored for her troubles.

The wolf flicked its eyes over her again, and over the sled and the shiny blanket that encased Peter, and then it went back to staring at the four dogs. It kept its head the same height, extended at the shoulders, for a few seconds more. Then it turned off the trail, taking one last, measured look at them before bounding away across the wind-whipped snow, only occasionally breaking through. For all its mass, it weighed less than any of her dogs, Hannah realized. No one fed this wolf specially prepared meat and vegetables after a hard day of hunting. She suddenly had the disturbing thought that, to the wolf, she was just a warm hunk of meat moving around, and only the size of her pack had dissuaded the wolf from making a different decision. She was not a threat; only the dogs were. She felt light-headed.

The whole episode had lasted less than a minute, although her drumming heart and the fatigue creeping through her already exhausted body told her that what the encounter had lacked in length was made up for in intensity.

Peter had not even spoken, but as the wolf disappeared, she heard him let out his breath in a whoosh. "Holy crap," he said.

Hannah shook her head. "That was a wolf, right?"

"Oh, yeah," he confirmed. "Way too big to be a coyote. Beautiful, wasn't it?"

Mentally, she tried to stick the word *beautiful* between *calculating* and *killing machine*.

"It was something," she said. "God, and I thought the moose was scary."

"Yeah. A pack of those wolves, they would have pulled that moose down no problem. Right now they have the advantage."

Hannah thought of the wolf running on top of the snow, and then the moose, labouring through the drifts, and shuddered.

"I wonder why it was on the trail, though," he continued, shifting to look around. "Those grey ghosts don't normally go anywhere near people."

"Probably the same reason as us," said Hannah. "It's easier. I mean, if a moose wants to use it, why not other animals?"

He nodded. "I guess, yeah." She watched him scan the side of the bush where the wolf had gone.

"What are you looking for?"

He craned his neck to look behind them. "More."

Hannah turned her head so fast she saw spots dancing on the snow in the empty trail behind them. "Shit!" she said.

"Yeah, they don't work alone, especially in the winter," he said. "And sometimes they'll send out a decoy and sneak around behind you."

"Are they all that big? It was so *big*." Hannah could hear the disbelief in her own voice.

"I don't know. I haven't seen that many — maybe four in my whole life. It sure looked big."

"Maybe it was the leader."

"Maybe. All I know is, where there's one, there's usually more. Let's get out of here."

Hannah called up the dogs, and they started off again,

slowly, hesitantly, still looking around. But they ran. When the trail began to angle down, Hannah rode the drag mat.

The trail then turned leisurely again, and there were more downhill sections as they left the wide-cut blaze. The trees thickened again as they descended, but Hannah could see all the way down the hill to where the trail came out on a large open area again.

"The lake!" shouted Peter, sitting up.

The sled rode easily down the hill, and the lake beckoned.

In no time, they were past the treeline and rushing across the ice.

CHAPTER TWENTY-SIX

The lake was a silent field of ripples scoured clean by the blizzard's winds. Hannah saw where the ice had ground up against itself, creating ledges that the sled lurched over, causing Peter to wince and swear.

The dogs pulled strongly, and Hannah handled the sled without even thinking now, leaning hard on the runners to turn it, talking the dogs through the leaning of the sled. And the dogs talked to her through it, responding to her commands. It was as though she were running with them. Bogey grew surer of himself the farther they went, and the team followed. The wolf's low killing stance faded from their memory, and they saw only snow and ice, the white layers piled on top of each other.

But suddenly, just ahead, the ice dipped and its rutted surface ended, replaced by a smooth, clear concave area, the water underneath visible and looming in a dark amorphous circle. Hannah felt the sled tilt a tiny extra bit to the left, saw Nook swing her head up and let her line go slack, and heard a muted crack at the same time. The hairs on Hannah's neck rose, and the kernel was suddenly there, not with a memory or an idea, like the other times, but linking her directly to the shrouded winter world itself — to the snowpack and the wind and the poplar trees, to the chickadees and the wolf trotting away, to the fish on the far side of the lake in the cold depths of coves, safe and silent and sluggish. Her world expanded to an impossible degree, and she flew through it, through the bindings and pins on the sled and through the gangline and the bodies of the dogs and then up, up, up, to look down and see the fault line that ran over the lake, through the weather-softened ice beneath them.

The kernel held her there for only the briefest moment, enveloping her in calm and distance and clarity; then she fell back to earth, to her body, to *the next thing*, and her arm flexed and her hand was grabbing the snow-hook and she threw it into the firm, still-thick ice at her feet, stepping on it hard as the ice changed from a thick, opaque white to a muddy, see-through brown. She drove it deep into the winter mantle of the lake and then jumped off the runners and landed roughly on her knees on the ice, yelling as the sled continued forward, propelled by the speed of four dogs who loved pulling and running and who were finally on packed ground, not wading through snowdrifts.

Fast.

The snowhook line unravelled quickly and was three feet away from stopping them safely when Bogey fell through.

His powerful shoulders did most of the work when he pulled, and now they thrust his sharp nails into the rotten ice below, acting like picks, piercing the skin of it and sending him crashing through in an explosion of ice shards and water and his sudden panicked screaming.

A second later, the snowhook line snapped taut. The sled, the team, and Peter lurched forward, then snapped back as the hook held. The ice around them cracked; she could see a large white rent snapping along underneath the sled. It was like watching lightning skitter across the ground; it moved so fast that she couldn't tell where it started or ended, hidden beneath cloudy swirls of snow. The snowhook held fast, keeping the sled crosswise to the widening gap.

"Get out get out get out!" she screamed, a sloppy terror overflowing her heart as she ran toward them. "Peter, *GET OUT!*"

The ice cracked again, ripping up in watery spouts of ice at other spots farther in toward the centre of the lake. The crack under the sled was not the crack that Bogey had fallen through. He had merely weighed too much and been in the wrong place at the wrong time. Around him, the ice thickened considerably, but he didn't know how different kinds of ice smelled, how thin ice was dangerous, how thick ice was safe. Now he was in the middle of the hole, paddling frantically through the floating chunks and churning up the water, panicking.

If it had been Sencha, Hannah knew, there would have been no hope. But the big brown Labrador lived to swim, and his thick double coat and otter tail were made to do exactly this: survive in frigid waters.

But suddenly Bogey went under, and the gangline pulled everyone and everything toward the open water.

"*BOGEY!*" she screamed. Hannah was still ten feet from them, and the rough ice tore at her boots, making her fall again. It felt like a dream, the stumbling and the pain in her legs, the terror in her heart. Sencha and Rudy and Nook had all begun to bark, pulling back from the open water. All of a sudden, Bogey's head resurfaced, half-smothered in the lines of the dogsled and his own harness.

The next thing, Hannah thought: *Get in the water, get the harness off.*

She quickly pulled off her toque and scarf and gloves, dropping them as she went. She would get Peter to pull on the gangline, she would support Bogey, and they would get out. She took hold of her zipper to take her parka off.

A long, flat rope sailed right at her head and she ducked, instinctively catching it with her left hand. She turned and saw that Peter had gotten out of the sled, his jacket and sweater were shucked off, and his torn pant leg was flapping behind him as he half ran, half hopped over to the open water. The other end of the rope was tied around his chest, just under his armpits. He was pulling his hand from his pocket and Hannah saw him flick open his pocket knife, holding it low and ready in his fist. He turned to her and yelled one word before throwing himself onto his good side, sliding toward the open water as though he were sliding into home base. "*Pull!*" he yelled.

Then he was in the water. The panicked Lab made right for him, trying to climb on top of him to get out. Peter yelled and knocked him away, and Bogey turned weakly, now trying to make for the other side of the hole to climb out. With his back to Peter, the lines were easy to get at; the knife flashed, cutting through the ropes. The other three dogs fell back when the tension was released; they scrambled to one side of the hole and onto the thick white paste of ice that would easily bear their weight, pulling the sled to the side but unable to move forward because of the snowhook. They were pointed at the shore now. Sencha's tail was curled right under her body, and she shivered in terror, trying to back away even farther from the frigid water.

Hannah was five feet away now. She threw her jacket down and stopped running, pitching herself down onto all fours to keep her weight distributed over more of the ice.

"Bogey, Bogey, come," she called, and the Lab turned to her, his eyes wide with panic and pain.

He swam to her and she grabbed his collar, pulling as Peter pushed up from behind with one arm, the other holding on to the ice.

"Hurry," said Peter. "I'm going numb."

He was eighty pounds of wet, terrified, panicking dog, and he did not listen well; he yelped and snarled and tried at all costs to keep his head above the water and his back feet down, but he was too heavy for Hannah to pull him out head first. She felt around until she had a hold of his harness. She pulled on it hard, listing him parallel to the water. Slowly, the heavy Lab came up sideways, his head dunking under the water momentarily as Peter pushed his rear end up first, the lighter end.

The flailing, scrabbling dog dunked almost as much water on Hannah as if she'd gone in herself, but finally he scrambled out, heaving up onto solid ice and bolting over to the other dogs, still crying. Hannah lay spread-eagled, her cheek on the ice, and tried to will warmth back into her limbs.

The cold crept all around them, wetting down the edges of the ice and making her ungloved hands freeze to the surface, ripping off chunks of skin when she lifted them to grab Peter's arm. He slipped out of her grasp again and again, kicking weakly with his good leg. Her arms were heavier than lead; they no longer felt attached to her, just frozen chunks with fingers that couldn't bend. Her teeth were chattering and the wet sides of her hair fell forward, already icy and sharp.

"Stop, stop," gasped Peter as she pulled futilely on the rope under his arms. He clung to the side of the ice with his hands, no longer able to pull himself up, his head barely above water. She couldn't pull over 140 pounds straight up, with no help. In the distance, the snowhook rested, humped up against a crack in the lake, holding the sled fast. She lifted her head off the ice, more skin ripping off, this time from her cheek.

She stumbled, her legs screaming in frozen agony, but she ignored them, she ignored everything but the glinting snowhook and the next thing. She lurched along the ice, moving across the thickest ridge, pulled the hook up, and raced back, calling the dogs as she ran.

"Nook, Rudy, Sencha — get up! Get up!" she hollered. The three dogs stood, alarmed and confused; she was calling them to go one way, but running the opposite. Nook pointed her head toward the shore, then back to Hannah.

"Nook!" yelled Hannah. "Nook, get up now! Get up! Sencha, go! Get up, go go go!" She threw herself back down at the mouth of the water and passed the line of the snowhook through the end of the rope, tying it off in a slipknot, still yelling at the dogs to start.

Nook, still in her place as wheel dog, shook herself off quickly and started forward, but the other dogs did not understand and did not pull, and soon she stopped.

Hannah grabbed Peter's arm; he had almost no grip left, and his lips had a bluish tinge to them. He looked sleepy, lolling in the water like it was the height of summer. Hypothermia was setting in.

"Get up, guys, let's go let's go!" yelled Hannah. Out of the corner of her eye she saw a brown blob move forward: Bogey, padding out to stand a little in front of the gangline, his cut traces dangling down, useless.

But he could still lead. *All the other dogs need is someone to follow. A leader.*

"Bogey!" she yelled. She put all her remaining strength into her voice. "Bogey, good boy, that's right, Boge, get up, get up, let's go, get up!"

And he moved. A few steps, then some more, then he broke into a trot, aiming for the treeline and the distant trail. Nook followed immediately, and Sencha, happy to be moving away from the water, and finally Rudy, pulling hard because that was his job.

The gangline tightened and the sled began to move. Hannah wedged her arm over the edge and into the water, putting her other arm around Peter and holding on, trying to act as a buffer against the hard sides of the ice. She set her knees and pulled and twisted, and the sled moved and so did Peter. He woke up and began to pull himself weakly, using her back as support.

His bad leg came up last, scraping over the edge of the hole, and then they were out and on the thick, safe ice near the shore. She pulled the knot on the rope free with numb fingers and set the snowhook, cramming it into a small crack and calling the dogs to halt.

Hannah and Peter lay on their backs, wheezing and coughing. The sun shone down with a freezing grin, but at least there was no wind. Her lips were raw, her hands felt like and looked like hamburger, and her arm was badly scraped now from Peter's body dragging it across the fissured ice as he was hauled up.

Peter turned and lay face down, breathing heavily. Finally, he coughed again and spat up some phlegm.

"Hannah," he said.

"What?"

"That. Sucked."

CHAPTER TWENTY-SEVEN

Hannah lay on her back, staring up into the sky. "Get up," she said, willing herself as much as Peter to follow the instruction.

"Just gimme a minute," he said.

"Peter, we have to get up. We need to get warm."

"I just need to rest a minute." His voice was still slurred, and his blue lips barely moved when he spoke.

"Get up," she repeated.

With agonizing difficulty, Hannah sat up. Neither of them had their coat on, and both of them were soaking wet and about to freeze to death.

No amount of common ground is going to get us out of this one, Mrs. Dowling, she thought.

But in a flash, she heard Mrs. Dowling's *I always know the answer* voice: "With the right kind of encouragement, a good leader and their team can overcome any obstacle."

Hannah almost laughed out loud. What kind of encouragement could possibly help right now?

"Peter, come on, get up!"

"Shut up," he slurred. "Ashhole."

Encouragement, my ass, thought Hannah. *Wanna see some leadership, Mrs. Dowling? Watch this.*

"Hey," she said. "Hey!" She shouted it this time, her voice roughened by the cold. She poked Peter's wet, prone body.

"Whaaaat."

"Pansy-ass!" she said.

"What?"

"I said you're a pansy-ass. Get up!"

He opened a bleary eye. "What?"

"Quit screwing around and get off the ice, you stupid hick!"

"What is your problem? I just saved your stupid dog." He turned on his side. His expression was confused.

"Oh, come on, you only went in the water because you were too dumb to use the snowhook, like I did."

"Are you *kidding* me?" Peter's face pinched as he squinted at her, and she realized he had lost his glasses — and his knife, probably — somewhere in the lake. That made her feel terrible.

She glared at him. "Kidding that you're too stupid to figure stuff out? No. You can't even work the stove properly."

He pushed himself up to a sitting position. "What in the hell is your problem?"

"*You* are! Now get up and get your stupid coat!"

"I can barely walk, for God's sake."

Hannah waved her hand in a *whatever* motion. "I just saw you sprint fifty feet. You can walk just fine. You're just lazy." She hauled herself to her feet and casually set off in search of her own discarded gear, trying to keep her teeth from chattering too loudly. "And by the way, could you get any fatter? It was like hauling a whale out of the lake."

"I'm going to kick your ass, you know that?" he shouted as she walked away.

"Whatever." She grabbed her coat. It took all her will-power not to wrap it around herself immediately. If she did, the water from her wet sweater would soak right into it, making it useless. She bent and picked up her toque and put that on right away, along with her scarf and gloves.

When she turned back, Peter was getting to his feet, hauling himself up with the strength of pure rage. He took a few hobbling steps and grabbed his own coat, hat, and gloves. "You get back here, you little —" He stopped midsentence and stared at the things in his hands. "Did you just make me mad on purpose?"

"Well, yeah."

He glowered at her. "I was going to get up, you know."

"No, you weren't."

He stared at her, shaking his head. "Unbelievable. You are such a shithead, you know that?"

She grabbed the snowhook and began coiling the line to put it away. "Whatever you say, chicken."

Their biggest obstacle now was building a fire, and the fact that they had no extra clothes. Hannah's pants were mostly dry, but her sweater and undershirt were soaked. All of Peter's clothing was starting to stiffen into chunks of ice.

When he'd thrown himself out of the sled, the emergency blanket had been torn to pieces, skipping away in the light wind that blew across the lake. She went to the first-aid kit, took out the last emergency blanket, and gave it to him.

Peter stripped down to his underwear, put his dry coat on, and sat in the sled basket wrapped in the emergency blanket. Hannah took out the makeshift coat she had fashioned for Sencha — which was just a dirty undershirt, anyway — and put it on. Then she put her scarf and jacket on. She pulled Bogey's frozen harness off, and the other dogs', too. She got four portions of dog food from the sled and fed them, roughing up the fur of each dog as she did. They ate so fast that she was pretty sure none of them even chewed. Then all four dogs settled down immediately and fell asleep, Sencha wedging herself in between Bogey and Rudy. The Labrador was already dry, due to the fact that his oily coat shed water like a duck.

Hannah slapped her arms on her sides to warm herself and placed all the wet, frozen clothing in a pile near where she was going to start the fire.

"Okay. So how do I make a fire?" she asked.

"What?"

"You know, what do I do? I need birch bark, I remember that …"

"Are you kidding me? You can make slipknots in the middle of a disaster and run dogsled teams, but you can't make a fire?" Peter laughed so hard the sled shifted, waking up the dogs momentarily.

He sent her off with instructions and teased her mercilessly the whole time she was tromping around gathering things. She came back with the first load, and he got off the sled and hobbled to the spot she had picked, using his remaining snowshoe to dig out a firepit while she went for more wood.

By her fourth trip, he had the fire going well. She dumped another armload of dead branches in the pile and turned to get another. "There's lots of wood there," he said. "You don't need to go so far." She paused, looking back. He was pointing at a large tree nearby. The front of it was almost obscured by a raft of snow, the trunk sticking out like a mast.

"Where?" She looked at the snowbank and the dead branches that started at twice her height off the ground.

"Go around the snowbank. I bet there's all kinds of stuff behind it."

She went around it, and sure enough, the snowbank had acted like a winter beaver dam; the snow was trapped on one side, while the other was dry and filled with branches and driftwood and old grass. She hauled armload after armload of it back to the fire. Peter took select sticks and made several teepees to drape their frozen clothes over. He set them close to the fire to dry.

"You could have told me that earlier," she said.

"What, and miss out on the fun?"

"It's really not funny, Peter. I'm starving."

They both were. The last energy bars had been eaten as soon as they had stopped shouting at each other.

"I'm sorry. You can stop. That's more than enough wood for the night."

Hannah dropped the last armload and went to the

sled. She pulled out four more portions of dog food and was unwrapping them when Peter called to her. "Hey, what's in that?"

"In what?"

"The dog food. Why does it look like that?"

"It's special," she said. "Dad makes it for them for sledding, then he freezes it so it'll stack up nice and neat."

"Well, what's in it?"

"I don't know, meat and stuff."

"Is there any, like, real dog food in it?"

She understood that he meant kibble and shook her head.

"No, there's peas and carrots and oatmeal and stuff. Blueberries, I think, but mostly meat."

He looked at her and grinned. "Like beef?"

"Yeah."

"Sounds like stew to me, Hannah."

Her stomach smacked against her spine with a resounding *yes* that overrode the smaller part of her brain that said people didn't eat dog food.

But they had lots of dog food. Lots and lots.

Peter dangled the largest pot from his hand. "Toss some over."

She tossed two of the bricks over, then got two more, woke the dogs, and fed them a second time. They ate this meal just as quickly as they'd eaten the first. Sencha's sides heaved as she chewed and ripped at her meal, her ribs and muscles showing clearly. Hannah went back to the fire to see the first two bricks of dog food sticking out of the pot. Peter was adding snow around them.

Soon, the meat and vegetables melted, and the snow melted, too; the dog food watered down with snow began to look less like lumps of brown junk and more like … stew. It smelled like stew, too.

Dog food stew.

Finally, Peter quit stirring and used his poker to grab the steaming pot from the fire, and then they feasted. Hannah burned her tongue and lips, but she didn't care. After three days of half-frozen powdered meals and energy bars, the richness of the stew was like eating chocolate, honey, caramel, freshly baked bread … every good thing she'd ever eaten in her life paled in comparison to that stew.

Peter ate even more quickly than she did. He built up the fire, tossing larger branches on until the heat of it started to make them sit back instead of leaning forward. The fire spat up far into the sky, the flames as tall as Hannah and getting taller.

Peter opened his emergency blanket a bit, took his glasses out of his jacket pocket, and put them on.

"Hey," said Hannah, "your glasses!"

"Yeah?"

"I thought you lost them in the lake, like your knife."

"I'm not going to lose my glasses over your stupid dogs. And you owe me a knife. That was a good one, too."

"My stupid dogs are feeding you."

"No, I'm feeding you with their food."

She lowered her head in mock surrender and they ate some more. They finally slowed down on the third bowl. Peter added more snow and now it was like a soup; the salted meat and root vegetables still made it taste like the world's best broth.

Hannah turned her spoon upside down in her mouth and sucked it clean.

"I can't believe you jumped in the water," she said.

He picked up the poker and stabbed some coals. "I just wanted to do something brave, like you."

Her hands gripped her bowl hard. "Brave? I was screaming the whole time."

"But you got us out. You figured out about Nook. You got us through the blizzard, too."

"Barely."

"You still did it."

"Yeah. Okay."

"That's all I meant."

They stared at the fire for a while.

"What's the temperature?" he asked. "It feels really warm."

"I know. I guess about minus five or so?" she said. "The radio was in the other bag."

"Oh."

"You know what?" said Peter, coughing.

"What?"

He reached over and bopped her shoulder. "I really hate winter."

They watched the embers of the fire shift, sending sparks up into the twilight. The sky darkened quickly this time of year. It didn't alarm Hannah anymore. Somewhere behind them were Jeb and her mom, but Hannah couldn't save them in the next eight hours, and she knew that pushing now, with the end so near, was just asking for trouble. No, they would stay by the fire, be warm, then go to sleep early.

Ugh. As soon as I put up the tent. And get the water ready. And check Peter's wound.

Groaning, she rose, went to the sled, and pulled out the tent and their water bottles and the first-aid kit before she had a chance to think about it and feel too full and sleepy. The ground sheet had been in the bag that got lost, so she just put up the tent and the fly and threw the sleeping bags inside. She left the supply pack tied to the sled. The sky was still clear, with a few stars already showing, and she could feel that the weather was light, even on her ice-burned cheek. There would be no snow for a little while, and no danger of being buried again.

Even though she was practised now, it seemed like she was moving through a vat of glue as she set everything up and pulled the first-aid kit to the fire. Her arms felt like they weighed a hundred pounds each. She gave Peter the last of the Tylenol, then they unwrapped his bandages and dried off his leg. The wound was puffing up in places now, but whether it was from the freezing water, from infection, or just from healing, she couldn't tell.

"I don't know if that's good or bad," she said, pointing at the deepest part of the cut, which was turning purple all across his calf and heaving up much like the ice on the lake had. The flesh was swollen and angry-looking. Some parts still leaked blood sluggishly.

"I think it's okay," said Peter. "The water washed it out and I've had it near the fire. I mean, it feels like it's on fire, anyway."

They could do little more than apply the antibacterial ointment and cover it back up with the same bandages. Hannah could feel heat coming from the wound as she rewrapped it, and she tried to keep her face calm. Peter hissed and made faces, but didn't swear, leaning back on his hands and looking at the sky when she had to tug especially hard.

"What do you think Jeb is doing now?" Hannah asked.

Peter looked sykward. "She's probably recovered by now, and worried sick about me," he said. "She knows I can take care of myself, but I try not to leave her alone for long when the weather is dodgy like this."

"My mom is probably worried sick, too," said Hannah. "Not just about me — she has to take care of Kelli, too. And my dad is probably still away." She paused. "They're going to be so happy to see me when I get back … but I'm going to be in so much trouble."

She and Peter sat quietly for a moment. Hannah's stomach ached from so much food after days with so little, and her shoulder smarted from being dragged over the ice. So did her knees and shins. But at last, everything was done. She put away the first-aid kit, lashed the pack closed, and secured it to the sled, then took off her snowshoes, went over to the fire, and slouched down beside Peter. She tugged her jacket open to let in the heat of the flames and clasped her hands around her shins. Finally, her body began to relax, and she stared into the red flames, dreaming with the fire.

They sipped water and stared at the embers as the night drew in around them. Hannah added more wood to make the flames leap high again, and they drank in the heat. The dogs moved and shifted and slept, the fire crackled, and Hannah's belly gurgled, digesting the stew.

Sometimes Peter coughed. After a while, he handed her the poker, and she stabbed at her side of the fire, sending up more sparks that disappeared into the sky, their red glow fleeting against the sharp diamond white of the stars.

She handed the poker back after the fire had been poked to her satisfaction. "You know that book, *The Hunger Games*, where all these kids have to fight each other or be killed?" she asked.

Peter grunted. "Yeah."

"Have you read it?"

"It's a girls' book."

"It's not a girls' book."

Peter looked like he was going to argue — his mouth opened in a flat, long way, like he was about to do the piercing finger whistle that boys loved to do so much — but then he stopped. "I didn't read it. But I saw the movie."

"You know the part where they're in the big city and all the adults are telling them about how hard it is, about how they'll face adversity?"

He smiled at the fire. "And then they have to do a parade and get dressed up and all that stuff. Matching outfits."

"And makeup."

Peter snorted again. "Yeah."

She paused for a minute, because she liked the book, and she wanted to say it right. She didn't want to make something else small just so that she could be big. And what she wanted to say seemed so funny; she couldn't really stop the smile that started to tug at her lips. She picked up her smoke-blackened bowl and looked down at the hole in her snow pants. Then she looked at Peter. He had a blotch of grease across his forehead from wiping away sweat with a stew-covered hand. He scratched at scraggly patches of black hair growing on his chin and along his jaw, and one side of his glasses was fogged, the other a blurry smear. She looked down at herself again, and when she looked up, she was smiling so hard her cheeks hurt.

"I don't think that adversity has makeup artists."

He had that look again, like she was crazy, and who could blame him? They were talking about books in the middle of a winter night on the shore of a lake he had almost drowned in. But he began to shake his head, and then his shoulders, and she realized he was laughing, and then she was laughing, too.

Sencha sat up in case she was missing something interesting, but in the end decided to stay with her team. She lay back down again, burrowing in close to Bogey's flanks. Hannah looked up at the stars. One shone brightly right at the horizon — she pointed to it. "Is that Venus? The Evening Star?"

"I don't know. Could be a satellite. I think it's moving."

They both watched, and it seemed as if the star did move; it flickered and disappeared for a moment, reappearing a little distance away, but somehow bigger.

"Must be a satellite," Peter decided.

Hannah watched as the light hovered along the tops of the trees on the other side of the lake, blinking out now and then and reappearing. After a while she could tell it was definitely getting bigger, and nearer.

"I don't think that's a satellite," she said, rising from her seat. "I think that's something else."

"Like what?" said Peter, craning his neck.

Then the light dipped down and winked out for good.

Hannah peered into the darkness, but the light did not return, so she sat back down. A minute later, a movement caught her eye outside the circle of light from the fire, and she turned her head back to other side of the lake. The light was back, and this time it was pointed right at them.

CHAPTER TWENTY-EIGHT

The light was accompanied by a sound, then it disappeared again but the noise remained, and then both the noise and the light broke the edge of an embankment, and she saw the dark, hulking shape of a snowmobile. It coasted to the edge of their campfire light, and then the light winked off and the engine cut out. The dogs began to bark, but Hannah could identify their voices almost individually now and was not worried. Each of them was barking the *hello/pay attention/ we are here* bark, not the wordless growl of being confronted by a true predator, the way they had with the wolf.

"Hello!" called a voice over the barking.

"Hello?" Hannah called back, standing up with her bowl still in her hand.

"I saw the fire. I live on the other side of the lake. Are you okay?"

For a moment Hannah was at a loss for words. She turned and glanced at Peter, who was still sitting and had his spoon halfway to his mouth.

"We're okay," she finally called.

A bulky shape rose off the machine and walked toward them carefully, snowshoe-less feet sinking in the snow. The dogs lay back down and went to sleep, even Sencha, who was still wedged between Rudy and Bogey.

"I would have been here sooner, but I couldn't come across the lake — ice is rotten from this crazy weather."

"We know," said Hannah.

Beside her she heard Peter laugh, then cough, spitting out phlegm. "That's the understatement of the year right there," he said. It seemed like the understatement of her life.

Hannah watched the man as he walked into the light of the fire. He was wearing a long dark-green parka with fur around the hood. It had many deep pockets on the outside — a woodsman's jacket. His mitts were the snowmobile kind, with wide ends that fit over his jacket to keep the wind out. Beneath his hood and above the snow goggles he wore, Hannah could see the edge of a brown knit toque.

The man stopped and took in the scene. Hannah imagined how the two of them looked to him: filthy from wood smoke and from gorging themselves, their noses running and their eyes red from leaning too close to the fire, still bedraggled from their icy dunking. His eyes flicked over the packed sled and the four dogs before coming back to the fire and the snow-filled pot beside it, then the water bottles that sat open-mouthed, waiting to be refilled. He took a step toward them. Silently, Nook and Bogey rose, their tails slightly lifted, and Nook raised a lip in silent warning. The man saw the dogs' movement and stepped back, putting his foot into its previous footprint. He left his hands hanging and lifted his chin in the greeting that locals used, pointing it at them.

"What are y'all doing out here?" he asked.

"She has to get to Timmins," said Peter. "Her mom's sick."

"And he has to get home," said Hannah. "His aunt needs him. But he fell on a plow, so he needs to see a doctor first."

Peter nodded and pulled back his tattered wool pants to expose the long white bandage spotted with blood. "It'll need stitches, I'm pretty sure."

"Looks like it," said the man, crouching next to the fire, but on the other side from them, not too close. He pushed back his hood and removed his goggles. His face was lined the way faces are when they spend a lot of time outside: deep creases around the eyes and the skin under his chin hanging slightly away from his neck. His expression was focused and unsmiling, though Hannah thought that wasn't its natural state. It looked like a face that smiled more than it was serious.

"Is that why you're out here?" continued the man. "To get help?"

"Yes," said Hannah.

"How long have you been going?"

She calculated quickly — Jeb's, the shortcut and Jonny Swede's, the quarry and the storm. "This is our fourth night," she said. She pointed down the shore the way he had come. "That's the way, right? To Timmins?"

"Yep, that'll take you to Timmins."

"How far is it?" asked Peter. He leaned forward, balancing his bowl on his good leg.

"Not far. Maybe twenty minutes by snowmobile. More on that, I'd imagine," he said, gesturing to the dog sled.

Peter looked at Hannah, and his eyes were glowing. "We're almost there! My other aunt lives in town. Aunt Peggy. She has a car."

The man looked at them, his eyes widening. "Peggy Purcell? You're Scott's boy?"

"Yes. I'm Peter."

The man nodded. "Your aunt, eh? Jenny, is it? She's the veteran."

"How did you know?" asked Hannah.

"It's a small town," he replied. "And who are you?"

"Hannah. Ha-neul Williams."

The man whistled. "Scott and George's kids. Your mom's sick?"

"Yes, she needs insulin."

"Oh, that's not good," said the man immediately. "By Jesus, kids, you've been outside all this time? You need something warm in ya, I'm betting. Are you hungry?"

Hannah and Peter laughed together this time. "Nope," said Peter. "Want some stew?" He held out his bowl.

The man looked at Peter, who was still laughing and coughing, and then at Hannah.

"And what's *your* name?"

"Me? Oh shoot, I'm Darren. Hubbard. Darren Hubbard."

Hannah glanced over the dogs. At his movement, they had turned and now sat watching him. None of them had a hard stare that said *you don't belong — danger!* Now and then, one of them would lift their nose to quest for scents, but their postures were relaxed. Nook met her eyes and then looked back to the edge of the light, where the trail continued. This man was no threat, and she was not interested in him or his machine. She wanted to run.

Hannah turned to Peter. "Do you know Mr. Hubbard?"

"No, but I've heard of him. You're a mechanic, right?" he asked the man.

The man shook his head slightly. "Small engines, lawn-mowers and stuff. I'm retired. I work at Len's, down by the cop shop."

"I think we'd better go with Mr. Hubbard," she said to Peter. "You need dry clothes, and a hospital."

Peter nodded.

She turned back to the man. "We'll go with you," she said. She inclined her head to indicate the team and the sled. "And the dogs, too."

He reached up and took off a glove and scratched the side of his head, looking at her with an odd expression.

"How old are you?" he asked.

"Fourteen."

"Fourteen going on forty," he said. She remembered that her father had said that about her, too. But Mr. Hubbard hadn't said it the same way her father had; he said it like it was something to be proud of.

Hannah helped Mr. Hubbard to gather Peter up and put him on the back of the snowmobile. Peter swayed on the seat, grinning and still holding his empty bowl. She took it gently from him.

"I'm going to be a doctor," he said to Mr. Hubbard, grabbing his arm to keep balanced on the long, plastic-covered seat of the snowmobile. He had his arm slung around Hannah, as well, and she felt him squeeze her shoulders. His face was flushed, but not with embarrassment; she could feel waves of heat coming off him, and his eyes were unusually bright. It wasn't just the reflecting firelight.

"He has a fever," she said to the man.

Mr. Hubbard looked at him, took his glove off, and felt Peter's head. "Poor kid." He got Peter settled with the emergency blanket around him and a heavy wool one over that, leaning him against the small seat post at the back of the snowmobile. Then, by the light of the dying fire, he helped Hannah take down the tent and pack it into the basket with their other gear.

He eyed the dogsled, the gangline straight with the dogs sitting or lying quietly, ready to go. Sencha's white and brown flanks stood out starkly against the thick gradient fur of the huskies. He craned his neck a little to take in Bogey's square haunches, his dark-brown fur almost lost in the darkness. "Wow. *Two* stringers?" He meant the house dogs; stringers were bad dogs, dogs that didn't like to work, didn't know what to do.

"They're not stringers," she said. "They're a team. They're good."

"Okay," he said, scratching his neck again. "Well, I'll take you and Peter to my place so we can get to the hospital, and then I'll come back for them, okay?"

Hannah gathered up the few things that were still out

and placed them in the packsack in the basket of the sled. She zipped the pack shut and tied it down firmly.

"No," she said, pulling on her gloves. "You go ahead. We'll follow."

He nodded hesitantly with that same strange expression in his face that she suddenly realized was respect and moved off to his own sled, starting it up with the press of a button. The sound was hollow and odd after so many days of hearing only runners and dogs and herself and Peter.

She dug the snowhook out and called the dogs up, and they stood. She ran her eye over each of them and saw that everyone was calm — no shoulders shifting uncomfortably, no paws being favoured. It didn't matter that it was nighttime or that they had run all day. Every ear was up and canted forward, ready; they were eager to work again. She waved to the man, who had turned to watch her, making sure she was with him. He raised a hand and turned back to the lakeside trail, thumbing the throttle of the snowmobile and pulling away, leaving the smell of gasoline and oil.

He went slowly, but he didn't need to; she knew they would keep up. They would follow the freshly groomed trail and the winking red tail light back around the lake to warmth and strangers with no trouble. She was strong, and her team was strong: they could keep up with anything.

EPILOGUE

As promised, Mr. and Mrs. Hubbard drove Hannah and Peter into Timmins that same night. They took Peter to the hospital emergency room. He still had a fever, and his wound was ugly, but Hannah had done a good job keeping it clean.

Driving past the local coffee shop, Mr. Hubbard saw the dull green Forces trucks. He drove over and inquired, and personnel directed him to the right spot, and Hannah and her dad were reunited. Mr. Hubbard told her father the story of how he had found Hannah and Peter — but he was careful to make it sound as though they had everything under control, perhaps to save her from getting in trouble.

She watched her father's face change and change again as he heard about the ice and the lake and Bogey, about the dog food feast and the fire and Peter's injury. He hugged her hard, and went in search of Scott, to tell him his son was at the nearby hospital, as well as to find an officer, to let them know about Jeb.

Mr. Hubbard offered to lend them a snow machine to get home, for the back roads had still not been cleared, and would not be cleared for days or weeks still. The crews would start in town, repairing downed lines and removing trees, before moving on to the outer areas. He had a wood sledge with high sides as well, and they put the four dogs into it.

The cabin looked the way it always had, squat and dark on the north side, the outhouse, the tarped-over snowmobile, the verandah neatly shovelled. They came down the driveway slowly, and the door opened. Kelli stepped onto the porch, then Hannah's mom, and then everything was okay and Hannah felt the breath she had been holding since they had seen the cabin let go. She was suddenly so tired she could barely stand.

Hannah got off the sled, unzipped her jacket, and handed over the box that held the new vials of insulin before apologizing. She had to hitch her snow pants up with one hand when she got off. Her mother, too, had lost weight, and for the first time that Hannah had ever seen, Mina began crying.

Hannah found that everyone listened to what she had to say more carefully, now; her parents and Scott, even Jeb. She had earned their respect, and she tried to keep it; she was more careful when she spoke, and she let silence speak as well, the way Peter had at night by the fire.

In the end, Hannah and her team had mushed almost one hundred kilometres in four days, forty of them through unbroken snow almost two feet deep. She knew because the next summer, Hannah and her mom retraced her journey, this time on an ATV, all in one day.

And every winter, for many years after, Hannah raced dogsleds, at first with Sencha and Bogey, and later with other dogs. She did short races and long ones, and the snow swirled behind her as she slipped over it, and she named it skirting snow. She won some races, but mostly she just loved being outside again, in the cold, feeling winter, returning to one thing, and then the next — and to find the kernel. She understood now that it was a skill, this kernel, and that was why she raced, to keep the skill in use ... she owed herself that.

ACKNOWLEDGEMENTS

You need a large pack to make a book, and like Hannah, I also have no stringers: Sharon and Heather (the superhero group), Robin, Craig and Zoe (the Aussie group), Hazard, Keats, Chelsey, Jenn Lowe (mush on, lady), Maggie, Reason, Tammy, Journey, and Karma. Thank you one and all. And to EJB, who was my Nook the whole way through — you're my favourite.